P9-CFC-092

A Shortcut in Time

A Shortcut in Time

Charles Dickinson

A TOM DOHERTY ASSOCIATES BOOK
NEW YORK

FORGE®

This is a work of fiction. All the characters and events portrayed in this novel are either fictitious or are used fictitiously.

A SHORTCUT IN TIME

This book is printed on acid-free paper.

A Forge Book
Published by Tom Doherty Associates, LLC
175 Fifth Avenue
New York, NY 10010

www.tor.com

ISBN 0-765-30579-8

First Edition: January 2003

Printed in the United States of America

0 9 8 7 6 5 4 3 2 1

FOR DONNA, LOUIS, AND CASEY

■ ■ ■ ■

FIRST TRAVELERS

ACKNOWLEDGMENTS

Support for this book came in many different forms.

Thanks to David Hartwell and Moshe Feder at Tor; my agent, Robin Straus; head cheerleader, Rose May; Norman Gawron, Dr. Wayne Bartholomew, Joan Dickinson, Toni Rubino, Lucy Hoy, Mitch Dydo, Jim and Nancy Barnes, Bonnie Moos, Rex McGee, Mark Jacob, Rich Cahan, Dave Nichols, Rich Wronski, Chuck Berman, Allison Colonero, Tasha Sahs, Natalie Valliere-Kelley, the Spicer boys—Bill, Butch, Andy, Rob, and Tom—and Burt Constable.

A Shortcut in Time

1964

This story began with a broken promise. It began in water over my head. It began with me, Josh Winkler, flying through the streets of the only town I had ever known, Euclid Heights, Illinois, six zero zero zero one.

I was in a hurry because I didn't want to disappoint my kid brother. Again. I was old enough to know that you don't get a lifetime of second chances with people. Especially with people who don't really need you. And Kurt didn't need me. He'd jumped out of bed at dawn to complete an Eagle Scout project with his best friend, Vaughan Garner. They were teaching retarded children to swim and Kurt had asked me to steer the kids back if they wandered away from where he and Vaughan mimed the Australian crawl in the shallow end.

I'd heard my brother get up that morning before his alarm clock went off, heard him wash, organize his clipboard, nudge me, whisper, "Josh, it's time," and hurry away in the dark.

Next thing I knew, mom was shaking me, knocking the sleep out of me, the sun so high it shined on the floor of my basement bedroom.

"You promised him, mister," she said.

The Euclid Heights community pool was next to the American

Legion baseball diamond and as I tore on my bike across the outfield grass I looked ahead through the chain-link fence for some sign of my brother, or Vaughan, or the retarded kids, some way to gauge how badly I'd let them down this time. But no one was in sight.

Before I could worry or even think about this, Jack Ketch—Jock Itch to those of us who hated and feared him—came toward me on his bike from around back of the poolhouse, riding with his head down, pumping so furiously that a rooster tail of dew sprayed out behind him. He was a flat-topped bully, all blackheads and cruelty. He'd made more boys cry than *Old Yeller*.

Jock Itch answered to no one. He had the law on his side. His father was Sheriff John "Jack" Ketch Jr., himself the son of a lawman of the same name. Imagination was not a Ketch family trait. Wielding power was. Itch's dad was half again his son's size and treated the town kids—his son included—with glancing disdain, like a lion that had just eaten. In that year, an election year, Sheriff Ketch was running unopposed for a third term.

He gave his son the pick of the town's impounded bikes and that morning Itch was on a spaghetti-tired English racer, his mind—such as it was—evidently elsewhere. I was pretty sure he hadn't seen me. He was producing this weird squeak—like he needed oiling—and we were about to pass each other without incident when he swerved his confiscated bike in front of me. My front tire slid across his rear wheel. I went down head over handlebars.

On my knees, my mouth full of grass clippings, I recognized the squeak he'd been making. It was "Wink. Wink. Wink." He turned up the volume as he circled me. *"Wee-ink! Wee-ink! Wee-ink!"*

I righted my bike.

"Is Winker all wet now, too?"

He threw something—a small, blue stick—at my feet. I stepped on it without bothering to determine what it was. It snapped under my foot.

I took a step toward him but we both knew it was nothing serious. No one really wanted a piece of Jock Itch. He was bigger and stronger than any two kids, and impervious to pain in that way the thickheaded and unreflective were. That morning his T-shirt was damp and wrinkled, like someone had recently grabbed a fistful of it and held on for a while, then thought better of the enterprise.

"You're too late, Wink," Itch said, then he was on his bike and gone.

Coming up on the poolhouse, I was struck again by how quiet it was. The retarded kids usually made a huge racket. They liked how their voices echoed off all that tile.

At first I thought I was just so late that the lessons had finished and everyone had gone home. It was a Sunday and the pool didn't open until noon. Kurt and Vaughan had been entrusted with a key. On summer evenings, they ran the pool's concession stand. Both of them were slightly small for their age. Vaughan was student council president, tops in his class. He had a smile that he used with kids, a smile with a little of the devil in it, a smile that he kept separate from the smile he used strictly with adults. Kurt liked to build things from scratch and won bets with kids by multiplying four-digit numbers before someone else could figure the answer on paper.

Inside the poolhouse, I saw a sign on the cashier's cage. *No swimming. Pump broken.*

That explained why the retarded kids weren't there.

But Kurt's bike was chained to a bench.

Shower steam hissed in the boys' locker room. I stuck in my head. One shower was running. I tiptoed across the wet tiles and shut off the water. It just made the place seem emptier.

"Kurt!" I yelled, startled by how scared I sounded.

A towel trolley sat in the center of the locker room. It was about the size of a big, deep bathtub on caster wheels, with canvas sides and a hinged, wooden lid. It was half full, a small mountain of towels piled next to it on the floor.

"Kurt!" I yelled again. "Vaughan!"

Nothing.

The surface of the pool water was absolutely still. The lane floats had been pulled out and lined up along the deck. I went and stood at the entrance to the girls' changing area.

"Kurt!"

I waited a few seconds, and then entered. Everything in the girls' locker room was the same as the boys' except that the tile floor was dry.

"Kurt?" I said to establish my reason for being there.

My mom didn't swim and Kurt and I had no sisters. Vaughan had a sister named Flo, short for Flora. She was my age, pretty enough, I guess, behind her glasses, but with a perpetual frown of concentration on her face. She was, like her brother, the top student in her class, but being number one didn't appear to give her any enjoyment.

"Vaughan?" I said, in case she was there, searching for her brother, too, and wondering what *I* was doing in the girls' locker room.

When I finally went back out by the pool, the day had altered fractionally. A cloud across the sun improved visibility into the water. Down in the deep end was a shape that registered immediately as horribly out of place. I hurried around the pool's edge, the blue-on-cream tiles spelling out 5 FT., then 8 FT., then 12 FT. The cloud passed. A flash of sunlight off the water made me cover my eyes. I examined the shape at the bottom of the pool indirectly, half afraid to confront what was there.

It was a towel trolley, right side up at the bottom of the pool's sloping floor. Its wooden lid was closed. A baseball-size bubble escaped from it and wobbled to the surface.

Then I was diving down through the water, wishing I'd taken a bigger gulp of air. The water squeezed my head as I went deeper and I felt vital passageways in my brain begin to slam shut. With a final, exhausted kick I got close enough to grab the edge of the trolley's wooden lid. It was varnished and slippery, but I expected it to open easily. It didn't budge. I yanked harder. Nothing. Another bubble—shaken free—broke against my chin.

Then I saw that the lid was locked, a ballpoint pen lodged in the latch. The pen was blue, with gold printing along the barrel. Removing it was easy enough. I tried to put it in my shorts pocket but it slipped out of my hand. When I grabbed for it I lost my grip on the trolley lid and bobbed to the surface.

Someone—a girl—was running from the poolhouse. I didn't get a good look at her. I could only scream—"Ambulance!"—and kick back down.

The water pressure on the trolley made it hard to lift the lid. A school of small bubbles fizzed past my face. The first thing I saw inside the trolley was a blue-white hand. As I lifted the lid higher I saw that the hand belonged to my brother.

I reached out in a panic and grabbed a good chunk of Kurt's cheek and pinched. Hard. I knew he hated when I did that and I hoped the pain and outrage might travel down to whatever cold grain of life remained inside him and make him angry enough to return to me.

He didn't respond. The imprint of my finger and thumb remained pressed into his skin like a dent in clay. He was folded into a fetal position. His eyes were half-open. I was pretty sure he was dead. A million times over the years that followed, I wished that he had been.

I got my hands under his armpits, got my feet balanced precariously on the edge of the trolley, and lifted. He came free easily enough. He was a shrimp, light and cold. A strand of pearllike bubbles trailed out his nose as I carried him toward the surface. I felt a slushy thump in his chest as we ascended.

The girl was kneeling at the pool's edge. She'd lost a high-heeled shoe. The tail of her blouse had come loose and there was a rip in the knee of her nylons. From far away, too far away to be of any immediate use, came a siren. The girl pushed her glasses higher on her nose, then grabbed the back of Kurt's trunks and dragged him out onto the deck, her eyes locked all the time on the trolley at the bottom of the pool.

Then she put her hand on my face and pushed me back under.

"Vaughan!" she screamed.

Vaughan Garner hadn't moved. He reminded me of a kid sleeping in a bed he'd outgrown, his knees to his chest, his toes scratching against the trolley canvas. The only sign of something wrong was the nail of his left index finger jutting out perpendicular from its roots, torn almost off in his panic.

I reached in and grabbed the back of his swim trunks. He came loose easily. He felt inert—empty—as I struggled with him to the surface. I delivered him into a flurry of activity. A firefighter went feetfirst over my head into the water, and then down, not knowing everyone was accounted for. Others worked on Kurt.

The girl in one shoe stood off to the side. She chewed the tips of her fingers, but she didn't cry. I learned soon enough that this was Vaughan's sister, Flo Garner. She had come to the pool when her brother was late returning home.

A spark of life was found almost immediately in Kurt and he was borne away.

Vaughan was taken away, too, finally, but there was no hurry.

The police interviewed me just once, in our house at 1112 East Collier Street.

"The latch was held shut with a ballpoint pen," I insisted.

The cop held up the pen he was using to take notes. "Like this?"

"It was blue."

"You're sure?"

"Yes."

"Where is it then?"

"I had it and dropped it. Did you check the bottom of the pool?"

"We followed the drain all the way out to the street."

"It had gold writing on it."

"What did the writing say?"

"I don't know."

The incident was ruled an accident, the tragic consequence of two young men just goofing around. Nobody listened when I said that Kurt never goofed around.

Flo Garner stopped me in the hall on the first day of school.

"How's your brother?" she asked.

I shrugged. "Not great. My dad's already started complaining about the hospital bills."

"Can I ask you something?"

"Sure."

"Did you bring Kurt up first because he was your brother?"

"No. He was on top."

She touched my arm. I thought she was going to thank me for at least trying.

"I wish I could believe that," she said.

Mom was the only person Kurt recognized. He was an anxious, demanding new presence in the house. A curious, contemplative kid had been replaced by a young man who could not sit still for thirty seconds. He went into the hospital a boy. He came home needing a shave. He prowled the house inch by inch. Then he did it all over again.

Mom grabbed me a week later. "Teach him his address," she said.

"Why?"

"I can't hold him. I can't keep him cooped up forever," she said, like she was revealing a shameful secret. "When I let him out I want him to know where his home is."

It took a day of repetition, but Kurt learned his address.

"One one one two East Collier Street, Euclid Heights, Illinois. Six zero zero zero one." His voice was flat, machinelike.

The next day, he started walking.

Flo Garner came to our house on the first anniversary of her brother's death.

"Want to revisit the scene?" she asked.

I didn't, not really, but I also didn't want her to leave without me.

As we crossed the baseball field, I remembered something from that hot Sunday morning that I had forgotten almost the moment it happened.

I tried to find the exact spot where Jock Itch had knocked me off my bike. It was easy, once I had the moment in mind. I hadn't given much thought to the minutes immediately before I found the towel trolley at the bottom of the pool. Fifteen minutes, maybe, tops, between when Itch knocked me off my bike and when I hauled Kurt to the surface. It felt like the events happened in two different lifetimes. The details of one never added up to the consequences of the other. Rehashing the details wouldn't change anything.

Then I told Flo to stop.

"What?" she asked.

It was a long shot. An entire baseball season had been played since that morning. The outfield grass had been mowed several times. I started where I fell, in right field. I began to search it inch by inch.

Flo, still straddling her bike, came up behind me.

"Do you think it's horrible of me to have derived some benefit from Vaughan's dying?" she asked.

Without lifting my head, I mumbled, "No, I guess not."

"Because—frankly—since Vaughan died my dad has really been a much better father to me," she said.

I wasn't paying attention. "Yeah?"

"Before—it was Vaughan, Vaughan, Vaughan. The golden son," she said. "He was the doctor-to-be. The star. But now—"

Something sparkled in the grass. I knelt and retrieved a strip of gum foil folded carefully into an arrowhead.

"Now I'm the star," she said. "By default."

"Huh."

"I've decided a star by default is still a star," Flo said. She didn't wait for me to answer. "I'm just as smart as Vaughan. Maybe smarter. But he was *the boy*."

She didn't say anything for a couple minutes. I walked back and forth over the grass.

"Why aren't you in any of my classes?" she asked.

"Because you're going to be a doctor," I said, "and about all I like to do is draw. Preferably in the margins of my homework."

She didn't laugh.

I expanded the area of my search. When I lifted my head to ease a crick in my neck she was a hundred feet away.

"I *do* miss him," she called to me. "Don't think I'm a horrid person."

I came back to her. "I don't," I said.

She nodded. "Good."

I followed her nod down from the point of her chin, down her body, down her long leg to the tip of her tennis shoe, which pointed precisely at what I was seeking. It was the barrel half of a ballpoint pen, half of the blue stick Itch had thrown at me.

Printed on it in gold letters were the words

REELECT SHERIFF JACK. HE'LL "KETCH" CROOKS!

I didn't explain to Flo the significance of the pen. Nothing I said would bring her brother back. Kurt was gone for good, too. And—to be perfectly honest—I was afraid of Itch and his father. So I just put the pen barrel in my pocket and we continued on to the pool. When we got there she held my hand.

ONE

Sticks figured in the summer of falling trees.

Booming thunderstorms—real inky monsters out of the southwest, with wrenching winds, apocalyptic lightning strikes, and blinding rains—swept across the months of June and July. One a week, it seemed. More than we deserved, certainly. The storms terrified my daughter, Penny—who was old enough to know better, but who nevertheless fell shaking into my arms when the shutters flapped. I didn't mind. She was too old to let me hold her, otherwise.

The worst storms always seemed to knock down a tree, like the weather was imposing a fine, or taking a bribe to leave more important things alone. First a sycamore fell. Then it was a red maple. Then a weeping mulberry. My wife paid cash to have the remains removed.

In August it wasn't even a storm, just a few drops of rain and a puff of wind, but I was interrupted in my studio by an old man's querulous voice, his passage on the perp walk alongside our house impeded by a branch that had fallen from the only apple tree on our property.

"I have a right to pass," the man said when I came outside. "It may feel like I'm intruding on your privacy, but this is a public way."

He was right twice. It felt like he was standing in my backyard. And he was free to stand there forever.

Perp walks were unique to my hometown, near as I could tell. The town fathers who laid out the streets of Euclid Heights were eager to convey honesty, forthrightness, and rectitude in all public dealings, and so hewed to a grid of squared-off lots and right-angle streets in the neighborhoods closest to the downtown business district. The only divergent line was the railroad, which cut off a corner of the town square on a northwest-southeast angle, and linked the town to Chicago. Several blocks east of downtown, where my family lived, the grid was more rectangular, with long north-south blocks intersected only infrequently by east-west streets.

Early in the 1900s a lawyer and surveyor named Peter McDeedle held the office of mayor. He projected the image of a family man, married to his childhood sweetheart, devoted father of several children, virtuous upholder of the public good, but his true love was a woman who lived on the edge of town, a brisk walk to the east. To reduce the time spent traveling from his office to his lover's embrace—and also to attempt to hide what he was doing from his constituents—Mayor McDeedle ignored the public roads and walked with his head down and his coat collar up, following the straightest line the town's topography afforded. He took this shortcut so often that he wore a path—between houses, through orchards, and across fields. The citizens of Euclid Heights knew the mayor's secret, of course, and disapproved. However, they found the mayor's shortcut to be useful in reducing the time required to get from downtown to the east side, and back.

Being a lawyer and a surveyor, Mayor McDeedle acted to make his shortcut an official feature of the town. Being a politician, he took credit for something positive that grew unforeseen from his general lack of personal character. His wife, however, was one of many people not fooled by his extragovernmental activities. On the day McDeedle stood for reelection, his wife bought train tickets to Chicago for herself and her children. Her husband—emerging from the town jail where he had just cast a vote for himself—watched as his family boarded the train across the square. His vote for himself was one of the few he received. He never saw his family again.

The paths he had made were known as perp walks because they lay perpendicular to the long, unbroken north-south blocks. The walk alongside our lot linked Clover Street—which our house faced—with Chapman Street, a hundred paces to the east. Across Clover, the perp walk continued west through the shadowy gap between one house's vine-covered slat fence and its neighbor's long row of rattling sunflowers.

I loved how the perp walks went against the grain of the town. They were unexpected and subversive in a playful way. They sliced through what ordinarily was hidden. We had lived for years next to the walk but someone appearing on it unexpectedly—like the old man blocked by the fallen apple tree branch—could still surprise me.

I phoned Flo from my studio.

"Dr. Winkler's office," she answered. It was too early for her assistant to be there, so Flo handled her own phones.

"More tree damage."

"Can you call?"

"Sure. Is Penny there?"

Flo's office was at the easternmost tip of the long east-west leg of our L-shaped house. My studio, created from our old garage space, was at the extreme tip of the north-south leg. I could see Flo in her office across the intervening space, talking to me while skimming a journal and jotting notes about her day and probably completing a couple other jobs in her head.

"She ate and ran," Flo said.

"Where to?" I was making small talk, but also I perversely enjoyed that my daughter was not in Flo's office, prepping to join her mother in the medical field.

"Corey's house. With Regan and Holly. Then the beach," Flo said. "Emmy's here."

Emmy Fontaine, Flo's assistant, strode up the brick walk from the parking lot that faced Chapman Street. Flo had laid the bricks in the walk herself. She'd arranged the bricks closest to the back door in our initials—JW FW PW.

Flo had saved money by knocking out the walls herself when we added her office wing. With the first sledgehammer blow she heard glass shatter inside the wall. Old panes of green glass leaned between each of the studs she exposed. A man named Portmanteau had built the house in 1910. He had amassed a small fortune in the wing-collar business before becoming convinced that his neighbors could read his mind. To reduce others' opportunities to intrude upon his thoughts, he bought the house and the lot to the east, and then leveled the building. His efforts to purchase the properties to the north and south were fruitless, so he inserted hundreds of panes of glass into the walls on all sides of his house in the belief that the glass would block the transmission and reception of his thoughts.

I stacked the panes in my workroom. They served as material during my Glass Period. They were wavy, pocked with air bubbles, and cracked under the slightest pressure. On a clear, summer night I lay on my back in the grass with a pane suspended over my head on the arms of two lawn chairs. My brushes were in my mouth and tins of black paint and white paint balanced on my stomach. My plan was to paint the sky. Flo appeared as I sketched the moon. Where she stood placed her perfectly in the painting. The moon rode on her shoulder. I knew she never would pose for me so I worked quickly—wordlessly—to get her in. Moon. Stars. Flo.

The result was the only piece I kept from my Glass Period. It was one of two pieces of my work I was certain that she loved.

Later that morning a long, gray State of Illinois van pulled into the rear parking area. Eight children tumbled out. When Flo started her practice she had signed a contract to care for a certain number of state wards. Now, even though the mothers of Euclid Heights and surrounding communities went gladly on a waiting list to put their children in the care of Dr. Flo, she renewed her deal with the state every year.

The kids reminded me of billiard balls on the break. They variously ran away from or advanced aggressively toward Dr. Flo's office. Some performed handsprings in the grass. Others simply whirled in circles, gleeful to be free of the van. One little boy whimpered into the ample waist of Hilly Cutter, who was both the driver of the van and the woman in charge.

Flo came outside to greet the state kids and to help Hilly herd them inside. She had a scale in her office that announced each child's weight in a voice of unpredictable goofiness—squeaking mouse, droning robot, buzzing space alien—and the kids loved it and demanded to be weighed again and again. Flo allowed one extra weigh-in per child, and then swept the child off the scale if the child was small enough to be swept. The scale was an extension of the voices Flo did to put the kids—and herself—at ease during her first years of practice. She'd felt like a kid, too, feverish and nervous. Silly voices made the kids laugh and took the attention off her. For Flo, going to work was like going to the doctor herself, where you wanted to hand your fate over to a more knowledgeable stranger. Flo believed in herself as that receiver of children's trust only after Penny was born. A restless confidence seized her and she borrowed money from her father and bought out the woman who had brought Flo into the practice. Soon after, the wing was added and Flo brought her practice home.

The new arrangement had taken some getting used to. I had always had Penny to myself during the day. She made messes alongside me while I worked, and as she grew she began to take on an artist's air of carefree effort. Having Flo nearby changed that. Penny drifted from my side into the new space her mother had created—and occupied. I would lose track of her and then the phone rang and there she was, in her mother's office, waving to me across the space that separated us.

When Penny was fourteen, Flo began to pay her $10 an hour to help out in the office. She measured kids, cleaned the bathroom, filed, diverted the attention of a sick child's jealous sibling, and lobbied her mom to be allowed to do actual medical procedures. Flo's injection of money into the equation felt unfair to me. In the undeclared war to shape Penny's future occupation, money was Flo's secret weapon. All I had to offer was the sporadic satisfaction of creativity.

Now she was with neither of us. Corey, a cute boy who lived over on Holt Street, had all her attention. He was like a fever Flo couldn't fight.

My phone rang. I checked across the yard. Nobody was in the window.

I picked it up. "Hello."

"Winker."

The familiar voice made my head pound. "Itch," I said.

"I'm calling about Crazy Kurt, Winker. For the millionth time—Kuh-razy Kurt."

"Where is he?"

"Where do you think? Get him in fifteen minutes or his homeless ass goes to jail."

"Isn't the jail being moved today?"

"That's why he isn't locked up yet."

"So, basically—Officer Itch—I can ignore you because you have no place to put Kurt anyway."

"You know me, Winker. I might do *anything*."

From Clover, the perp walk led west to Tinker Street, then across Tinker to Cottonwood, Cottonwood to Pine, Pine to Pincoffin, and finally Pincoffin to Greencloth, which I took north into the center of town, where a chaotic, loose-animal atmosphere prevailed.

Men in red coveralls swarmed at the intersection of Violet and Mottle, each one armed with what appeared to be a fifty-foot-long shuffleboard stick. These were used to lift any wires clear of the old Euclid Heights Jail as it was transported inch by inch atop a sixteen-wheel tractor-trailer from its location on the town square to its future home on a small plot of ground next to the Euclid Heights Historical Society. Its departure made the square look like it was missing a tooth.

Kurt sat on the front steps of 1112 East Collier Street like it was still our home, like he was waiting for dad to get off work. One of his thin, grimy wrists was handcuffed to the banister. Jock Itch squeezed out of his squad car when I arrived.

The current owners of our old house had made changes over the years: aluminum siding, a new roof of greenish shingles, awnings over the downstairs windows, planters that need watering on the porch steps. No amount of change, however, could erase the house's irresistible hold on Kurt. It was home. It always would be home. The location and address were lodged somewhere in the deepest, most protected region of his brain. The apartment we'd moved to after our father died and we lost the house had no hold on Kurt. If the house were put on a trailer and carried away like the jail, Kurt would still return to 1112 East Collier Street and try to live in the hole that was left behind.

My brother was always happy to see me. Life was forever fresh to Kurt. Big, wet teeth glistened in his dirty face. His beard had a lot of white in it. He was a homeless man heading alone into his late forties. I still remembered when he was smarter than me.

"Is this really necessary?" I asked Itch, jangling the cuff chain.

"Didn't want him stinking up the car."

"I bet the Corbetts like him being cuffed to their porch."

"They aren't home," Itch said.

"Who complained, then?"

"One one one two East—"

"Hush, Kurt." To Itch I said, "Who?"

"*They* did. Then they went to lunch," Itch said. "I told em Crazy Kurt'd be gone when they got back. They're *real* tired of this, Wink."

Kurt liked the sound of the rattled cuffs. "One one one two East Collier—"

"Shut up, Kurt," I said. "Did he try to get in again?"

"No. Just rang the bell about a thousand times."

"One one one two East—"

"Shut your hole!" Itch roared in his face.

"Hey!" I actually slapped Itch on the shoulder with the back of my hand. I knew he'd let me. He'd grown up to be a tall, stocky man with a big butt and fleshy lips and pitted, potatoey skin. He was a bachelor cop skating along on the backwash of his father's power. He would never be in charge, like his father and grandfather had been. And he would never be called to account.

"I can yell at him," I said. "*You* can't."

"This is gonna stop, Winker."

Yeah, yeah, I thought. "Kurt," I said, sharper than I meant to. I always sounded sharper than I meant to with him. "We don't live here anymore."

"One one one—"

"Kurt. Stop."

Itch produced the cuff key. I noticed with undiminished satisfaction that the knuckles of his right hand still bore the disfiguring grooves I had inflicted on him. Not that they made up for anything.

"I think he should live with you," Itch said with malign innocence.

"One one one two East—"

"He's your only living relative," Itch said. "Living in the street."

He hadn't unlocked the cuffs. We both knew what would happen when he did.

"One one one two—"

I put my hand over Kurt's mouth. His breath moistened my palm. I spun—freshly, endlessly enraged—on Jock Itch.

"Why don't *you* take him home?"

"Not my problem, Wink."

"No. Not your problem."

He shrugged, smug. He inserted the cuff key. He had enough experience with Kurt to know to unlock the wrist cuff first. If he unlocked the banister cuff first he'd lose the set, because when Kurt was loose he was gone, off the porch and around the corner so quickly I was perversely proud of him. He was homeless and brain-damaged, but with breakaway speed.

"Stay away from here!" Itch yelled, but he and I knew it was futile. "A change has got to come, Winkler," he said, going coplike and imposing on me.

"Shut up, Officer Itch," I said, and headed for home.

I took Greencloth Street back south to the perp walk, and then followed it east to home. The apple tree branch had been removed. The torn stub had been sawed down to the trunk and smoothed off. Squashed apples, bits of broken leaf, and twigs were scattered on the walk. The tree produced wizened, sour apples that were a bit of a disappointment to us. We never ate them. I could barely be bothered to pick them up.

I noticed a stick of apple wood impaled in the ground. It was about a foot long, with a small fork at one end. Stripped of bark, it had the grainy, smooth texture of wood dead for a while. Its shape reminded me of something. I turned it this way and that. Something. Someone. I stuck it in my hip pocket.

I went into the house for a broom and dustpan, and then began to sweep up what remained of the branch. I wouldn't tell Flo about the latest Kurt episode. I had a rule of thumb: I told her approximately one of every four Kurt incidents. She didn't deal with the helplessness as well as I did. I was good at ignoring the problem. She always wanted to *do* something, repair the irreparable.

Her solution was always for Kurt to come live with us. She imagined in Kurt's comfort and stability in our home a parallel comfort for her brother, cold and blue at the bottom of the swimming pool. In rescuing my brother she would also do something I'd been unable to do for her brother.

I was kneeling to scoop up the small pile of twigs, leaves, and bad apples I had accumulated when movement to the east drew my attention. A young girl came running toward me down the perp walk, a laugh cut off in her throat and transformed into an exhalation of confusion.

She stopped dead. She was maybe a little older than Penny.

"What—?" she began, mystified.

She looked all around. She wore a gray dress that hung to just above her ankles, over it a voluminous blue apron with large pockets outlined in white, and no shoes.

And she was soaking wet.

She took one step toward me, fixing her attention fully on me for the first time. It was an intense—almost frightening—experience.

"What have you done with Dash?" she asked, her voice quavering.

I stood up. "What?" I said.

When I stepped toward her she ran back the way she had come. At Chapman Street she looked both ways, then back at me. She had left wet footprints that were already fading on the walk. Then she turned north. She didn't appear to be lost, just bewildered, and upset, but also a little curious. Her soaked state made me want to help her, but each step I took toward her compelled her to take a step away from me. I kept her in sight until she turned off Chapman, onto Collier, heading unerringly toward downtown.

I found Flo sipping a mug of onion soup, leaning against the kitchen counter in an unbuttoned white lab coat, one ankle crossed over the other. She did not allow herself to sit down in the course of her long day. Sitting invited ease, which opened her to the fact of her tiredness, which would be dealt with at a more convenient time.

I told her about the wet girl.

" 'What have you done with Dash?' " Flo repeated.

"That's all she said."

"Maybe Dash isn't a person. Maybe she meant, 'What have you done with zest?' Charisma. *Joie de vivre.*"

"What? I killed charisma?"

She smiled and kissed me on the cheek. Four cars were in the rear lot. A mother dragged a reluctant child up the brick walk.

"Make something zesty for dinner," she said, and was gone.

Penny might know a Dash. But my daughter was at a kid's house—a boy, no less—the exact location of which was a mystery to me. Some dad I was.

I checked the pantry. I needed potatoes. I left a note to that effect and set off on my bike. I pedaled east on the perp walk to Chapman, then down Chapman to Collier, hoping to see the wet girl. No luck. When I reached the 1100 block of Collier I jogged north to avoid our old house.

A white, double-wide trailer had been rolled onto the town square to serve as the interim police station and jail. Work on the permanent structure had already commenced. A sign read

FUTURE HOME OF
"JACK" KETCH JR.
POLICE HEADQUARTERS

Itch's dad, retired but still imposing, a yellow hardhat balanced like a thimble on his head, stood with the current police chief and pointed out something in a blueprint scroll. I ignored him, as I tried to ignore his son.

The grocery store was across the tracks. I bought potatoes, nutmeg, black pepper, and sausage. I got my pack centered on my back and headed home.

Passing a house on the perp walk between Pincoffin and Pine I was set upon by a dog I had never seen before. Squat and muscular, he charged at me so headlong and ferociously that he snagged—and maybe chipped—a tooth in the fence that surrounded his yard, the pain and indignation only intensifying his outrage at my presence. The dog then turned and galloped along the fence—parallel to me—with such single-minded snarling that I was afraid he had lost sight of the fact that the fence corner was approaching.

Some memory of the dimensions of his world must have wormed through his fury because he turned his head, made a questioning sound like "Proof?" and then to avoid being strained through the mesh hurdled the fence in a leap that surprised the dog only slightly more than it did me.

He stopped. He licked himself. He might have been wondering if he had gone too far, jumping out of his safe, reliable enclosure.

Then he remembered the reason he had jumped. Me.

I had at most a half-block lead, pedaling flat out, faster than I had traveled on a bike in my life. The dog caught me before I reached Pincoffin Street. I streaked across without slowing down. The dog snapped at my tires, at the bike chain, at my pedaling feet, at the handlebar streamers Penny had put on when she was nine.

I drifted to the right, trying to rub the dog off against the fence of the yard we were passing. He wasn't fooled. He slowed enough to get behind me, and then come around on my left.

Side by side we barreled across Pine Street.

I considered pacifying the dog with the sausage. I weighed the physics of reaching behind me, opening my backpack, tearing the sausage wrapper with my teeth, letting the juice dribble onto the dog's muzzle, dropping the entire package if necessary.

No, dammit. It was my family's dinner.

Then we were across Cottonwood Street and back onto the shadowy walk. I was about out of gas. My legs were shot and my lungs shredded. As we came up on Tinker Street I felt something break loose inside me. Some vital sac burst in my brain, or heart, or soul, I couldn't tell which exactly, but it released a liquid heat that was both pleasurable and disturbing.

The world went silent and serene. For a moment I wondered: *Have I had a stroke?* But my body was working fine. I knew who I was. I felt great. I could pedal forever.

Then I figured out why it was so quiet.

The dog was gone.

I rolled to a stop. Up ahead, a car went by on Tinker Street. I checked all around me. No dog.

My breathing slowed.

I recited my phone number, address, Social Security number, various account numbers and PINs, the president's name, the alphabet, Flo's and Penny's birthdays.

Nothing felt amiss. I evidently hadn't had a stroke.

The dog had just disappeared.

The sensation of spreading warmth had melted away. Up the path behind me, a string of dog footprints came out of a wet spot thrown by a lawn sprinkler, and then faded.

The air ticked with heat.

I went on my way. At Tinker, I slowed, checked the street in both directions, and crossed.

Approaching Clover Street, I met the dog coming the other way. He stopped when he saw me. I stopped, too. I expected him to resume being the enraged cur, but he just sat and stared at me, panting. When I moved toward him he turned and ran. When I crossed Clover he was already halfway down the perp walk toward Chapman, running and looking back, running and looking back.

TWO

Penny was on the phone in the kitchen when I returned, the receiver lodged between her ear and her raised shoulder, leaving her hands free to drum with a pair of Flo's tongue depressors on the countertop and the rim of a large mixing bowl. She'd broken eggs into the bowl and arranged the shells like a little village of dome-top huts on a piece of paper towel.

I held open my backpack so she could see its contents. She waved me away. She had other plans. She had not said a word to the person on the other end of the line.

I took a seat at the kitchen table, which was a six-by-twelve-foot oak slab with so many drawers that it absorbed every loose object that landed on it. At present, the table's surface was covered with the official flags of four nations: Iceland, Denmark, Sweden, and Canada.

Penny had gone through a flag phase when she was eight years old and Flo in her zeal to encourage any and all passions exhibited by her daughter—and to ease the guilt of being fifty feet away, but gone all day—managed to acquire nearly a hundred flags from the nations of the world. The M.D. letterhead on the queries she wrote gave her a success rate approaching ninety percent, plus several requests that she bring her excellent U.S.A. medical training to countries short on doctors. One island nation a thousand miles southeast of Manila offered her a plantation that amounted to ten percent of that country's arable land. They had also sent a photo album of every child on the island, each one in an identical pose: smiling, waving with one hand, beckoning with the other. They reminded me of a nation of trainee traffic cops.

The inundation of flags, the colorful mountain they made on the floor of Penny's bedroom as she snapped each flag free of its mailing carton, inspected both sides, and let it fall, killed her interest in them. They had become her mom's project.

When the flags underfoot began to feel disrespectful of the nations in question, the two of us—Penny and I—folded the flags of the world and piled them neatly inside a cedar hope chest, which was then rolled deep into her closet. Flo didn't ask what became of them.

Then last winter, at the first snowfall, Penny unfolded the flags of Brazil, India, Mali, and Panama. When the temperature fell below zero she replaced those flags with Fiji, Niger, Saudi Arabia, and Sri Lanka. Now, in the middle of stormy, steamy August, she had laid out the flags of cooler climates.

She slung a plate of scrambled eggs in front of me. Four triangles of toast rimmed a yellow mountain. She cracked her gum and listened to the other end of the phone conversation. She still had not said a word.

Penny had gone through a waitress phase, too, a period Flo was reluctant to encourage. She feared her daughter finding some deep satisfaction in serving food to strangers for money. But then she recalled her life before her brother drowned, when she felt her own passions went largely unnoticed, fleeting as they might have been. So she bought Penny an apron, an order pad, a name tag, even an order ticket carousel. When Penny told Flo that she envied her her waitress name, Flo began to pay Penny to help around the office.

When the waitress era ended, Penny used the carousel to make short, primitive films, fastening an image to one clip, the same image slightly advanced in the next, and so on. Then she gave the carousel a spin. She made one of herself smiling, of a flower opening, a snowman melting, and finally a finger rising out of a fist.

She abruptly hung up the phone.

"Who was that?"

"Corey and Holly."

"You didn't say anything."

"I wasn't supposed to be there," she said. "It was a three-way."

"You were spying?"

"Holly was checking out how much Corey likes me." She scowled. "She didn't ask any of the questions I would have asked."

"Do you know someone named Dash?" I asked.

"No. I know a Dot. Dotty Muller. Why?"

"I met a girl on the path today. All she said was, 'What have you done with Dash?' I thought it might mean something to you."

"Sorry."

She sat to my right, her back to the window, and began to eat. Her table manners were a little casual and bits of egg spattered about. Flo would have called her on it. I was happy just to have her sit close to me. It was possible for two people to share that table and feel on opposite ends of the room from each other.

"I had a friend named Dott," I said. "Two *t*'s. Todd Dott."

"Two *t*'s in Todd, too?"

I laughed. "No. But we did call him Ta-Todd. Like a stutter. Reversing his last name. Ta-Todd. Dot-ta."

I hadn't thought about Todd Dott in years. He'd had a large head so pale it was nearly translucent and an air of breakability that made everyone anxious to steer clear of him. Jock Itch nicknamed him Bulb Head and the kids who were afraid of Itch took up the name.

"Kids made so much fun of him," I said, "they pretended they could see through his head."

"What?"

"Yeah. His head was very pale. You could see all his veins."

"Hydrocephalic?"

I blinked at her. She smiled. "I learned that from mom."

"What have you learned from me?"

"Oh, daddy." She jumped up and swept away our plates.

"Seriously. What?"

"Marry rich," she said, to shut me up. "And keep my brushes clean."

"And?"

"And my mind and options open."

"Good." I nodded. If she became a doctor it wouldn't hurt my feelings. She would at least be on equal footing with the man she married. I patted my stomach.

"Your mom asked me to make dinner. Now I'm too full."

"Work it off washing the dishes. I'll see you."

"Where are you going?"

"Corey's," she said, and was gone again.

Mention of Todd Dott got me to thinking about how Kurt and Vaughan Garner met. I used to follow Kurt around more than was probably customary for an older brother. Usually it's the kid brother making a pest of himself, pleading to be let in on the big brother's life. The fact was, Kurt always found interesting things for us to do. Two summers before the swimming pool incident he'd led me into the Dragon Hills, the ritzy side of Euclid Heights, where huge, new houses sprouted like toadstools in the cool tree shadows the builders were required by law to maintain. A patrol of busy women, some clutching infants, some tennis rackets, scurried from construction site to construction site making certain no tree was felled that had not been agreed to.

Kurt had led me up Pincoffin Street into the Hills, where grilled-meat smoke hung in the trees, and the ringing hammers and power saws had gone quiet—by law—at five o'clock.

"What's the hurry?" I asked, as we half walked, half ran.

"I was here yesterday," Kurt said. "For some reason they've stopped work on this one house."

A dove-gray Cadillac glided past. The mom at the wheel and the three kids in the back seat gave us the pivoting evil eye. I didn't want to be there. At school, kids from the Dragon Hills were largely stuck-up snots, like they had earned the money to afford that life themselves.

Even Jock Itch, dumb as sand and the son of a glorified municipal employee, lived in there and possessed the Dragon Hills sneer. I don't think Kurt even noticed any of that stuff. I know he'd never mentioned it.

Kurt veered off the street, into a shadowy grove. We came to the edge of a basement excavation.

"Something's wrong," Kurt said in a soft voice. "It was exactly like this yesterday."

A small park was across the street. Kids were playing baseball on the far side of it. Plenty of daylight remained out there. My stomach tightened when I realized one of the kids was Jock Itch, wrenching the bat out of some poor slob's hands. I was pretty sure he hadn't seen us.

When I turned back, Kurt had climbed down into the basement hole.

"It's like the pyramids!" he said excitedly.

"How?"

"It's like archeology. *Come on down!*"

"How are you going to get out?"

He pointed behind him. "There's a big root. It's like a step," he said.

The excavation was eight feet deep. I lowered myself over the side, but before I let go I hung with my feet in the air, my eyes at ground level looking out of the shady building site toward the sunlit baseball diamond, where Itch was pounding the kid who'd been reluctant to give up his bat.

I let go and fell.

Kurt was in the corner nearest the street. The foundation wall loomed above us. There was little direct light down there, but from somewhere he had produced a small flashlight.

"See?" He ran his fingers horizontally along the wall. "See the layers?"

I did see faint striations in the dirt, but to my eye they were only slight variations of dark brown. Kurt touched the wall, delicately, reverently.

"It'd be so neat to find mastodon bones. Or arrowheads. Or something someone a thousand years ago dropped on their way home."

I felt the lengthening pit shadows creep across our heads. I was ready to get out of there. Kurt, however, stepped closer to the wall. He'd seen something.

"Hey," he said. He pulled me to him. "Boost me up."

I laced my fingers together, he set his foot in the step my hands formed, put the flashlight in his mouth and his hand on my shoulder, and I lifted him.

He'd seen something in the wall, about a foot below ground level, and as he reached for it I saw it, too. It was small and black, blacker than the dirt that held it, and with a curve that was out of place in the wall, which was shaved flat and polished by the bulldozer blade's sliding bite. Kurt touched it. He wet his finger and rubbed it.

"It's not dirt or rock," he said, thrilled. "It . . . it's sharp!"

"Hurry up," I said, my arms coming slowly out of their sockets.

"I need a brush," Kurt said. He leaped out of my laced hands. "I need a brush and something with a fine point on it."

I found a bent nail on the ground. "Here."

"We have to close this site down and mark exactly where we found the specimen," he said. "Then we have to take it out from above. Dig down to it. There're probably more specimens around it that we can't see."

"Kurt—"

"You know what it is, don't you?" he asked in a hushed voice.

"What?"

"A saber-toothed tiger tooth."

"I thought I saw you fairies," came a voice from above.

It was Itch.

"Speaking of pyramids," Kurt said to me, "here's one made of flesh."

I couldn't help laughing. Itch did appear awfully wide-based from our angle, his head way up there coming to a point.

He kicked a stone down at us. "Didn't your mommy warn you not to play around big holes in the ground?"

"You're the only hole she warned us about," Kurt said.

"You fairies want company?"

We didn't exactly know what he meant. He stepped out of sight for a minute. I hoped he was gone. But we heard a scuffle, and then Itch reappeared with a small kid he casually flung down into the hole.

The kid hit the ground and went to his knees, throwing out his hands to stop himself. He was big-eared and bony-kneed, with glasses he kept on with a strap around his head, and tears washing down his face.

This was Vaughan Garner.

Itch watched us for a minute, like he expected us to mate or something. We gave the kid some privacy while he gathered his dignity. Itch threw a couple rocks to try and stir us up, then lost interest and left.

"That's a saber-toothed tiger tooth," Kurt told the kid, shining the flashlight up on the wall.

Vaughan didn't pay any attention. He'd wiped his face off with his T-shirt, but he still looked unutterably sad.

"Itch is gone," I said. "He won't bother you."

Vaughan flared at me. "I don't care about him! Marilyn Monroe is dead!"

"She is?" I said.

"Who's Marilyn Monroe?" Kurt asked.

Vaughan laughed disgustedly, like Kurt was hopeless. He removed something from his pocket, unfolded it carefully, and held it out by his fingertips. It was a photograph of a naked woman, blonde, smiling.

"*This* is Marilyn Monroe."

Kurt regarded the picture with only mild curiosity, his mind more on saber-toothed tiger teeth. I was older, and desired a closer examination, but Vaughan folded the picture carefully away.

"I got it from my dad," he said.

"What if he finds out it's gone?" I asked.

"He sees naked girls all the time. He's a doctor."

Kurt tapped my shoulder. "Make a step again," he said.

I relaced my fingers and Vaughan stepped close and did the same. Kurt had the bent nail, and when we'd lifted him to the height of the tooth in the wall he began to pick at the dirt with it. Grains, then clods, fell on us. It didn't take long to dislodge the object.

Kurt displayed it in his hand for us when he got down.

"Saber-toothed tiger tooth," he said. It was black, about a half-inch square at its widest point, and curved to a sharp point.

"Why isn't it fossilized?" Vaughan asked.

"Who said it isn't?"

"Doesn't look fossilized." He reached for the tooth, but Kurt pulled it away.

"My dad could tell us if it's fossilized," Vaughan said.

"I *know* it's a saber-toothed tiger tooth," Kurt said.

"My dad says every idea has to stand up to scrutiny—or you don't know what you have," Vaughan said.

"I don't need to know if it's fossilized," Kurt said.

"I can see from here that your head is," Vaughan said.

We all laughed. Vaughan lived another two years, but those were the last words I remembered hearing him speak.

A thunderstorm from the southwest that afternoon rolled the sky up greenish and hissing. The emergency sirens tripped, at first a tentative moan swallowed by the wind, then a full-throated wail of impending apocalypse.

I went outside to watch the trees fall. Four children were in Flo's office, three of them with mothers, and one, a boy getting a high school football physical, unescorted. Flo watched the sky tumble past her window. I waved to her, but I guess she didn't see me.

One mom, son in tow, made a run for her car. The wind tore a White Sox cap off the kid's head and sent it cartwheeling like a ground ball across the yard to me. The kid didn't even notice. The cap's band was warm and damp. The logo was old-fashioned—the *s* snaking around the *o* and the *x*—from the 1919 Black Sox.

A marble of rain smashed so hard into my cheek that it caused one of my teeth to ache. A foamy curtain of gray-green rain advanced on us from two houses away. It blurred the details of everything it touched and then it washed over me.

The mother and her hatless son returned, double-time, the boy in the lead coming back, pushed along by the wind and the sheets of rain.

At the door to Flo's office the mother stopped and glared at me. She pointed emphatically toward the parking area and screamed something that sounded like, "Ock!"

I followed the brick walk through the downpour, in the direction she had pointed. A large branch had snapped clean off and fallen behind her car. I almost laughed. Flo should've just hired a tree guy to live at the house, in the room she kept half-ready for Kurt.

The blocked mom's thwarted journey got everyone else in Flo's office all in a tizzy. She herded the moms and the kids into the basement, finding places for everyone to sit in the southwest corner. Two towels warm from the dryer were draped over the shoulders of the mother and boy. I put the kid's cap back on his head and he shivered at the fresh chill, but said nothing.

David Harrison, the kid who had come for his football physical, watched the water rise in the window well. It was already three inches deep. It would start to leak into the basement any second.

"Hey!" David exclaimed. He tapped a finger on the glass.

A mouse in the window well struggled in the rising water, its little snout thrust up desperately into the pouring rain. David reached up and for a moment I thought he was going to open the window to save the mouse—and flood the basement—but he only pressed his finger to the spot on the glass where the mouse helplessly scratched.

When I touched his shoulder he jumped like he'd thought he was alone. "Come on," I said. I jerked my thumb upward, a general indication of ascent.

"I hate storms," he said.

His confession reminded me of Penny. Storms terrified her, too, and I couldn't picture her safe at Corey's house.

I found a strainer in a kitchen drawer and went outside. Rain drummed cold on my head.

Two little girls and Flo now had their faces up close to the window well glass, their eyes on the mouse in the rising water. The girls were out of scale, tall as Flo, and I realized she was holding a girl in each arm up to the window to witness the daring mouse rescue. The girls' cheeks were pressed to Flo's. Their mothers watched somewhere back in the basement shadows.

Flo caught my eye.

Then she winked. Not a wink of encouragement, or a consoling wink, but a wink to transmit an understanding of a shared joke.

I dipped the strainer into the water and scooped up the exhausted mouse. It might have been confused by the suddenness of its rescue, because as soon as I tipped it out onto the grass it made a beeline back to the well. I had to block it with my foot or it would have jumped right back in. Finally, it gave up and scurried away, hugging the wall of the house.

The storm's ferocious leading edge had moved on. I went back down into the basement, passing mothers and kids who followed Flo up. Water had begun to trickle into the basement from around the window well glass.

I handed David Harrison an empty wastebasket. The phone rang.

"Bail out the window well!" I said.

"It's still storming!"

"The worst is over," I assured him, just as a bolt of lightning silvered the water I wanted him to remove.

The kid peered hopelessly into the empty wastebasket.

Flo tapped me on the shoulder with the phone. "Penny," she said.

I took the phone, then grabbed Flo's arm to hold her in place.

"Bail out the window well and Dr. Flo here will give you a free physical."

I didn't wait for either the kid or my wife to respond.

"Hello!" I yelled into the phone.

"Come get me, daddy?" Penny asked. She sounded close to tears.

"Sure, sweetheart. Where are you?"

"I don't know."

A worm of impatience curled into my mind, a reaction I was instantly ashamed of.

"Are you at Corey's?"

"No. I'm at someone's house."

"Who's there?"

"A man," Penny said.

A crack of lightning struck simultaneously outside the house and at the other end of the phone connection. She gave a little scream.

So she was nearby.

"Ask him—"

"He says he's Mr. Burton."

"Let me talk to him, sweetheart."

Mr. Burton sounded affably nervous, probably just a guy who gave a pretty girl shelter from the storm, then discovered her to be more of a handful than expected.

He lived over on Holt Street. He told me the address.

"She's okay here until the storm ends," Mr. Burton said.

"I'll come now."

"I can drive her home."

"I'm on my way."

David Harrison was on his knees in the grass beside the window well, shoulders slumped, water streaming down his face. Next to him were three dead newborn mice, arranged like pink shrimp appetizers on the grass. He'd found them floating in the water. I touched his wet head but didn't have time to stop and talk.

The fallen tree that had prevented Flo's Black Sox fan and his mom from leaving had blocked me in, too. I'd forgotten an umbrella and I didn't want to waste time going back for one. Out of touch with Mr. Burton, I was less confident of his innocent helpfulness.

I plunged across Chapman Street, then down the next link of the perp walk. Strips of green plastic blown out of the fence on the south side of the path slashed at me as I sprinted past. My forward motion only intensified the pounding of the rain. Within a block I was exhausted.

I forgot to check for traffic on Spinney Street until I was halfway across, and then didn't bother. On the perp walk connecting Spinney and Holt that sac of liquid warmth that I'd felt when the dog was on my heels burst again in my head, and because I had lived through it once I gave in to it unreservedly. For the space of five steps I felt like I could run forever.

Then the rain stopped. It didn't peter out or drift away. It stopped like a tap closing.

The wind fell away, too. The sky threatened, though, a wall of thunderheads tumbling in the southwest. The municipal sirens played their opening notes.

The perp walk was dry.

I stopped running. My breathing came in gasps, but I couldn't tell if I was exhausted or merely astonished.

I'd reached Holt Street. Mr. Burton's street. His house was just north of the perp walk's mouth.

I stood for a minute on his front porch, watching the storm approach, my mind trying to fit together a puzzle of a few very odd pieces, but never putting them together in a shape that made any sense.

The wind was new, cool, and on the rise.

I rang the doorbell. A man answered. He was polite, but wary, the normal response to an unexpected visitor as a storm approached.

"Mr. Burton?"

"Yes?"

"I'm here to pick up my daughter," I said.

He frowned, but solicitously. Thunder rumbled behind me.

"I'm sorry," he said. "You must have the wrong house."

"Her name's Penny. She called me—" My voice trailed away.

"There's no one here but me," he said.

The pieces of the puzzle shifted and locked. I decided not to fight against the conclusion. I apologized to Mr. Burton and walked back into the street.

I saw no sign of Penny. She was somewhere nearby, though, maybe still at Corey's house, maybe not knowing the storm was so close, but already on the path toward her intersection with Mr. Burton.

If you're going to travel through time, you should wear a watch. I had never replaced the one I ruined when I dove into the swimming pool. I couldn't be absolutely sure, but my sense of time and the status of the approaching storm led me to estimate fifteen minutes.

A quarter-hour gained. Regained.

I had an overwhelming desire to see my wife. I hurried back toward my home, back down the perp walk links. When I reached our yard the wind was up strong and the first cold drops of rain burned through my shirt.

I watched the tree branch at the rear of our property snap off and fall behind the cars in the lot.

I watched the rain sweep in again.

Everything again.

The mother and her son hurried down the path toward the rear lot. The wind tore off the kid's Black Sox cap but I wasn't in position to field it.

The oddness froze me there in the backyard. I felt like I was wasting a gift, a talent I didn't understand well enough to use. Given a second chance, all I could do was watch the fifteen minutes unfold again. I also felt a strange pity for Flo, her patients, Penny, Mr. Burton, everyone, as they all lived through that gift fifteen minutes just for my benefit. I felt in control of them only because I knew what came next.

Still, what a waste. Such a lost opportunity. I hadn't even been able to keep the kid's hat on his head.

I saw movement in the grass behind our house. It was the mouse, running through the rain toward the window well. I got in front of it and diverted it with my foot. The mouse climbed over the toe of my shoe and resumed its headlong rush. I blocked it again. It went around my foot. It wouldn't give up. It was determined to go over the side into the water.

I remembered the newborn mice. They were why the mouse wouldn't quit. They were the lives I could save, the destinies I could alter. But when I looked down into the water I saw them already afloat, pink fingerlings washed out of their beds.

An adult mouse swam among them. I thought it was the mouse I'd just seen, that somehow it had slipped past me and plunged over the side, but a second adult mouse watched over the lip of the well in an anguished spectator's pose.

It dawned on me: This was a family. A parent to run things at home, another to handle things in the larger world. I imagined the pregnant mother falling into the well by mistake. The babies were born down there. The father watched from above. It was a sort of life. Probably not the life they would choose, but better than the family whose father was snatched into the air by a hawk, or whose mother couldn't outrun a cat.

When I looked again the water was up and the outside mouse was hopping away. Down through the rising water I saw Flo step forward holding up the two little girls, cheek to cheek to cheek. I waited on the wink, and although I was ready for it, it bothered me when it came: so un-Flo, cynical and manipulative.

A lot could happen in fifteen minutes, and at the same time, not much at all. I felt myself catching up to the present. Soon I would be living through time I hadn't lived through already.

I went into the house. I felt as wet and helpless as I had that long-ago day by the Euclid Heights pool.

David Harrison was there in the kitchen. I handed him an empty wastebasket.

The phone rang.

"Bail out the window well," I said.

I didn't offer the kid a free physical. We might need the money. He opened his mouth to speak but I cut him off.

"I don't care if you *are* afraid of storms. Bail."

Flo, from somewhere nearby, held out the phone to me.

"Penny," she said.

THREE

I waited until the following day before I told Flo about my quarter-hour journey back in time. I ventured into her office after her last patient had gone home. It felt important that I meet her on her own turf, considering the story I had to tell. A relaxed, satisfied quiet of completion was the mood of the moment. No office windows faced west, so an early twilight was in force, and Flo had switched on at least one light in every room. Penny was out with her friends, all fear of the previous day's storm gone in that way children can be rid of such things until such things return.

Flo was changing the roll of paper on an examination table. I took a seat on a four-wheel stool, which put my head at the level of her waist, and gave her a straightforward account of the previous day's events. I was prepared for the scientist side of her personality to dissect what I said, but she didn't interrupt. I wished she had. As my story spun out she stopped what she was doing. By the time I finished she was motionless and staring at me.

"Time travel," she said.

I had to smile, shrug.

"Fifteen minutes at a time," she said.

"We were having dinner last night after the storm, just the three of us, everyone safe, talking and laughing," I said. "And I thought—I want to relive *this*. I was so happy. You and Pen getting along. I wanted to see it again."

"That's why I live each *moment* to the fullest," she said, leaving the room.

I went after her. "You sound like an infomercial."

"You *can't* live your life over," she said. "Once it's gone—it's gone."

"But I did."

"I want you to get an MRI." She whipped out her prescription pad.

"No, Flo."

"I'll call Sherm Paperink. He's a neurologist." She wrote rapidly on the pad. "He'll give you a straight answer fast."

"Flo."

She tore off the script and handed it to me. For the moment she wasn't my wife. She was my primary care physician, the worst kind of sawbones passing a hopeless case on to the next level.

"Something—" she began. She paused for breath. "Something caused you to believe you went back in time. The warm liquid feeling. Your thinking it was a stroke. Maybe it was. But it should definitely be checked out."

She put a cool hand on my cheek, my wife again, checking for fever.

"Do you remember when you winked at me through the basement window?" I asked.

She shook her head and grimaced. "What?" she said, dumbfounded.

"I should've kept my mouth shut," I said.

"No," she said. "I believe you *think* you experienced what you said you experienced. Then you ask if I remember winking at you. It's such a non sequitur."

"You were holding up two kids," I said. "I was saving the mouse. When you saw me you winked. Both times."

"Both times," she said skeptically. "Okay. So I winked."

"I didn't like you then."

"Oh?"

"Because your wink said, 'Look at me pretending to care about these two kids. But my wink lets you know that you and I both know I am only doing this so their moms will tell their friends what a warm-hearted, caring doctor I am.' "

"All that from one wink?" Flo said coldly.

"Yes." Again, I should have kept my mouth shut.

"So I'm not as genuine as you thought," she said. "Deal with it. I don't even remember winking—but maybe I thought I could share a little of my evil side with my husband and he'd understand and accept me."

"I do."

"You can't accuse me of not caring about my patients."

"I don't."

"And it's easy to criticize when *you* don't *need* good word of mouth."

For the space of a long-ago heat wave, in our third-floor apartment, I had taken to painting on Flo as she slept. She was in the middle of her pediatric residency at Children's Memorial Hospital. Her father mailed us a monthly check, addressed to us both, which Flo always opened. My watercolors on her belly or thigh or the backs of her knees made her smile when she awoke—still exhausted—to go back to work. She claimed to not be aware of my painting on her, but the brush was wet and cool, and often she would stretch languidly in her sleep and open the canvas of her skin to me.

She refused to allow me to photograph my paintings, and each little masterpiece went down the shower drain. My more permanent work struck less of a chord with art show shoppers and browsers. I exhibited in and around Chicago, in parking lots, on sidewalks and closed-off streets, one time in a cavernous, concrete municipal garage that was so chilly even in summertime that my feet went numb through my shoes, and I tracked in oil when I got home.

A show was a success if I earned back the booth fee.

After one such show, as I packed up, Flo's father appeared. He was a self-assured, impatient man, always in a coat and tie, his utter lack of self-doubt making him extremely hard for me to be around. Without a word of greeting he began to simultaneously help me pack and examine my work.

"You removed the price tags," he noticed.

"Bad luck to leave them on," I said. "They might start thinking they aren't worth what I asked for them."

"They?" he said. "Them?"

I shrugged. We worked together in silence for a minute.

"I never thanked you, did I?" he said. "For trying."

I understood what he meant, but not how to let him know. So I gave him a moment's privacy while I slid a watercolor into a protective sleeve.

"It always feels *wrong* somehow that you and Flo are together."

I wasn't sure I had heard him correctly.

"In a way, unhealthy," he said.

"I never thought of it like that."

"You're like two wounded animals trying to live together. You should each be with a healthy person."

I laughed, too flummoxed to be angry.

"You both witnessed the worst thing that ever happened to the other one," he said. "Good marriages have been built on less, I suppose. Which one—" He spread his hands over the pieces both packed away and out in the open. "Which one is the most expensive?"

"I can't tell you that," I said.

" 'Can't' is the operative word in that sentence."

When Dr. Garner visited our steaming apartment, and Flo was at the hospital—as she almost invariably was—he went from room to room dispensing advice and platitudes of self-fulfillment. He was confident that it was only a matter of indoctrinating me in his system of self-confidence before I was hanging in the Louvre and the Art Institute, my every doodle fought over with fistfuls of cash.

"Success is like painting a picture," he said. "You've got to see it in your mind first. If it isn't in your mind—it won't be in your life. Can't.

Couldn't. Never. Wouldn't. Those are the words that will cut you off at the knees every time."

"Okay," I said.

In answer to his question about my most valuable piece, I unpacked the painting that—aside from the pane done in my Glass Period—was Flo's favorite. It was a watercolor of her father, napping on the couch in our apartment, his large hands folded on his stomach, his necktie taut, vest buttoned, the stone jut of his jaw not relaxed even in sleep. I called it *Doubtless in Dreamland.* The first thing Flo asked when I returned from every show was, "Did anyone buy it?"

"Is that me?" he asked, leaning in, adjusting his glasses.

"Yes. It's Flo's favorite."

"When did you paint that?"

"At our apartment."

"I've never gone to sleep there," he said, sounding harried and accusatory.

"Once."

He straightened. "I don't care for it."

"She says she's never seen you asleep."

"That's nonsense," he said. "I've tried to be a sentinel in my children's lives. But of course I have to sleep."

"That's what she said."

"How much?" he asked.

"A million dollars."

He raised an eyebrow. "That's a little high, even for me."

"She doesn't want me to sell it. So I charge a million."

He turned the painting to catch better light. I had sat in an adjoining room and painted him from a distance. He'd had a dainty snore. I'd worked an hour before he awoke, and finished it from memory.

"Is there any give in the price?"

"For you—half off," I said, and waited for him to laugh.

He didn't. It gave me a thrill of fear that I might have come into his price range, both for the possibility of that much money, and because I didn't know how I would explain it to Flo.

"It's like I'm laid out for a funeral," he said.

"Kind of."

"Is that how you dream of me? Out of the picture?"

"Of course not."

"I'll give you five thousand for it."

"I can't. Not even for you."

"You ever sold anything for five thousand dollars?"

I lied. "Yes."

"What's the most you've ever been paid for a painting?"

"It's Flo's favorite. It's as close to being not for sale as I can make it."

"Ten thousand. And I'll give it to Flo as a gift."

I wanted to bring home ten thousand dollars. At the show in question, I'd sold enough to only almost make back the booth fee. Ten thousand would be an unexpected contribution to the baby we wanted to have.

"That's one percent of the asking price," I said.

He had his checkbook out. I glimpsed the tasteful, embossed checks that came in the mail, made out to Mrs. Flora Garner Winkler. I was being bought off on a monthly basis, but at least I had a middle-person to route the money through. That cushion would be gone if I took his money.

"That's too much of a discount even for you," I said.

So I had the MRI done. Flo's connections got me in the next day. But there was no hastening the results.

"If it's a terminal diagnosis," I said, "I can just keep going back fifteen minutes to avoid receiving it."

Flo didn't smile. "I have patients to see."

"If I do have, say, a tumor, and I'm able to keep reliving the same quarter hour—"

Her expression went fixed and perturbed. "You wouldn't be reliving the fifteen minutes," she said. "You'd just think you were."

"Right. But. Okay. Fingernails. Hair. Tumors. Any part of the body that grows. If you go back fifteen minutes—would you reverse the growth of those parts of your body?"

"I don't know," she said impatiently. "Maybe. Technically."

She had moved to her office door. She was standing in the shadows and hard to read.

"I'm going to work a little," I said, hoping to impress her with my industry.

"I don't think anything has ever happened that wasn't supposed to happen," she said. "People dying. People meeting and falling in love. Or not meeting. A car turning left or right. You—me—people are *not* supposed to go back and mess with that stuff."

"I agree. Or I did."

The front doorbell sounded. A man was there. I recognized him at once. Flo consulted her watch.

"Fred Burton," the man said. We shook hands. I introduced Flo. I expected her to make her excuses and return to her office, but something pending in the situation kept her there.

"I've been thinking," Burton said. "Since the storm?"

"Yes?"

"Penny's okay?"

"Oh, yes. Thank you," Flo said.

But Burton did not look at her. Only at me.

"She was such a basket case," he said. "I'm glad I was home to help her."

"I think if she could just get through one of those storms on her own, she'd be okay," I said. "But she's like me—not good in a crisis."

Burton chuckled politely.

"The thing is," he said, "I can't figure out how you knew to come to my house."

"You called us," Flo said.

"No," Burton said, his eyes on me. "The first time."

I tried to formulate an answer, even as Flo's curiosity increased to match Burton's. This was a wrinkle in the story I hadn't told her.

"What's he talking about?" she said to me.

"Yes," Burton said, encouraged to have someone on his side. He directed his words to Flo. "Before the storm hit, before Penny came to my door soaked and crying, your husband rang my doorbell and said he was there to pick up his daughter. Said her name was Penny. A stranger asking for a girl I'd never heard of. I told him no one was there. He leaves—and just a few minutes later there she is. Penny." He held out his arm. "Gooseflesh, even now. It was kind of like seeing a ghost."

I had a thought: Go back fifteen minutes and don't answer the door when Burton came calling. But he would still be out there, with his suspicions, his eyewitness's conviction.

"See, the thing is," I said, Burton's expression avid and hopeful. "You've lived in that house how long?"

"Nine years."

Longer than I would have liked, but since it was a length of time less than Penny's age, I could work with it.

"Penny had a friend who lived in that house before you did," I said. "When she was five we picked out safe houses on each block—places she could go if she ever got in trouble. Her friend's house—your house now—was the safe house on Holt Street. We never had to use any of them, luckily. When the storm hit, I just had a hunch. It didn't occur to me that her friend no longer lived there."

"A hunch," Burton said skeptically.

"Yes."

"Why go to the safe house on Holt, though? Why not the safe house on some other street?"

"She'd told me before she left that she was going to visit a friend on Holt."

Flo evidently felt I had matters under control. "I've got to go to work," she said.

"What do you do?" Burton asked politely.

"I'm a pediatrician."

"Where's your office?"

"Right here." She pointed toward her distant chambers, but reluctantly, as if afraid to reveal too much to this man.

"I didn't know this neighborhood was zoned for business," he said.

"For a number of years," Flo said.

"How fortunate for you," Burton said.

I took the stick of apple wood I had found on the perp walk and positioned it upright in the vise on my workbench, protecting the spongy, washed-out wood from the vise's pinch with a sleeve of foam rubber. If past experience was any guide—and it usually was—the nature of what drew me to the stick would become clear only when I was finished with it.

The stick took a coat of green watercolor paint so thirstily that only the faintest algae tint remained when the wood dried. Slightly more of a second coat clung to the surface. Four coats of green and the green finally held, but in a color closer to olive drab, which did not feel right for whatever it was I had in mind.

I immediately switched to a tempera red. Then a golden yellow that came out tawny on the stick. Nothing helped me understand what I was seeking.

I was called to dinner. Flo and Penny were dishing take-out Chinese. I washed my hands, then took a plate and scooped food onto it. The twilight amazed me. The sun had been high and hot when I had last paid attention to it.

"I saw you in the backyard," Flo said. "Then you were gone."

A tone in her voice made me stop eating. I glanced at Penny. What had Flo told her?

"Did you think I'd gone back in time?"

Penny did not appear to be listening.

"No. Into the future," Flo said. "For stock tips." She gave me a cool smile.

"What are you guys talking about?" Penny asked.

"Nothing."

"Time travel?" she said.

"Your father said he went back in time fifteen minutes," Flo said.

Penny turned to me. "You did?"

"Yes."

"Cool! When? How?"

"During the storm. I was running to get you from Mr. Burton's house. You'd called. Remember?"

"The guy creeped me out."

"What else do you remember?"

"I was mad at myself because I should've stayed at Corey's. But I was trying to be brave—then this like gigantic bolt of lightning hit right next to me and I just lost it. And the guy was right there. In his garage. Staring at me."

"Like he knew you were coming?"

"I guess."

"In a way, he did."

She gave me a doubtful smile. "So—can you go into the future?" she asked, half teasing, half curious.

"I don't know. I don't even know how I went back."

"I thought you needed like a machine or something."

"You need a really vivid imagination," Flo said, "which we know your father has."

"Or a tumor," I said, to hurt Flo by scaring Penny.

"You have a tumor?"

"No. That was your mother's diagnosis when I told her."

"She *is* a doctor."

"Don't I know it?"

"Well, that is *so* cool," Pen said. "So now, if you say something that makes mom mad you can go back fifteen minutes and unsay it."

"Or phrase it better," I said.

"You can edit your life."

"Well, it's not like I can just hit a button."

My plate was clean. Much usable daylight remained.

"I'm going downtown." I tapped Penny on the shoulder. "Want to come with?"

She glanced at her mother. Something unspoken existed between them.

"Mom wants me to help out in the office tonight."

"I have state kids coming in," Flo said. "Some Penny's age. I want her around—sort of as an example of what is possible."

"You mean what is possible if they had two parents, no kids of their own, and no crack habit."

"These kids aren't like that," Flo said. "They have a little hope to build on."

The perp walks sped me past watering men, through citronella smoke, and the earnest gabble of a lawn party. No sign of the dog between Pincoffin and Pine. I rode on into downtown.

On the square, Kurt waved to me. He was with another man and my impulse was to wave back and keep moving.

I couldn't, though. Kurt's guileless wave triggered a memory.

I had been a sophomore in driver's ed, behind the wheel of a car stuffed with a PE teacher named Mr. Furfooz and four students, when we drove past Kurt on the shoulder of the highway. He was striding along with his T-shirt off.

"Hey!" came a voice from the back seat. "It's Kuh-razy Kurt!"

Jock Itch jabbed a stubby finger between the seats and into my ribs and cackled so close to my ear that I felt a mist of spit. Worse was my impulse to flick the wheel, lose control in a way that would be excused in a sophomore driver's ed student, and run my brother down. Free him from himself. Free us from him.

But I swept past and everyone in the car but me turned to stare back at Kurt, who waved, enjoying the attention. He was fourteen and free to roam. A truant nobody bothered to hound.

"What happened to him?" a girl asked.

"Yeah," Itch said. "What *did* happen to him?"

At Euclid High I jumped out and opened the car's rear door like a gentleman and when Itch grabbed the frame to pull himself out I slammed the door so hard on his hand that the latch caught.

"Sorry, Itch," I said to the shrieking kid. "I don't know what happened."

Kurt was a year younger than I was, but now he looked fifteen years older. Life without reliable shelter had frozen and thawed him so many times that the skin on his face was permanently chapped, cracked over the sharp hollows of his cheekbones, setting off the hard blue of his eyes. Incessant walking and a haphazard diet kept him lean. His hair was mostly gray now, and grown halfway down his back, bound with an Indian bead belt I remembered giving him for his birthday the year of the swimming pool.

When I stepped close to him and his friend I caught a whiff of onions and engrained cigarette smoke.

"Buy one one one two East Collier Street, Euclid Heights, Illinois. Six zero zero zero one," Kurt said.

His friend had an anticipatory twinkle in his eye. "He wants to live in his old house."

"It's not ours anymore."

"Buy one one one—"

"It's not even for sale," I told Kurt. "And you stay away from there." I felt like a bully, pointing a finger at him.

"My old house is on Quail," the other man said. "One oh six North." He said it with such longing.

"What happened?" I asked.

He shrugged. "You know. Bad turns."

"Buy one one one two East—"

"One day I just wasn't welcome."

"What's your name?" I asked.

"Doug Vug," he said. "I was in freshman algebra with you."

"You were?"

"The year Mr. Butterwright's dad died."

I didn't remember anything about that.

"I got an A," Doug Vug said.

"I'm pretty sure I didn't."

"Buy one one—"

I faced Kurt. "That's not gonna happen."

"We need a place to stay," Doug said. "Winter's coming."

"Did you put this idea in his head?" I asked him.

"It's always been in his head."

"Buy one one one—"

"Your wife's a doctor, man."

"My wife—my life—are none of your business."

"Buy one one—"

"Kurt! *Shut! Up!*"

"Hey, he's your brother, man," Doug Vug scolded.

"You got an A in algebra," I said. "*You* buy it."

"But you've got the doctor wife."

FOUR

I returned home, my reason for going downtown forgotten. Kurt and Doug Vug were like a wall I'd hit, and the truest bounce was back to my family. I returned by a telltale route, very Euclidean in keeping to long lines and right angles, which consumed a little more time, but did not deliver me a quarter hour out of step with the rest of the world.

The state van was in the parking lot. Flo was with the wards, her office wing ablaze with light. The kids were older in that night's group. They could be a tough, sad, sullen bunch, and I wondered if they noticed that Flo left them no dark places to hide, no shadows where they might lurk. They were almost always girls. Sometimes they brought babies, sometimes they brought questions about menstruation, or condoms, or Ecstasy, questions about the nutritional value of Reese's Peanut Butter Cups, about mean streaks in boys, about the bruises they carried and when they could be expected to fade.

The lights were turned off in the other half of the house. I heard the ebbing rumble of a flushed toilet. Penny was not in her room, but stick-on stars on her ceiling still held their glow. The light was off in my studio, but the glow-in-the-dark switch plate still emitted a faint green pulse. I felt like I was tracking a trail of fading clues through the house.

I flipped on the light and crossed to my worktable, where the painted stick remained carefully upright in the vise. I appraised the color. It had faded further. I was reminded of my thwarted errand. Unhorsed by my brother and his friend.

Then I saw the girl in the mirror.

She stood in the corner behind the door. Her arms were folded across her chest and her eyes were closed. I wondered if that was her way of hiding, thinking that if she couldn't see me then I must not be able to see her.

But she was only protecting her eyes from the sudden light. Little by little she got them open and fixed plaintively on me.

"My—" I said, putting a hand on my chest. "You scared me."

She was on the brink of tears, waiting for the worst. She was about Penny's age, pale skinned, no makeup, looking horribly uncomfortable in denim coveralls with a homeboy sag in the crotch, shredded knees, an Insane Clown Posse T-shirt and Dr. Martens with the laces removed, like she was a suicide risk. Maybe she was.

"You want Dr. Flo," I said.

"She sent me to talk to you."

As she stepped toward me, her movement jarred something loose in my memory. I glanced at the door. Where was Flo?

"She said you would know what happened to me."

"What happened," I repeated.

"Please," she said. The tears she'd been holding in began to fall. "It rained terribly hard. We stayed under the trees too long. Dash chased me."

It came to me, finally: "The wet girl!"

She blinked at me.

"Dash," I said. "Who *is* Dash?"

"My beau. Dash Buckley."

I offered her a seat but she declined. I tried to arrange my questions in a coherent order. There were too many to know exactly where to begin, I decided. Best to start asking and let her answers point the way.

"What's *your* name?"

"Constance Morceau."

"And you live around here?"

"I don't know. I *did*." She drew a deep breath. "I *believe* I did. But I can't go anywhere in Hickory Hill before—"

"In where?"

"Here. Hickory Hill."

Three questions in and I was lost. I gathered myself. "Tell me about Dash."

She brightened and wiped her eyes. "He's the dearest young man. I miss him terribly."

"But he chased you."

"We were in the orchard," she said, a blush warming her face. "I had made up my mind that I would allow him to kiss me. When the lightning crashed he thought my father had caught us."

Voices sounded outside the house. I checked the window. Three people walked down the path to the state van.

"Don't make me go with them," Constance pleaded. "They've put me in this awful house full of strangers. They made me change the diaper on this pretty Negro baby. The next night this dreadfully filthy little boy with sores and a shiner was delivered to them. I had to wake up and read to him." She began to cry in earnest. "I want *my* family back."

The studio door opened and Flo was there, aglow in her white lab coat. She carried a single, thin file folder.

"You found him," she said to Constance in a friendly voice.

"She doesn't want to go with the others."

Flo folded her arms. "I see."

"How did the state get her?" I asked.

"The police picked her up."

Constance nodded. "They found me on the porch of Dash's house."

"Dash has a house?"

"He rents a room. I had to pee but the privy was gone." Constance went to the studio window. "That's one of our trees," she said, pointing to the apple tree next to the perp walk. "Where are the others?"

"I don't know," I said.

Flo read from a police report contained in the file folder.

"Subject persistently uncooperative in interview. Possible runaway. No family on record. Place in foster care."

"I *have* a family," Constance said.

"When is your birthday?" I asked.

"All Hallows' Eve."

Flo and I exchanged a glance.

"What year?"

"You won't believe me."

"*I* will," I said.

"I know what year this is," she said like a warning.

We waited.

"Do I look a hundred and six?"

"You're well preserved for a hundred and six," I joked.

She didn't smile. "I am fifteen years old. I was born in 1893. I have a mother and father, a beau, a life." The tallying up of what was important brought her to tears again. "And I want them back!"

Penny shyly knocked on the doorway. She also wore a white lab coat, with yellow rubber gloves almost to her elbows.

"Hilly's looking for her." She nodded at Constance.

"Don't make me go," Constance begged.

"We have no legal right to keep her," Flo said.

"Wait here," I said to Penny. "Keep her company till we get back."

I steered Flo out of the studio, free of Constance's subjective presence.

"What do you think?" I asked.

"I think she's one of the finest young actresses I have ever seen," Flo said.

I pushed past this. "Can we get custody of her?"

"Why should we *have* custody of her?"

"She strikes me as genuine. Some of the things she says."

"Beau."

"Right. And privy. And All Hallows' Eve. Who talks like that these days?"

"Someone who's trying to con someone," Flo said.

"In light of what happened to me . . . don't you think—?"

Hilly Cutter, put out and perspiring, found us.

"Dr. Flo," she sputtered, "I have a schedule to keep, as I'm sure you are aware."

"I'm sorry, Hilly."

"Where has our Constance Morceau got herself to?"

"She's in my studio," I said. "She doesn't want to go with you."

"*None* of those children want to go with me. I don't particularly want to go with them. *Nevertheless.*"

"She's made accusations," I said.

Hilly's eyes narrowed. "Against . . . ?"

"Not you," Flo said.

"Against . . . ?"

"Where's her foster family?"

"Right here in town."

"She doesn't like them."

Hilly let out a roaring sigh. "They've been in the system seventeen years without a complaint. They're very strict but loving folks. They've adopted three of their foster kids over the years. One of them works for us now. They won't let our Constance lollygag, but they're fine."

"Do you know her?" I asked. "Constance? Has she been in the system before?"

"Me, personally? No." She consulted a file. "She's new to us. But that doesn't mean anything."

"Can she stay here tonight?"

"Absolutely not. I signed that child out. If I don't *return* her, that's a black mark on my record. And I don't abide black marks. So please produce Mizz Morceau."

"There isn't a form we could sign?"

"Oh, I've got forms of every shape, size, and color you could sign," Hilly said. "But none of them will keep that girl here tonight."

We returned to the studio. The light was on, but Constance and Penny were gone.

"Penny!" Flo said, a general hailing.

No answer.

"That girl has put me so late I have to start all over figuring out how to spend what little time I've got left on this Earth," Hilly complained.

"Penny!" I called. I was suddenly uneasy with the idea of my daughter on the loose with that strange girl.

"Constance Morceau!" Hilly barked.

We stood listening at the center of the house.

"And I was in such a good mood that I was going to treat the kids to ice cream on Illinois's dime. *Constance! More! So!*"

Hilly stalked back into my studio, whipped open each closet door in turn, gave each overloaded space enough of a glance to determine that no girl was hiding within it, then slammed shut the door.

"You some sort of camp counselor?" she asked me.

"No," I said, nettled.

"You're heavy on all this *crafty* stuff—pipe cleaners and paint and clay and stuff. Like you're fixing to keep kids shut up and busy on a rainy afternoon."

Flo broke out laughing, a laugh so full of delight that Hilly joined in.

"I say something?" she asked.

"She's just never heard my life boiled down so succinctly."

"Hey, be proud." She poked a finger into my chest. "You got a sweet deal working here." She walked back out of the studio. "*Constance Morceau!*"

"What?" came a small voice.

We found the girl standing on ground we had already covered. She came across all innocent and inconvenienced.

"The others sent me to find you," she said.

"I'm sure!"

"They want ice cream on Illinois's dime."

"Uh-huh." Hilly waved goodbye, then walked to the van.

"Where's Penny?" I asked.

"Inside," Constance said. She gave us a little curtsy. "Thank you for listening."

"Come visit," I said. "I'd like to talk about your situation."

"My situation is that I want to go home."

■ ■ ■ ■

Flo returned to her offices and I went inside to see Penny, to get her take on Constance. A note was on the kitchen table, white paper against Sweden blue. *At Corey's. Back soon. P.*

It maddened me, her casual confidence in the future. I would have warned her to stay off the perp walks.

Flo found me an hour later sitting on the front porch. She'd hung up her lab coat and brushed out her hair.

"Pour me a glass of wine?" she said.

"I'm waiting for Pen to come home."

"I thought she was."

"She went to Corey's."

"Corey," Flo repeated. She sat down beside me.

"What's the story with him?" I asked.

"He's a good kid. Dad's in computers. Mom sells radio ad space. She should be home by now."

"She's fifteen."

Flo smelled of the soap that she used at the end of the day to wash herself clean of the least trace of what she did.

"If she was a hundred and six, I'd still worry," Flo said. We both laughed. "This is crazy, you know?"

"I'm just sitting on the porch waiting for my daughter to come home."

"You know what I mean."

"It's unusual," I said. "I'll grant you that."

"There's something—some sort of trick being played," Flo said. "It may not be apparent now, but it's there." She patted my knee, stood and stretched. "And *you* will have to figure it out. I don't have the time. I want some wine."

"I keep thinking about her family. How do they explain her just disappearing?"

"No one has to explain anything," Flo said. "Time travel doesn't happen. Fifteen minutes or a hundred and six years. We have to slog along in the time we have. It has features to recommend it."

"I'm not—I'm not longing to live in a different time," I said. "I like it here."

She leaned over, put her hands on my shoulders, and kissed the top of my head. "Remember, you've got a sweet deal working here," she said. "Now. Wine."

I stayed put while she went into the kitchen. I witnessed three cars pass on Clover, then a truck, a sputtering pickup that drew no attention to itself beyond the fact it had an old silhouette, a bulky 1930s roundness, a sense of being out of place. I told Flo about it when she brought out the wine, a basket of warm pretzels, and a tub of honey mustard.

"Don't," she said, abruptly grave. "An old truck is not proof—or even an indication—of a rip in the time-space continuum."

"Isn't it awfully coincidental?" I said. "I go back fifteen minutes—then this girl appears."

Flo sipped and chewed.

"I think it had something to do with the lightning," I said.

"Like *Back to the Future*?" she scoffed. "No. Listen. It wasn't the lightning. It wasn't the rain. It wasn't you running really fast or pedaling your bike at the speed of light. It was just a couple coincidences that lined up—I will admit—in a pretty otherworldly way. But it *wasn't* time travel."

"I thought you'd be more open-minded."

"Don't start."

She poured more wine. I ate a pretzel. It really was a beautiful night.

"Why would you want to go back into the past anyway?" Flo said. "That's where all the trouble starts."

"I didn't *try* to go back in time," I said.

She put a hand on my knee, then leaned around in front of me to plant a kiss, her lips soft with wine. I checked her watch. We'd waited half an hour for Penny to return.

"This is the kind of time travel I like," she said. "Sitting here with you. One second following another."

I couldn't disagree.

"Kurt wants to buy back our old house," I said.

"Why?"

"It's home."

"Is it even for sale?"

"No. But you're a doctor."

"If people only knew what I clear—"

A movement at the corner of the house stopped her. Penny emerged from the perp walk, walked right up to us, natural as can be, lifted my wine glass out of my hand, and sipped.

"Did you turn twenty-one when we weren't looking?" I asked.

"I traveled into the future to when I was twenty-two and stole my driver's license from me." She handed back my glass. "Wanna see it?"

"What are you like at twenty-two?" Flo asked.

"Even more perfect," Penny said, cutting a pose. "My tongue ith pierthed."

"Who was at Corey's?"

"Regan and Holly."

"Were his parents home?"

"His mom was."

"Don't use the shortcuts anymore, okay?" I said.

Flo rolled her eyes.

"Why?" Penny asked.

"I don't trust them."

"But they're such good shortcuts."

"Did you talk to that girl tonight? Constance?"

"A little," Penny said. "I was *so* busy emptying mom's wastebaskets and putting away toys—all those *doctor* things."

"She came from almost a hundred years ago."

"*Said* she did," Flo clarified.

"She loves the bathroom," Penny said. "I could hardly get her out of there."

"Well, she got lost here by running on the shortcuts. Or where they'll be—eventually," I said. "So, please, for me?"

"Okay."

"I keep thinking about her family not knowing what happened to her. And her stuck here." I shuddered. "It's just the loneliest feeling."

"If I wear a rope around my waist when I'm on the walk—would that reassure you?"

I played along. "Why?"

"If I went back in time you could pull me back."

"My thin grasp of this time travel thing leads me to believe that the rope would go with you. There'd be no pulling you back."

"But you'd come after me?" Penny asked. Her teasing tone was gone. Something about the subject had become real to her.

"How would I know where to search?" I asked. "Yesterday? An hour ago? A hundred years from now?"

"But you'd try," Penny persisted.

"Absolutely I'd try. Just don't use the shortcuts."

She scampered up the stairs and into the house. The noises of occupation she made were tremendously reassuring. I leaned my head on Flo's shoulder.

"Now I can sleep," I said.

FIVE

Constance Morceau was waiting for me at breakfast the next morning, and seeing her there sent me back to check on my family's whereabouts. Flo was in her office. Penny was asleep in present time, a breathing, substantive creature whose warm shoulder was firm to my touch.

Constance had lost the hip-hop outfit, replaced it with the dress and apron she had had on the first time I saw her. She'd kept the laceless boots.

"Your wife let me in."

I nodded.

"I'm ready to go."

"Go where?" I asked.

"Back. To 1908." She swallowed. "Back to Dash and my parents."

"I don't know how I can help you."

She did not seem to hear me, but plunged ahead. "We must find the precise spot where I was when Dash—when I disappeared."

"I could estimate."

The perp walk was already warm from the sun, bees doing business with our apple tree; Constance's father's last tree, if she was to be believed. I examined the path in both directions, remembering how I had at one time loved every inch of those paths, their eccentricity as much as their utility. Now I felt like I lived on the edge of a cliff, with the wind picking up.

"You weren't wearing shoes," I said.

"Really?"

"You left wet footprints on the sidewalk."

She kicked off the boots.

A door slammed next door. The noise made Constance jump.

"It's so crowded here," she complained. "So compacted and *hurried*."

"You should see Chicago."

"Oh, I have," she said. "We went on the train when I was twelve. I shook hands with President Roosevelt."

I gaped at her. That would be President *Teddy* Roosevelt. I recalled what Flo had said: One of the finest young actresses she had ever seen.

I found a spot on the walk that felt right. We were close enough to the apple tree that Constance reached out and plucked an apple.

"It's full of worms and rust," she said, but then took a bite—like it was an act of loyalty—and chewed. A bee swooped at her, even bumped her cheek. She idly waved her hand across the spot it hit. She was accustomed to bees. I would have to remember to tell Flo that, like a scrap of evidence.

She had finished the apple by the time we reached the end of the perp walk at Clover Street. She set the core in the palm of my hand.

"Thank you," she said.

"It was your apple."

"For believing me."

Before I could respond she was off, pivoting in her bare feet and sprinting hard back up the walk toward Chapman Street. She had long, strong legs and youthful grace, and when she was halfway down the walk I had a sudden conviction that she would make it, that she would be there one moment and gone the next, back to Dash and her family, back through the hidden door.

At the far end of the walk she was very much present, hands on her hips, breathing hard. I went to her. She lifted one foot to dislodge a scrap of apple stick imbedded in its ball.

"I don't—" I began.

"I'm here forever, aren't I?"

"I don't know. This is as strange to me as it is to you."

She used me for balance as she stepped back into her black boots.

"Where do they keep the records?" she asked.

"The records?"

"Births. Deaths. I want to find out what happens—happened—to my family. And to Dash."

"I don't think that's a good idea," I said. "If you know that—and get back—you might alter what happens."

"Daddy isn't much of a businessman. I'd love to help him."

"You can't go changing the past," I said, sounding petulant even to myself.

"Of course I can. If I knew things and didn't use them? What a terrible waste."

Euclid Heights kept the vital records of its citizens on microfiche in the subbasement of City Hall, but those records only dated back to 1920. Anything prior to that was in its original form at the Euclid Heights Historical Society, a building hardly larger than a garage on a quarter-acre of fenced grounds. The little stone building was dwarfed by the newly arrived old jail, which still balanced on the stacked railroad ties and trailer that had transported it from its location on the town square.

Constance and I took the long way there. No perp walks. She said the dense trees made everything appear more substantial, less like a prairie town staked down in the wind off the flatlands.

"So many houses," she said as we walked along. "And no one has any land. All the gardens are so small and pointless. But the privy smell is gone. Everything moves so fast. And not a soul has said hello to you since we've been out."

"I've lived here all my life," I said, "and I can go weeks without seeing anyone I know."

She stopped short in front of the library, aligning the coordinates of her memory with what she saw in front of her.

"The orphanage is gone," she said.

She pointed across the intersection, to a block of substantial houses.

"I work there when daddy doesn't need me," she said. "The kids make me stop cleaning and read to them."

She walked without hesitation across the street and up to the nearest house, a redbrick Georgian with the sun in its windows. She put a hand on the house's corner, then flicked an ant away.

"They built this house right off the orphanage gate," she said. "See?" She had me step back. "The bricks of the gate post are older than the bricks used for the rest of the house."

She was right. The corner of the house, going up almost to the second story, was constructed of bricks more weathered, roughened, and darker than the next bricks over. The builder hadn't done a particularly careful job of splicing the old bricks with the new, and gaps had opened, some of these patched with sloppy worms of mortar.

"They love me there," Constance said. "They hate when I leave. They're always certain I'm never coming back."

At the Historical Society—around back of the library and across the street—a sign announced the building was open, but the door was locked. I knocked. The building was a former power station built by the WPA in 1935. Phased out of its electric job in 1959, it was converted into a bomb shelter. The rusted sign declaring its function in time of nuclear attack was still bolted high on the corner of the wall facing the street.

The door—a heavy metal slab—groaned open like we were imposing upon it. A small man of about eighty greeted us—his pure white hair standing in a thick shock—with the effusive friendliness of someone rescued after long years of solitude.

"Young people! Goodness! Come in! Come in!" He stepped back, bidding us welcome with a courtly sweep of his hand. "I am Henry Hinsdale," he said, bestowing fierce handshakes.

I could almost reach from one wall to the wall opposite just by spreading my arms. A heavy black rotary telephone sat on a table, next to a chair, which had a cardigan sweater draped over its back, and a small pillow that bore the skinny imprint of Henry Hinsdale's butt.

"I'm a retired metal fabricator and I started volunteering here when my wife—Louise—passed on," he said. "I've been here almost a year and you"—he lightly tapped Constance's arm—"are by a long shot the youngest person to set foot in here." He winked at me. "And *you're* relatively spry yourself."

"We're looking for family records from around 1908," I said.

"You've come to the right place." He wiggled the switch on a heavy-duty lantern, shaking it until the reluctant beam burned true. "Follow me."

He pulled a chain of keys from a roller disk affixed to his belt and unlocked the only other door in the room.

"Biggest drawback to the job? No can on the premises," he said. "No can do-do. Gotta cart my carcass over to the library. Which isn't such a big deal—but I've got to lock up and while I'm gone I always wonder: Is someone pounding on the door while I'm out walking my prostate? And if a bomb fell during the Cuban missile crisis and people came down here for a hundred years until it cooled off topside—where would they do their business? Not a lot of thought went into this. Watch your head."

Down a staircase we went, following Henry Hinsdale's bouncing lantern beam. The air cooled as we descended. A dry smell touched my nose and I sneezed.

"G'bless you!" Henry yelled back, his voice echoing. "Power's out. Ironic, ain't it? Been out since that big storm in June. Village doesn't want to spend the few bucks to fix it. Can't be good for all this old paper."

Henry had a second key ready for the door at the bottom of the stairs.

"You remember when they converted this?" he asked. "Spring of '59?"

"I was a kid."

"Uncle Sam paid for the conversion. Everyone was positive the Soviets had a missile with our name on it. Remember the old Nike base? They started digging as fast as they could. Down and down and down. Then—" he got the door unlocked "—out and out and out."

We entered a room that even in pitch-darkness conveyed a sense of impressive dimension.

"Too bad the juice is out," Henry said. "This room does go on."

He flashed the lantern beam into the darkness, where the space swallowed the light. Support columns gleamed white, each bearing reflective green letters and numbers, like a parking garage.

Henry Hinsdale removed a shoe.

"We don't want to get locked down here," he said, and lodged the shoe so it held open the door.

"We'd have plenty of distilled water and freeze-dried food, though," he said, setting off with a limp. "We could live for years—long as we didn't have to use the can."

We walked for a couple minutes before reaching one of the room's corners. Stacked there on wooden pallets were fifty-five-gallon drums, stenciled silver on black—DISTILLED WATER. PROPERTY USA. DO NOT CONSUME AFTER 2050.

Henry tapped the number. "That doesn't mean ten minutes to nine, either," he said. "Want a sip?"

A spigot was attached to one of the drums, and next to it was a column of conical paper cups. He filled one and passed it to me. The water tasted flat and tepid.

"Welcome to the future," Henry said.

Constance refused a drink.

"Down that way," Henry said, flashing the beam along the wall of black drums into the darkness, "are the C-rations. Korean War vintage. We lobbied for gulf war vintage, but no dice. We'll be eating fifty-year-old food for a while."

Henry veered away from the wall, out toward what I estimated was the center of the room. Ghostly pillars swam out of the darkness. Constance gripped my hand. Much of the space we traveled through was empty.

After several minutes we reached a tall, gray, metal filing cabinet, and from the angle we approached, it appeared to be the only one. But then Henry led us around front and I realized it was just the end cabinet of a wall of such cabinets and this wall ran out of sight.

"Here we are," Henry said. He shined the light. The cabinet had five drawers, each drawer labeled with a neatly typed card slid into a holder.

"These go about a hundred yards that way," Henry said, with a swing of his beam for effect. "What name are you looking for?"

"Morceau," Constance said. She spelled it.

"And what year did the event take place?"

"We're not sure," I said.

"It's divided by years," he said, cranky, the novelty of us wearing away fast. "You need to know the year something happened."

"What about land surveys?" I asked.

"Across there—" He flashed the beam. "But don't expect an easy time of it. Euclid Heights now and Euclid Heights then don't bear much resemblance to each other."

"Hickory Hill," Constance said.

"Used to be," Henry nodded, his curious examination of the girl obvious even in bad light. "Changed names in 1911."

"How odd," Constance said, almost to herself. "And death certificates?"

"In here," he said, slapping the cabinets. "You'll need the year. 1918—the flu year—takes up the most space. Some doughboys. But life was just harder then, you ask me."

"What's a doughboy?" Constance asked.

Henry Hinsdale shined the light full in her face. She took it with eyes closed, patient and steadfast. She was a pretty girl, I realized, beneath the fatigue and loss and dislocation laid like veils over her features.

"Why—a doughboy was a soldier in the Great War," Henry said.

"Was that the Korea war you mentioned?"

Henry addressed me. "One of the benefits of young people not coming down here is that I don't get exposed to the existence of this level of ignorance. Depresses the crap out of me."

Constance reached and turned Henry's light so it shined on a drawer as she pulled it open.

"Could you leave the light with us?" I asked.

"How will I get back?"

"Go with him," Constance said. "I'll wait here."

We left her standing patiently before the open cabinet, her hand thrust into the dusty records of the past. Or her future, depending on the year.

Henry knew the way back, thankfully.

"Who is she?" he asked, in a voice that made no allowances for possibly being overheard.

"A friend of my daughter."

"It breaks my heart to see someone who has no conception of the world around her," he said.

"She's more interested in the past than most kids her age."

"Can she name the presidents in order?"

"I don't know. Can you?"

"Sure can. I know the periodic table of elements by heart, too."

"That's why they put that stuff in books," I said. "So we don't have to memorize it."

"Spoken like a true boomer," he grumbled. "Here we are."

The door was still propped open with Henry Hinsdale's shoe. The faint light from the head of the stairs was inviting to me, proof of another world, and a way out of the one I was in.

"I'll need a shoe," Henry said. He'd put on his own.

I removed a shoe, then the other, to even out my walk. The floor was chilly through my socks.

Henry shined a light on his watch. "I have noon," he said.

"I don't wear a watch."

Henry's opinion of me notched lower. He might have been questioning the wisdom of even allowing us down there.

"Mine says lunchtime. Can you stay occupied for an hour?"

"I think so."

"You kids have real short attention spans, I know," he said, "so if you get bored just let the door close behind you."

He placed the light in my hands and trudged up the stairs.

It took a few minutes of calling to each other before Constance and I reconnected. Minutes later she had found the cabinet of birth certificates—and in it her own. A faded, browned sheet of paper was illuminated, so aged and brittle I feared it might combust just from the lantern light. Someone with handwriting even Henry Hinsdale would admire had recorded in black ink the birth of Constance Marie Morceau: "Healthy Baby Girl, 31st October, 1893, weighing 8 pound 8 ounces, 21 inches in length, daughter of Peter T. Morceau, 28, and Faith Wilkins Morceau, 24."

"You were a big baby," I said.

Constance didn't answer. She soaked in the reality of the document, as if up until that point she had doubted her existence. Or, possibly, the certificate cast in a harsher light her presence at that moment.

"Let's find the land surveys," I said.

"I want to find out what happened to Dash."

"That's a bad idea. And I have the light."

She returned the birth certificate to its spot.

"You'll get back to your time," I said, "and then you'll be glad you don't know the future. We aren't *meant* to know it."

"These records—" she began, then hesitated, working something out in her mind. "These records are based on the past without me in it. Right?"

"I would think that's true because you're still here," I said. "In 1908, life goes on and everyone thinks you're gone. You *are* gone, in 1908."

"So we could find out in here if I ever get back," she said.

"That's one of those things you shouldn't know."

"But if I found out I got back—it would be such a relief."

"And what if you found out you didn't get back?"

"At least I'd know," she said, but sounding unconvinced.

"You're going to get back," I said, turning the light away from her.

The land survey cases were five feet tall, made of steel, each containing several wide, shallow drawers. I rolled one open. A faint, blue-white glow seemed to radiate out as the maps caught the lantern light. The top map was three by five feet, and a quick glance at the street names located me immediately. The Dragon Hills. Just as there were no heights in Euclid Heights, there were no hills in the Dragon Hills. Or dragons, either. The map in front of me dated from 1955 and indicated sewer lines and individual lots, each lot bearing a code number. I saw something from my quasi-overhead perspective that I had never noticed at ground level. The sinuous layout of the streets resembled dragons coiling in the surf, and the lots resembled dragon fins.

"Too recent," Constance said.

The drawers were labeled with the years of the surveys inside. We backtracked to 1910, then 1905.

"Here," she said, her voice trembling. She slid open the drawer.

The map on top was noticeably browner, an area of town I couldn't place. In the lower right-hand corner a label read **HICKORY HILL, ILL.** And beneath that were the words **PETER MCDEEDLE, MAYOR.**

"Do you recognize this?" I asked.

"No." Constance thumbed through maps beneath it. "Here." She extracted a survey from the middle of the stack. Its edges were nibbled by bugs. She spread it out and shined the light on it.

I knew where it was. The grid was firmly in place. Tinker Street was there, and Cottonwood and Pine to the west. But east of Tinker there were no streets, and the area was labeled farmland.

Constance stabbed the spot with her finger. "Our orchard!" she said triumphantly. "I knew it was there!"

She squinted at the faded markings, turned the light for the best view. "See? Morceau!"

I saw it in faintest ink, yes, the printed name. Or thought I saw it. No harm in pretending to see it. That old blanket of paper freezing for eternity one specific sliver of the world was not going to help her return.

"Yes, I see it," I said.

The excitement went out of her like a breath. She began to cry.

"I'm never going back."

"Your being present—now—is so . . . inexplicable that I would never say there's no chance you'll get back."

She wiped her eyes with her sleeve.

"We can go now," she said. "I don't know what I hoped to find here."

I went to the 1915 drawer. In just ten years you could see the town change, the farmland reduced, the right-angle streets spreading. And the maps were labeled EUCLID HEIGHTS. The mayor was someone named Archer.

I found the map I wanted toward the middle of the stack.

"Our orchard is gone," Constance said, a catch in her voice.

The orchard was, indeed, gone. Clover, Chapman, Spinney, and Holt streets had taken its place.

"That isn't a bad thing, necessarily," I said.

"It's my family's life. It's gone. Something terrible happened."

The terrible thing that had happened was obvious to me, and no doubt to her.

"I've got to get back," she said. "I don't belong here."

And she left me there in the dark, in my stocking feet, taking the lantern and rushing off down a diminishing tunnel of light.

"Constance!" I cried.

I couldn't tell if she stopped, or even hesitated, but she didn't answer. The light faded like a flame running out of air, and then I was alone in the dark.

"Constance!" I tried one last time. Nothing.

I fumbled with the surveys, feeling that it was important to get them restacked as we had found them, and the drawers closed. Blind, I moved the papers with my fingertips, fitting the fragile sheets within the cold, metallic limits of the drawer. Then by moving carefully—one arm feeling out ahead, the other to the side—I progressed from pillar to pillar until I reached a wall. To my left were my shoes, not twenty feet away, propping open the door and letting in a thin slice of the most welcome light I had ever seen.

SIX

A bowl of flowers sat that evening on the flags of Iceland, Denmark, Great Britain, and Bhutan, and propped against the bowl was a white ten-by-twelve-inch envelope, addressed to me, by me. My heart sank.

Flo was reading a pediatrics journal and drinking iced tea. I poured out the contents of the envelope: a packet of slides of my work, and a rejection letter from the Illinois Arts Council.

I scanned it, my anger and disappointment racing ahead of my brain and rendering comprehension sporadic and selective: "regret," "insufficient," "record-high number of submissions," and "please try again."

"No dice," I said, cramming the letter and slides back into the envelope, rolling the envelope into a tight, lopsided missile and launching it across the kitchen in the general direction of the wastebasket.

Flo touched my hand, a finger marking her place in her reading. "You said yourself it's so subjective. And every year the list is full of teachers."

"You're better than all of them," Penny said reflexively. She retrieved my thrown bundle, read the letter to herself, and pocketed the slides. "These are the ones of me, right?"

"Yeah," I said. "I'd have liked to have kicked in twenty grand to the family pot," I said.

Flo regarded me across her reading glasses.

"That's five years' income," I said.

Penny's jaw dropped. "You make four thousand dollars a year?"

"Three some years. Five others."

"That is so cool! I didn't think you made *nearly* that much."

"Without your mother," I said, "we'd be able to live in this house about two months."

"If it was spread out right, it wouldn't matter," Penny said.

"I don't know what that means, but okay."

"Two months is sixty days, right? And there are fifty-two weeks in a year," Penny said. "So we live here one day a week and at the end of the year we've got a cushion of eight days."

"Then another four grand arrives," I said, playing along. "It might just work."

"Where do we live the rest of the week?" Flo asked.

"With Uncle Kurt," I said.

"Not funny," Flo said.

Penny returned to the meal she was making. Stir-fried scallops.

"And you could open a catering business to fill out our income," I said.

"Nah," Penny said. "I only do this to feed the family. I don't love it."

She pronounced it ready and I set the table.

"Or you could go back in time and keep living the sixty days over," Penny said, dishing out.

"How boring," Flo said, setting aside her journal.

"It wouldn't have to be the same each time," Penny said. "Would it?"

I hunkered down over my food. "I don't know," I said.

"While you're reliving the two months over and over again," Penny asked, "what's the rest of the world doing?"

"Reliving it with you," Flo said.

"So one person reliving time could basically stop the world in its tracks," I said.

Flo gave me a long, cold stare. I searched her face—unsuccessfully—for the slightest hint of amusement.

"From that person's perspective, the world would be stopped," Flo said. "But of course that person would be insane."

I said to Penny, "Isn't it great, having a scientist in the family? Maybe this life, this world, with all its humdrumness and routine and pointless repetition is someone somewhere reliving a chunk of time again and again."

"Good attitude, dad!"

"I took Constance to the Historical Society."

"Do I want to know what you found?" Flo asked.

"Her birth certificate."

"Proves nothing."

"I don't need proof."

"No death certificate?"

"She needs a date for that. And I told her she shouldn't know things like that."

"Smart boy."

We heard laughter outside the house, an infectious, fast-moving knot of merriment that drew Penny up from her seat and out the door to investigate.

"Don't fill her head with this nonsense," Flo said in a fierce whisper. Her face was the face of an adversary. I had a frightening thought: This is the face of a wife in a shaky marriage, the face of a woman who has begun to consider alternatives to her present situation.

The cost of pushing ahead was clear to me.

"It isn't nonsense," I insisted.

We heard Penny outside, laughing. I jumped toward the sound, remembering Constance lost in her own future.

Penny was draped over the fence, talking to a boy I didn't know and two of her friends, Holly and Regan. Holly had self-confidence, and Regan hoped to learn it from her. The girls were taller than the boy, and all of them were imbued with a painful self-awareness I was certain they couldn't wait to shed, but which I found their most endearing quality. All conversation ceased when I appeared.

"This is Corey," Penny said.

"Hi," I said to the kid. "Come and finish dinner," I told Penny.

"Did you really go back in time?" Holly asked.

"Holly!" Penny scolded.

I approached them. They arrayed along the fence as I drew near.

"I'm not sure what happened," I said, with a scowl for my big-mouth daughter.

"And it happened while you were running on this path?" Corey asked. His hair was spiked and dyed gold at the tips, his face dappled with zits, but open and friendly. I liked that he appeared to be harmless and overmatched by my daughter.

"Like I said: I'm not sure."

My unforthcoming mood killed their interest in me.

"Inside," I said to Penny, and retreated.

Flo watched me from the door. I went past her, deeper into the room, and then positioned myself so I could see what was happening outside.

"What is going on?" Flo asked.

"Time-travel fans."

"Oh, great," she said despairingly.

Corey and the two girls were out of sight. Penny remained at the fence, watching something to her left. A rolling ball of laughter approached, and in a moment Corey, Holly, and Regan sprinted past, hair flying, arms pinwheeling, down the perpendicular walk. Penny's head pivoted to watch them pass, then glanced guiltily over her shoulder into the house.

"I went back ten seconds!" Corey bellowed triumphantly.

"You did not!" Holly screamed, smacking him.

"I knew you were going to say that!"

Their laughter went on and on. Finally Penny said something and came inside, giving me a shrug and a scowl as she went past.

Flo angrily stabbed at the last scrap of food on her plate.

"I thought—" I began.

"This is a place of business," Flo interrupted. "I have a considerable investment—we all do—in the reputation that is attached to this address."

"Sorry," Penny murmured.

Flo was startled, evidently by Penny's mistaking the target of her anger.

"I thought it was clear that this was something that stayed within the family," I said, but unable to work up much outrage.

"I only told Corey," Penny said. "*He* told Holly and Regan."

"You shouldn't have told *anyone.*"

"Jesus. Okay. I'm sorry." She slammed out of the room.

"This fantasy of yours is already out of control," Flo said.

"What if one of those kids disappears?"

She made a noise that was somewhere between a grunt and a growl. Her office line rang. She picked it up on the kitchen phone and was off in fifteen seconds.

"A cancellation," she said ominously.

"You've had cancellations before."

"That was for a school physical. *Nobody* cancels those."

"It's just one," I said.

She froze me with that adversarial glare. "We can't live on your four thousand dollars a year."

I didn't sleep much that night and rose before sunup and ate eggs and toast on the back patio. The perp walk was empty but for one commuter hurrying through toward downtown, toward the train, her briefcase strumming against the fence, cigarette smoke streaming out behind her. Her grim haste filled me with gratitude for Flo, for keeping me clear of such a fate: the schedules, the travel, the raw addiction of just enough money, checking your watch by the light of the day's first cigarette.

Flo nudged me with her foot an hour later. I was asleep in the sun with egg on my pants. She was brushed and bouncy, with a sparkle in her eye until she got a look at me.

"I couldn't sleep," I said.

She sighed. "Any particular reason why?"

"I was thinking about Constance," I said. "She knows too much about her future. A little knowledge could have a huge impact. On us."

"This is getting really tedious," Flo said. "And a little frightening."

She turned on her heel and went back into the house. I gathered up my breakfast things and followed. I tracked her to the door of her office, even called her name, but she ignored me, ignored Penny, whose presence that early in the morning could only mean some momentous undertaking.

Flo slammed her office door in my face. I whirled on Penny.

"Who else did you tell?"

"No one!"

"I guess it's too late to ask your friends not to say anything."

"Why is she so mad?"

"She doesn't believe."

"I don't either, really. But I don't hate you."

"She doesn't hate me," I said, but remained open to confirmation.

Penny pursed her lips. "I was Holly's best friend the year her parents split up," she said. "Mr. and Mrs. Dearborn faked it in front of her friends. But the hate in that house—you could feel it."

"Do you feel that here?"

"Not *yet*. But something's definitely different."

"One canceled appointment doesn't mean the death of her practice."

"I was supposed to work with her. She canceled on *me*."

"I'm going into town this morning. Want to come with?"

She laughed. "You make it sound like it's a day's wagon ride away."

"I wonder . . . if Holly's parents could go back—what would they do differently?"

"Daddy—you're a little too into this time-travel thing."

"Yeah. And what could they accomplish in fifteen minutes?"

"I wouldn't bring it up with mom."

"But then I'd be keeping the most amazing part of my life from her."

"Daddy! Listen to yourself."

"What?"

"*I'm* the most amazing part of your life!"

There had been a time when she was absolutely correct, and a time when I had forgotten that what she said was true. But now I really cared. She had reached an age when her father was more impediment than ally in her plans. I blamed the boy—innocuous, callow Corey. He was not the first boy to have his head turned by my daughter, but he was the first to turn her heart around. Although my daughter didn't say as much, her actions told me Corey was the first person Penny thought might be able to replace me. He had made her a partner in secrets to keep from me.

She had been a different person the summer before, when I began to get my materials ready to apply for the Illinois Arts Council grant. I asked her to sit for me.

"Only if I can paint you at the same time," she had said.

This pleased me more than it should have. Although I sensed Flo's nudging hand in my daughter's stipulation, I was willing to fool myself into thinking Penny had no better plans for her summer vacation than to sit facing me easel to easel.

We began with charcoal pencil, and then moved on to watercolors. An afternoon slipped away. As the sun went down I said, "Tomorrow we should sit outside."

She huffed out her cheeks and I thought I had lost her. Her shirt—one of mine—was slashed through with black and pastels up and down the sleeves and across the front. She had dabbed paint on each shirt button—one color per button—and now they had dried and she didn't want to touch them for fear the little caps of color would break off.

She had matched me drawing for drawing. When I finished something she automatically declared her own done, as well. I didn't show her anything until the day was complete. She did likewise. At the end of the day we stood—still face to face—over matching piles of paper.

"I get to see yours first." She held out a hand.

I slid my pile over to her. I was pleased with what I had done that day. I saw progress in each succeeding piece. Penny had a heart-shape face and eyes that were most appealing when she was lost in thought. She was easy to look at and easy to draw.

She spread my work out on the table. As she examined each piece in turn she took her own pile and pulled it farther away from me, until she was done looking and had her own day's work pinched in her hand. When I asked to see it she hid it behind her back.

"No," she said.

"Tomorrow I want to paint you by the walk," I said.

"I might be busy."

"Just one more day?"

"I'll sit. You just paint."

"Let me see." And I held out my hand to her again.

"You'll laugh," she said.

"I won't!"

She wouldn't budge. She took everything with her when she left the room.

At breakfast the next morning I waited for her to tell me she had other plans. She might have been waiting for the same thing from me. I stood her on the perp walk in the apple tree's shade. The path was so verdant and shaggy to the east that it appeared to close off before it reached the vanishing point.

She lost patience within the hour.

"How long do I have to stand here?"

"You want to take a break?"

"I want to do something—anything—else."

"This is a big help to me," I said.

"You know—just because you're an artist and mom is a doctor—that doesn't mean I can only *be* an artist or a doctor," she said.

"I know."

"And if I'm as good a doctor as I am an artist—I might as well open a funeral home, too."

"You're not *that* bad." I laughed.

She flipped her wrist at me. "Go on. Paint. Paint."

I settled back in.

I wanted to get her eyes back to thinking about something else. "What do you *want* to do?" I asked.

She sighed melodramatically. "Now? Anything but this. In the future—no clue."

"That's not so unusual."

"The clueless part—or the part where I don't want to be here?"

"Both."

She bit her lip. "I'm leaning toward doctor," she said.

"That's okay." She watched my face for signs of disappointment. I didn't want her to see any. "I lean toward the doctor as much as she will let me."

"Daddy!" she giggled.

I set her free in the afternoon. She came around and stood next to me and examined the painting. It wasn't finished, of course. I had pencil sketches in the corners of the canvas, little miniature Pennys that I liked better than the one of her I painted in oils. In that one the path's lining of leaves reminded me a little of an ocean wave breaking behind an unwary bather.

"It needs work," I said.

"I know exactly who it's supposed to be," she said.

"Hah."

"I'll keep posing if you want."

There was something pitying in her tone. "Is it that bad?" I asked.

"Daddy! No!" She slapped my arm. "Stop it!"

I felt terrible for her. She shouldn't have to be responsible for bucking up her father.

"You can go," I said.

She didn't give me much of a fight. In fact, she was gone in less than a minute. I bagged the oil painting of her with a promise to myself to finish it later, when it meant less to me, when it wasn't the most important thing I'd ever done.

When I went to get her for dinner she wasn't in her bedroom. I would have stopped right there at the doorway if I hadn't seen the pile of sketches she had done of me the day before, rolled into the silver tube of her wastebasket. She came up behind me while I was going through them.

"Daddy," she said softly.

"I'm keeping these," I said.

"Whatever."

I told her they were wonderful. Neither of us mentioned they were better than mine.

I was halfway up the walk between Clover and Tinker when I remembered I didn't want to be there. Just habit. My heart raced for an instant. I was pretty sure I was safe. But then fifteen minutes ago was a lot like now.

Constance had come here across almost one hundred years. What had loosened her ties to her present day that she slipped so far from it? I wanted to find her. It was another day in the future for her. Another day away from her family. In 1908, neither of my parents was born yet. My grandparents were alive, but were they married? Had they met yet? In 1908 it was all ahead of them, there to be altered.

Constance Morceau returning to that world made me shudder.

I found her easily enough by the crowd she'd attracted. She was relaxed on a downtown bench erected by the city fathers to promote a neighborly atmosphere, but anyone who sat for any length of time was regarded with suspicion, someone with nothing better to do than just sit, someone with no better place to be.

The crowd was composed of eight kids forming a half-circle, some on bikes, some sitting on the ground in front of her like disciples. I wondered if they were wards of the state on an outing. No, I decided, they were too confident of their place in the world.

And that frightened me. They might already be more fans of time travel, part of a spreading secret.

Constance held a cigarette with grand, exaggerated flourishes of flung ash and smoke, but put it to her mouth only infrequently. When she saw me she broke free of her admirers and rushed over.

"Women can vote at eighteen!" she exclaimed.

"I know."

"And smoke tobacco in public!"

"Technically—because of your age—you're not supposed to."

"I'm a hundred and six!" She threw the cigarette into the street.

"There were kids outside my house last night trying to go back in time," I said. "Or forward."

"They might be sorry," she said, her mood darkening.

"I'd rather they didn't know about it at all," I said.

"Too late, I'm afraid."

"It might make it harder for you to get back."

"I'm not going back."

"Because you like it here so much?" I teased.

"I hate it here. Rather—I hate it now."

"Every age has something to recommend it," I said. "And things that don't quite work out."

"The only thing that matters to me is my family. And Dash. And they aren't here. So I have to make the best of it." She leaned closer. "Do you have a cigarette?"

"You don't want to go back to 1908 addicted to nicotine."

"To what?"

"Nicotine. The addictive ingredient in cigarettes."

"It gives me the most exhilarating sensation. I can see why men want to keep it for themselves."

"You're better off, believe me."

"Let's return to the archives," she said, pulling on my arm.

"You ditched me."

"I was upset. I apologize. Can we?"

A treasured feature of my life was that I never had anything specific to do, but I told Constance that I did, that commitments and responsibilities prevented me from accompanying her back into that lightless file room.

"I'll go by myself," she threatened.

That troubled me. If I was with her I might control the information she turned up, or at least be aware of what she had found. If she went alone I'd have no idea what she might take back with her.

"I'll go with you," I said.

"When?"

"Tomorrow."

"No. Now. You don't seem to realize this is all I think about."

"Okay. This afternoon."

"Why not now?"

"I have to buy art supplies."

"Do you remember Thaddeus Brine?"

"No."

"In 1908, he is the finest portraitist in Hickory Hill," she said. "Now, no one remembers him. You might want to keep that in mind."

"I will," I said, refusing to be baited. I had learned long ago and with some relief that artistic immortality was not a fate that awaited me.

"So wouldn't it be more fulfilling if you helped return me to my time? Rather than simply painting some silly picture that will just be forgotten?"

"This afternoon," I repeated.

"What time?"

"One o'clock. I'll meet you there."

"Let me go with you now."

"No."

"I'm interested in your art."

"No you're not."

She turned her back on me, playing hurt. I used the opening to hurry away. I found what I wanted not at the art supply store but at a hobby shop around the corner, one of those near-death businesses with dust on everything and the owner working all the hours to save the price of an employee.

Out on the sidewalk, holding my purchase, I expected to find Constance waiting for me to come around to her way of thinking. I was in a part of town that felt old enough to be familiar to her. In the window of a print shop next door was a sign:

READ ALL ABOUT YOU!

It was possible to purchase the laminated front page of the *Chicago Tribune* from the day you were born. It gave me an idea, an avenue of approach.

A line of homeless men and women sat in the shade on benches out front of the Euclid Heights Memorial Library. I scanned for Kurt and came up empty, but relieved. No sign of him inside the library, either. He'd no doubt be on the move. That compulsion to walk and walk came upon him as reliably as another man's itch to be up and at work in the morning.

I found what I sought in a cabinet by the window, which gave a view of the Historical Society grounds. The drawers contained microfilmed copies of the local newspaper—the *Daily Beacon*—on spools in cardboard boxes, each spool holding two weeks' worth of papers.

I put the reel for August 1–15, 1908, on a microfilm reader and began to spin through life in Constance's time. Mark Twain was alive. Teddy Roosevelt was in the White House. A man's new suit could be purchased for $2. Indian head pennies were in everyone's pockets. A debate raged over the possible damage to a young lady's nervous system if she crossed her legs in public.

The newspaper type was much smaller than the present style, with so much more news packed on a page. It seemed quaint. I had to remind myself that when that paper hit the street it was the height of modernity for the people who read it. Constance must not find out about those old newspapers. Legal documents in an unlighted cellar were not nearly as dangerous as direct word from the world she'd left behind.

I went to the edition of August 14, 1908, the day after she had appeared to me, soaking wet and barefoot on the perp walk. I carefully scanned each page as it rolled past, adjusting the focus now and then, a headache kicking in as I concentrated on the condensed type.

At the bottom of page 3, I found a small article under the headline

LOCAL GIRL'S DISAPPEARANCE CONFOUNDS FAMILY, SHERIFF

by E. Wayne Manger

An apparently innocent romp in a summer downpour took a mysterious turn yesterday when 15-year-old Hickory Hill beauty Constance Morceau vanished while running with a male friend among her father's apple trees.

The young man in question—Harold "Dash" Buckley—arrived at Sheriff Lloyd Horton's office with a perplexed expression and rain-drenched clothes to inform the constable that his fair friend had disappeared off the face of the Earth.

Presently Sheriff Horton and Deputies T. Murphy and J. Ketch accompanied the troubled beau to the site of Miss Morceau's evaporation. At this point, the girl's parents—Peter T. Morceau and Faith W. Morceau—returned from an errand to purchase "seed, muslin and a lady's delicates," according to Mr. Morceau, and intensified the general bewailing of the situation.

Young Buckley guided all present to that point among the apple trees where he reported last seeing the absent damsel. A man-high wooden staff was fetched and in a grim, steady rain the ground was fathomed for a sinkhole or forgotten well shaft or underground cavern that could explain the sudden disappearance. No such aperture into the unknown was found.

Sheriff Horton had no recourse but to invite Mr. Buckley to return to the Hickory Hill Jail for a more careful recreation of the incident.

I printed out that article, then scanned the August 15 edition. Nothing.

I threaded the August 16–31 reel onto the machine and hurried ahead. Constance's disappearance was not mentioned in the August 16 paper, either. I was baffled. A missing girl seemed like news to me. Then I saw a small item reporting a staggering 459 people had drowned the previous summer in lakes and rivers in and around Chicago. Maybe with people drowning left and right, the *Daily Beacon* wouldn't make a fuss over the missing daughter of an orchardman until she was officially dead.

The following day—August 17, 1908—she stared out at me from the front page. It was a sketch, obviously done from a photograph, but very true to life. It was also a year or two old, I estimated. Getting lost in the future had aged Constance. Her hair in the picture was bound up in two pigtails, a flat hat tipped back on her head. The artist (he'd signed the drawing TBrine) had left the hat indistinct, creating the hint of a halo around Constance's head. Beneath the drawing was a caption: *Young Constance Morceau, missing these three days.*

Beneath that was a headline:

HICKORY HILL ORCHARD UPROOTED IN HUNT FOR MISSING LOCAL LASS

by E. Wayne Manger

An intrepid battalion of lawmen, worried citizens and horrified family members spent the entirety of yesterday digging up the Hickory Hill apple orchard where 15-year-old Constance Morceau reportedly was last seen.

The young lady—whose unhinged mother, Faith W. Morceau, reports had dreams of a career in the law and who loved her family's annual Christmas pilgrimage to Chicago—was running in the summer rain Aug. 13 with Mr. Harold Buckley when—Buckley maintains—she vanished from sight.

Town Sheriff Lloyd Horton and his various deputies conducted a cursory search of the area of the reported disappearance, seeking a hidden underground space large enough to swallow up the unfortunate young lady. That probing search with a long staff reminded some observers of the gondoliers of Venice, another of the many exotic destinations Constance expressed a desire to visit, her mother revealed. The search unearthed nothing.

A second, more thorough examination of the ground near where Buckley said he last espied Miss Morceau was conducted in the fresh light of day, again without successful results.

Yesterday, a concentrated, organized effort by more than 100 men and women was made to sift every square inch of ground within a thousand paces of the point of the girl's alleged disappearance. The search also extended to the house and sundry outbuildings of the Morceau property.

Buckley, the girl's swain and best known by the sobriquet "Dash," directed the search of the orchard ground, in close consultation with Sheriff Horton. A palpable air of hopelessness attended this odious chore, for few any longer clung to hopes the missing maiden would be found with her high good health and sweet nature unaltered.

Alas, the day's search revealed only what the girl's father, Peter T. Morceau, has staked his life and livelihood upon: the fecund earth of his orchard is rich, loamy and unperforated by any sinkhole or cavern that could devour his blessed daughter.

The search was extended by lantern light, then called off when full darkness obtained. Coincident with the orchard search, an official examination was made of the room Mr. Buckley kept in a downtown home. Nothing incriminating was found, according to a source familiar with the search.

Two days followed without a story, and then another front-page account ran in the August 20 edition, accompanied by a TBrine drawing done in the style of Constance's earlier portrait. Its caption read: *Harold Buckley—Arrested in the disappearance of Constance Morceau.*

It was not a flattering likeness. His mouth, nose, and eyes were rendered in a way that—collectively—made Buckley appear fatuous and untrustworthy. A complicated, droopy bowtie at his throat and the first scatterings of a moustache gave him the appearance of an unkempt dandy.

ORCHARD WORKER HELD IN DISAPPEARANCE OF HICKORY HILL BEAUTY

by E. Wayne Manger

The "dash" was long gone from Harold "Dash" Buckley's demeanor as he sat pondering his fate and his future yesterday in the Hickory Hill Jail, officially accused in the Aug. 13 disappearance of 15-year-old Constance Morceau, who was reportedly last seen alive by Mr. Buckley in her father's apple orchard.

Repeated searches of the orchard have wreaked havoc on the season's bounty to such an extent that Peter T. Morceau, the missing girl's father, has reportedly expressed doubt about his livelihood's future financial viability.

Interviews with acquaintances of Mr. Buckley (who appears to have no close friends) revealed a young man of considerable charisma and personal ambition who earned the cognomen "Dash" for his quality of hurrying through life in order to sample as many of its delectations as possible. He was at once employed at the Morceau orchard, studying in Chicago to be an apothecary, and saving for a much-anticipated tour of the western states.

Buckley met the missing girl when he was hired to help tend her family's apples. He made no mention, according to people he knew, of any serious romantic intentions, and, indeed, Mr. Buckley's "Dash" was also said to be in reference to the speed with which he harvested the fairer sex.

Hickory Hill Sheriff Lloyd Horton reported that Buckley has been unfailingly cooperative in their frequent jailhouse interviews. He further revealed that Buckley sleeps only fitfully, has scant appetite, and a nervous stomach capable only of keeping down thrice-daily servings of Dr. Price's Wheat Flake Celery Food.

"The suspect gives all indications of being a man tied in knots over being charged with a crime of which he is innocent," the sheriff said.

SEVEN

I printed out another copy and was about to continue reading when I became aware of a presence behind me. For an instant I feared it was Constance sneaking up and seeing details of her boyfriend's future.

But it was only Kurt.

He held a book with both hands, a neediness in his bearing that was at once touching and repellent.

"What?" I said, sharper than I intended. I felt whipped out of a world whose questions were already answered, or forgotten, into one that was ongoing and demanding.

"Buy one one one two East Collier Street, Euclid Heights, Illinois. Six zero zero zero one."

He thrust forward the book he held. *My First Home*. I leafed through it. The terminology and charts meant little to me. Flo had handled the purchase of our home. I'd signed where she pointed.

"Can you read this?" I asked, handing it back.

"Buy—"

"Doug picked this book out for you, didn't he?"

"Buy one—"

"It isn't going to happen, Kurt."

I saw him pinch the book's plastic cover between his thumbs and forefingers, making the tiniest tear, the skin on his fingertips going bloodless with the effort of holding back his frustration.

Two years into Kurt's present situation, two years after Vaughan Garner drowned and Kurt's accusations were ignored as the ramblings of a brain-damaged nuisance, my mother yelled to me down the basement stairs.

"Follow him! He's different tonight!"

Different from what he had become might be a nice change, I'd thought. "He's getting away!"

He wasn't, actually. He had only made it as far as the end of the block, kneeling under a streetlight and picking up something and putting it in his pocket. Then, as if reassured that I had joined him, he set off in earnest.

Soon enough we were in the Dragon Hills. By then I was no longer following him but walking at his side. He didn't speak. The things he stopped to pick up were rocks. When his pockets were full he began to fill mine.

"Let's go home, Kurt."

Mom was right. He *was* different. He was more like his old self, the pre-Kurt, focused and organized. That glimpse of his lost self-reliance, the limitless kid he had been, made me miss him all the more.

Two years earlier we had gone—the three of us, me, mom, and dad—to the hospital where they took Kurt after he came out of the swimming pool. Dad could find nothing to talk about except the minute-by-minute accumulation of cost while Kurt was hospitalized. Kurt was conscious, a boy afloat on a green bed, staring at the ceiling, but it was clear in his eyes that the Kurt we knew was gone. I would have to learn to love an entirely new brother. I never quite did.

He was discharged just as autumn struck with wind and ice. The power went out in the hospital as they were calculating his bill. The lights dimmed and the woman tallying the expenses blinked, and then a generator somewhere kicked in and the adding-up continued. Issues of inadequate insurance—of payment denied—were in the air over Kurt's oblivious head. The total owed was at $52,440 when we brought Kurt home. The phone was ringing when we arrived. It was the hospital asking for their money.

Dad held them at bay for one terrible year. Kurt's condition—his dead eyes, his diminished capacity—was like a repudiation of the hospital's claims. They sent Kurt home like that and still they wanted $52,440.

A registered letter arrived. The hospital had placed a lien on our house. I didn't know how much the house was worth or how much we owed on it, but the official shackling of our fate squeezed some vital juice out of my father.

That terrible year stretched into two. The doorbell rang in the spring. Jock Itch was on the front porch, duded out in a skintight brown cadet suit, accompanied by a real cop who had Kurt in custody for refusing to vacate the country club fairway bunker where he'd been sleeping. Sugary sand glistened on the sides of his legs, shoulder, and cheek. He was transferred into our custody with a warning. We'd used up our favors with one.

Soon after, my parents put 1112 East Collier Street on the market. I was pretty sure Kurt had no idea what that meant. Mom confided to me that the money from the house would pay off the hospital bill and leave us with enough for a couple months' rent. Rather than view this as a calamity, my father, clear of the hospital debt, perked up. A deep wheeze of frustration that had rattled in his throat since Kurt's hospital bill arrived began to ease.

On moving day, Kurt discovered that he could make the rental truck's ramp bounce in an entertaining way. Dad sat on the porch steps, sipped scalding hot coffee, and watched.

Flo was there. She carried a box up into the truck, and on her way down took a couple seconds to bounce on the ramp with Kurt. I tried to sell dad on Kurt's talents. He had the perfect mover's disposition: strong and unreflective. We had most of the upstairs to be moved downstairs and out to the truck, with the day getting away, and mom crying while she packed. Dad was gray in the gills and I was already exhausted. Kurt was a wasted asset.

"Hitch him up," dad said. Then he went inside, down into the basement.

I led Kurt off the ramp and put a heavy box in his hands. He turned like an automoton and marched it into the truck. He came back and I gave him another. I felt like a cool breeze had come up. With Kurt working, the day no longer felt endless.

Flo had a gift for organizing the interior of the truck. She had a way of talking to my mother that dislodged her from the pockets of sadness that the rest of us allowed to overwhelm her. Kurt went back and forth without stopping. Mom cleaned out the refrigerator. Runny Jell-O molds, bread crusts, old croutons, uncooked rice, a cuttlebone from a long-dead parakeet, everything was thrown into the backyard. A motley collection of crows, squirrels, and chickadees watched this small mountain accumulate, but from a distance, like they were all waiting for someone else to go first.

"Where's your father?" mom asked me late in the day.

Time, which had stood still, caught up in a rush.

"He went down the basement," I said. I didn't tell her how long ago.

We found him in a dark corner, relaxing in an old lawn chair. His mouth was open like he'd been surprised and his glasses had slipped to the end of his nose. A puddle was beneath the chair. When the paramedics carried him out it seemed in a weird way to be part of the move.

Kurt returned the next day to help the new owners move in. They thought he was part of the crew. The movers thought he was the nutty side of the family. The police were called when Kurt lay down to sleep in his old room.

The snaking streets of the Dragon Hills bore names such as Aquitane, Wivern, and Foxglove. The houses exuded a self-satisfied twinkle of substance. My pockets were so heavy with rocks that I had to hold up my shorts by the waistband. I was about to stop and empty them when we reached Kurt's destination.

It was a house impressive even by Dragon Hills standards, two and a half stories, room-size bay windows, a four-car garage. Kurt slipped through the gap between this house and its neighbor. I made a grab for him, but I was too late. We were on private property with pockets full of rocks. The night had turned for the worse.

The rear of the house's top floor featured a succession of dormer windows, each one dark. The ground floor had patio doors and picture windows in profusion. Rock magnets. A thrill of foreboding turned my insides cold.

"Who lives here?" I asked in a whisper.

Kurt was on his knees, emptying his pockets by an in-ground pool, which was covered with a tarp.

"Kurt. Who?"

He heaved the first rock on a long arc out of sight over the house. We didn't hear it hit. He giggled, danced a nervous jig, shaking his hands like they were on fire.

He tossed me a rock underhand. "Catch," he said.

He spun, threw a rock at the house, and yelled, "Catch!"

The rock struck home with a great crashing of glass, which triggered so many alarms they were almost festive: lights, sirens, tape-recorded dogs, maybe real dogs.

"Come on!" I shouted, grabbing for my brother. But he deftly sidestepped me—laughing—and drilled another rock through another window.

A spotlight on the roof swept the yard and for a moment I was afraid we'd overlooked a guard in a watch tower. But three times in thirty seconds the beam had us cold, only to move on, and I realized it was a programmed pattern, a figure eight, infinity.

Kurt was cocked to throw again when I jumped him from behind. He fell on his pile of rocks, knocking out his wind, me on top. The rocks in my pockets crunched me painfully.

We lay like that for several seconds, me with my arms around his chest.

"Catch!" he said, giggling. Even in my grip he managed to flip a rock an inch toward his target.

A white spotlight as round as a gong pierced the gap between the house and its neighbor. It froze the rear fence in unforgiving examination. Next came the scratchy, impersonal voice of a radio dispatcher. A second beam of light appeared behind us, originating on the next block over.

Kurt giggled. I clamped my hand over his mouth.

"Shut up!" I hissed.

He said something. I removed my hand.

"Catch," he said.

I released him and got to my feet. I dispersed his pile of rocks with one kick. As individual rocks, not as a pile of rocks, they might conceivably be viewed as part of the landscape.

The siren in the house shut down, making the police radios easier to hear. The light on the roof stopped its big-house sweep. I duck-walked to where Kurt lay on his side, took him by the arms, and pulled him toward the pool's edge. He resisted less than I expected. I wondered if he knew where I was leading him.

The pool tarp was cinched tight around a lip of rounded stones. I pried it back. A strong chlorine smell was released and clicked with Kurt in a bad way. He tore free of me, fell back, kicked out, crab-walked away, whimpered.

"We've got to hide!" I reached for him, knowing it was hopeless.

I slipped feetfirst under the tarp. The water was warm but still a shock. The rocks in my pocket pulled me down. I wondered if I was going into the deep end, and I took a breath almost as an afterthought, but then touched bottom, the water just up to my chin.

Kurt watched me. I put a finger to my lips and winked. He smiled nervously. I waved him over but he refused. So I let him go. I pulled the tarp down over my head and worked it with my fingers until the edge was back in place. Fingers touched my head, pushing me down. I was reminded of Flo pushing me back under water, back to fail to save her brother.

Then I heard keys jangling and running boots thudding on the pool tiles. Radio voices were directly overhead. A gruff voice ordered Kurt onto his stomach. Beams of light found their way through the mesh of the tarp, and then moved on. I was proud of Kurt for not giving me away, and certain that he would at the next moment.

A voice I recognized brayed, "It's Kuh-razy Kurt!"

Someone got slapped. I heard Kurt giggle. "Catch," I'd thought he'd been saying. No. He had been saying "Ketch."

"Take the kid home," a new voice said. "Leave him cuffed until you're a block from his house. Scare him—but don't tell his parents."

"It's just his mom, Chief," someone said.

"Then don't tell his *mom,*" the voice said contemptuously. "Call Edmonds at home and have him wake up his carpenters. I want plywood on my windows." He listened to a muffled voice. "Yes, *tonight.* My jackass son here will pick up the glass."

The voices and the flashlight moved away. I stayed in the water another hour. While I waited, I emptied my pockets of rocks, let them fall one by one, clicking on the pool floor.

A police car was at the foot of our apartment building when I got home. A cop—not Itch's father—was sitting at the kitchen table with my mom when I walked in.

My wet clothes apparently did not tip him off. Mom gave me a hopeless look. Kurt was already gone again. I emptied my pockets in front of the cop. The contents of another ruined wallet—three ones—had been fused into a single bill. When I squeezed the water from this three-dollar bill, the drops splashed on the cop's shirt cuffs and folded hands. Still his suspicions weren't aroused.

"Go get him," Mom said.

The breath went out of me. I wanted to call Flo. I wanted dry clothes and time to myself.

But I went back out. It was easy enough to walk across town to find him. He was sitting on the familiar front steps. He probably had rung the doorbell four or five times.

When he saw me he smiled. "Catch."

"Come on home."

His face clouded. "One one one two East Collier Street. Euclid Heights, Illinois. Six zero zero zero one."

I sat down beside him. "Not anymore."

"One one one—"

"Let's go see Flo."

Kurt liked that idea. Flo paid attention to him beyond the glancing, impatient embarrassment his family adopted in order to be in his presence. She lived with her parents on the edge of the Dragon Hills, in a trim house that had some historical significance as the fourth-oldest house in Euclid Heights.

The way the sound carried through the empty street when Kurt rapped on the front door reminded me that it was late. A porch light came on. Flo opened the door. She didn't seem surprised to see us, just stepped back and let us in.

Someone was typing rat-a-tat in a room off the hallway. Flo waved us past, then through an arched passageway that contained a telephone nook arched to mimic the doorway. No phone, though, just a picture of Vaughan, smiling his smile for adults, caught in the act of sewing on his own merit badges.

In Flo's room, one light was on over her desk to focus all her attention on the piles of schoolwork arranged there. She flopped into her desk chair. I went to the floor. Kurt perched, hands and feet together, on the end of the bed.

"Organic test tomorrow," she said, elbowing an open textbook a half-inch out of its place.

Kurt giggled. He stared at the ceiling so intently he might have been looking through it.

"You remember Vaughan's room, Kurt?" Flo asked. To me, she said, "It's directly overhead. Mom's asleep up there now."

"Kurt stoned Itch's house tonight."

Flo clapped and howled.

"Catch," Kurt said.

"And what did *you* do?" she challenged me.

"I went with."

"Did you stone him, too?"

I shook my head. "I didn't know whose house it was until the cops were there."

Flo's eyes got big. "His dad caught you?"

"Catch!"

"He got Kurt. I hid in the pool."

"What pool?" Mention of a pool made her nervous.

"They have an in-ground pool."

She stood beside me and cupped a hand next to my ear, and with her other hand pushed my head over like she wanted to pour something from it.

"Dry," she said.

"I wasn't under water."

"You hid without going under?"

"The pool is covered."

Her hand was still cupped against the side of my head. It was warm and hummed like a seashell.

"You hid and let him be caught?"

"Catch!" Kurt said.

"He wouldn't come with."

She turned her attention to my brother.

"You didn't want to go into the water?" she asked in a gentle voice.

"Catch!"

"I don't blame you."

She got up and left the room without a word. I stayed put. Kurt giggled a little, but didn't budge. The typing went on in the other room. Overhead, a floorboard creaked. Then another, a short distance past the first. Kurt and I watched the sound progress step by step above us. It might have been Flo's mother awakening, but I was pretty sure it was Flo tiptoeing past her sleeping mom. The sound stopped at the spot near the outside wall.

"Catch!" Kurt whispered.

"You like Flo?"

"Catch!"

"Me, too."

The footsteps retraced their path across the ceiling, less stealth in the pacing, and out the door. Flo was back in a minute, at her desk, a preoccupied expression on her face.

"I thought mom was in Vaughan's room," she said. She was untangling the straps of a nose clamp, the horseshoe-shape kind that fastened to the bridge of the nose. She held it out for Kurt. "This was Vaughan's. You can have it."

He took it, examined it, not a clue what it was for. I was going to help him but Flo beat me to it. She looped the strap around his neck and pinched the horseshoe over his nose. He smiled doubtfully, mouth half open, his pinched skin turning white.

"Hatch!" he said adenoidally.

"Noseplug," Flo said. She pinched her own nose with her fingers. "Hoseplug!"

Kurt would have left it on forever but Flo removed it. Kurt tried to pull it over his head but she pressed it to his chest.

"Yours," she said.

He lifted it to his nose and sniffed. The chlorine smell in the rubber made him uneasy. He stretched the band out so far I was certain it would snap. If he was alone he would have panicked, but he was with Flo, and he let her push his hand back to his chest, easing the pressure on the straps.

"Come with me," she said.

We followed her into the kitchen and she had us wait while she went into a bathroom. She returned with an armload of towels. She found a flashlight in a drawer. Kurt watched everything she did with rapt uneasiness. Every time he tried to remove the nose clamp Flo pressed it back down around his neck.

She led us out a door off the kitchen, down a flight of steps to the backyard. It stretched away to the west, moonstruck.

She pushed the towels and flashlight into my arms.

"Shine it here," she said, pointing to a rectangular fifteen-by-thirty-inch window set flush in the house's foundation wall. She released a tension latch in the center of the frame and carefully tilted out the window. When it was at a forty-five-degree angle from the wall she lifted it out of the pivot brackets and leaned it against the house.

Flo directed the beam into the opening. She waved us over. I went more readily than I felt, just to trick Kurt into going at all. The light pierced a low-ceilinged space, a suspended canopy of cobwebs shivering faintly in the air that came in through the window. On the floor were several lengths of lumber and a coil of dusty rope.

Flo gave me back the flashlight, then took a towel and slithered through the opening headfirst, her legs following, first left, then right. A moment later her face was in the window, smiling—but doubtfully—like she was afraid we wouldn't follow her.

I stuck my head through but Kurt grabbed my waistband and yanked me back. He wanted to go next. He wanted to be close to Flo. His nose plug was in place. I gallantly waved him ahead of me.

Flo took back the flashlight when we were all squatted beneath the low ceiling. I wasn't eager to go on. Entering that space was adventure enough for me. I hated how the floor joists brushed the top of my back, and how Kurt's smelly body got between me and Flo's light. And I hated how the cobwebs snagged on my lips and eyes.

Luckily, we didn't have far to go. Flo stopped at the edge of a cement-sided water tank, eight feet in diameter, set into the ground. Her light shined on a rusty pipe that ran from the ceiling overhead straight down into the center of the tank.

"It's a cistern," she said, her words hollowed out by all the unusual spaces. "Rainwater collected down here and then was pumped up into the house. We don't use it anymore."

Kurt peered over the edge of the dark pit.

"Sister," he said.

"Cistern," I corrected.

I couldn't see how much water was down there. Flo had turned the light so it shined away from her, vaguely in our eyes, and in a flash she was out of her clothes and over the side. I heard a splash, a grunt, and a half scream, half laugh.

"It is *ice* cold," she reported. "Wooh!"

I picked up the flashlight.

"Don't you *dare* shine that down here!"

Her clothes were organized, shirt and pants atop shoes, with a towel alongside.

"Kurt," she asked, "you want to come in?"

"Sister."

"Sure, Kurt. I can be your sister." Her voice had a shiver in it.

"Why don't you come out?" I asked.

"He'll come in if you do," she said.

"How deep?"

"Knees."

I rocked back and pulled off my T-shirt, scraping my knuckles across the ceiling. A chill went through me. I kicked off my shoes and wriggled out of my jeans. Each fresh exposure of skin to the air made me a little colder until I was down to my socks and felt all puckered and vulnerable.

"Sister," Kurt said, his eyes wide with concern as I rolled off my socks.

I turned the light away, darkening the tank further, and let myself over the side.

"Yo!" I screamed when I hit the water.

Flo's laughter sounded sealed in a drum.

The cistern floor was covered with a cold slime. I clutched the center pipe to keep from falling.

Flo couldn't stop laughing.

The light overhead got brighter, like the moon rising, and then it shined full on us, held aloft by Kurt.

Flo was laughing so hard because she had covered her bets by keeping on her bra and underpants.

"Sister!" Kurt yelled, delighted.

"Yeah, sister," I said. "Get that light out of here."

Kurt ignored me. He played the beam all around, stopping on me and pointing and laughing, hurrying past Flo, but frequently.

"Ketch!" he said.

I jerked up my head, expecting to see the flashlight falling toward me. But Kurt was watching how the beam made a solid disk against the cistern's rim.

"Ketch!"

"You're right," I said. It did look like the spotlight that had hunted us earlier in the evening.

Flo's cool fingertips found my back. I shivered. She put her mouth against my shoulder and I felt her swallow a laugh. She touched my hip with her other hand.

"Thank you," she said, "for following me."

"Sister," Kurt said, noseplug on for safety, watching us over the lip of the outside world.

EIGHT

I made a point of going past 1112 East Collier Street on my way home. I felt safe knowing Kurt was somewhere behind me, reading or attempting to read the library book about owning his first home.

He'd never spent an entire night in the apartment we moved to after leaving the old house. I could hardly blame him. The rooms were compacted, gloomy, and difficult to move around in, like they had been pumped full of a sad gas that made forward motion difficult. Kurt was not one to spare our mother's feelings. Her grief, the fact of her dead husband, his dead father, did not drag on Kurt's pursuit of motion. He was out and gone.

A woman watched me from the door of 1112 East Collier Street. The brick wall I had nearly worn a hole through pitching a tennis ball against was visible beneath someone's shaggy idea of landscaping. I'd marked out a generous strike zone with four wads of baseball card gum. I still could picture the mediocrities I'd unwrapped in the packs: Tom Tresh, Jay Hook, Don Blasingame.

The woman came out on the front stoop. She was plump, in a pastel pink sweatsuit, holding a red rag and a bottle of Windex.

She seemed to know me. "Go away, now. We're not selling."

"I'm not buying."

She studied me more closely. "I thought you were that other one."

"That's my brother. We lived here."

"Oh, I've heard all the stories. You're driving my father-in-law to an early grave—you and your hobo friends."

"They're not my friends. He wants to buy the house. Not me."

"Yet here you are," she said.

She fired a blue mist at me from the Windex bottle and went inside. I laughed. Discharged like a bug. A smudge.

I stopped at the mouth of the first perp walk I reached. A hundred paces from one end to the other. Harmless enough. In 1908, Mayor McDeedle might be shaving precious minutes off his busy schedule. The walks might be thick with men and women hurrying to somewhere they were not supposed to be. For an instant I thought I could feel them brushing past me.

By then I had reached Pincoffin Street. My thoughts were on the microfilm reel. Constance's story—her future—was all there. The copies I'd made of the 1908 newspaper stories had left grainy ink smears on my fingers and were folded away in my bag. Did that physical manifestation of the stories set forever the actuality of the events described? It was August 20. Was it August 20 in 1908? A week since Constance disappeared. After a week, the search for her had probably been reduced to her mother and father picking through the grief they shared. They were inconsolably alone in what they had lost. Everyone else had moved on to laying blame. To thinking the worst. Attention had shifted to Dash Buckley, jailed, disbelieved, but sticking to his story.

A group of four kids—two boys and two girls—came out of the perp walk across Pine Street. They were Penny's age, undoubtedly modern, laughing and breathless.

"Who's the president?" one asked me.

"Lincoln, of course," I said.

For a shocked instant, they weren't sure.

"It's 1863," I said.

A car went by and the four watched it pass. They were so relieved.

"Ha!" one of the boys said.

"What would you do if it *was* 1863?" I asked.

"Tell Abe not to go to the movies," a boy said.

"Stop the Civil War," said another.

"How would you get back to now?" I asked.

"Run the other way."

"You're Penny's father," one girl said.

I nodded.

"Are you in the present now?"

"It feels like it."

"What's time travel like?"

"Didn't happen," I said. "I was teasing her. I never thought she'd believe me."

"But the other girl—"

"She's just like you. And me."

"I heard she's like two hundred years old."

I tried to laugh this off. I had the sensation of restraining them by the thinnest thread against flying off in all directions toward oblivion.

"That girl will believe anything," I said.

I stepped around them, fighting the impulse to oversell my casual conviction that time travel couldn't happen. Hadn't happened. But don't run on the perp walks.

Constance was waiting for me just ahead. She startled me, stepping out of the shadows. She had heard what I'd said.

"You shouldn't lie to them."

"I don't want one of them lost like you—fifty years from now. Or a hundred years ago."

She slumped against the fence. Exhaustion had cut deep lines in her face.

"Why are you here?" I asked.

"Nowhere else to go."

She fell in step beside me. I felt vulnerable being that close to her. She might possess some unexplained quality that eased her through time. Proximity to her could drag me along. I didn't want to be in 1908 any more than she wanted to be in my time.

I reached carefully into my bag. The copy ink still was on my hands, and the last thing I wanted was for Constance to see an official account of her disappearance. I withdrew the package I had bought downtown. She read the label.

" '*Têtes et mains de poupée.* Doll heads and hands.' "

Five doll heads, each an inch long from chin to brown hair, with blue eyes and a dot of red for lips. Each head came with a pair of hands, the nails adorned with pinpoints of red polish.

"They look like my mother," Constance said.

I tore open the bag. Each head's hair was bound in place with a clear plastic ring. Constance slipped the band off one head and fluffed the hair.

"If you could work this hair into a bun," she said, "it would look *exactly* like her." Tears came to her eyes. "We're still going back to that place, aren't we? That cellar of records?"

"What for?"

"It's important to me."

We had reached my house. The walk was clear of time travelers. Around back, Flo's parking lot was empty. She was sitting in the kitchen, a glass of iced tea at her elbow, paperwork spread before her. She gave me the coldest stare, started to say something, then saw Constance come in behind me. I was saved, but not entirely.

"That Mr. Burton was here again," she said.

"What did he want?"

"He's talked to some of the kids on the walk. Now he's fairly desperate to talk to you."

Constance, unbidden, had passed through the kitchen and stretched out on the couch in the family room, first kicking off her laceless boots and setting them side by side on the floor without bending over, using just her toes. She folded her hands on her stomach, perfectly relaxed, and closed her eyes.

"They won't let me sleep," she said, her lips barely stirring. "Wake me when it's time to go."

"Okay."

I returned to Flo. She hadn't moved.

"Aren't you curious why I'm not in my office being a doctor?"

"Check this out," I said in a low voice, pulling the newspaper copies from my bag. I unfolded them, put them in order, and slid them under Flo's gaze. Her eyes took in the first story so rapidly that someone who didn't know her would assume she was skimming. As she moved to the second article I waited for her to begin to turn to my side of the story, especially when she saw the drawing of Constance.

But she kept reading. She finished the third story and put them back in order.

"This has to stop," she said.

"What stop?"

"Two more appointments canceled. Both girls Penny's age."

"But I found these stories in the paper," I said. "From 1908! Look at the drawing."

"It resembles her," Flo allowed.

"*Resembles?*" I fought not to shout. "It's her!"

"She's working some sort of scam," Flo said. "Probably on me, ultimately, since you don't have any money."

I took a deep breath. "Your closed-mindedness on this is starting to disappoint me, Flo. I bring you evidence—"

"Evidence? She could've found these stories ahead of time—seen a girl who looked like her. Hatched her scam based on that alone. Then waited for you to find what was already there."

"And her scam is?"

Flo killed the rest of her tea, the ice crashing against her top lip.

"She's good. I've said so. And I can't figure her angle. But it's there. It *will* come out."

Constance slept deep into the afternoon, not moving, as if afraid to disturb someone or something beside her. She slept through the time we'd agreed to return to the Historical Society and I saw no reason to awaken her for that. I stayed close, painting sticks and examining doll heads.

She was still asleep when Burton returned, coming down the perp walk. I went outside to cut him off. He held out his hand. I reluctantly shook it. A spot of green paint was transferred to him.

"Can I ask you something?"

"My daughter has been spreading crazy stories."

He didn't appear to hear me. "I have a certain resilience of spirit," he said. "A spiritual side. I've come to believe in a lot of things that—even a year ago—I'd have told you were totally crazy. You probably heard about my wife."

"No," I said.

He was visibly disappointed, as if realizing this was going to be harder than he'd expected.

"She left me a month ago," he said. "Took the kids, the dog, the Astrovan, and cleared out one day while I was at work. I figured she'd go to her mother's. But she didn't show up there. That's when I knew she was serious. She's smart. But she'll make a mistake. Three people and a dog don't just vanish."

"I'm sorry," I said.

"Yeah, well." He shrugged, relaxed, the explanatory portion of his story behind him.

"When I—one day the phone rang. This was after the thing with . . . after your daughter stopped by." He gave me a look fraught with significance. "It was a friend of my oldest daughter. Vicky Something. She's about twelve. She'd left her bike at my house before my family disappeared. I told her my daughter wasn't home but she still wanted to come over and get it. I thought she'd bring her mom or dad, but she came by herself. What parents let a girl go alone to a man's house? But I was lonely and I—you ever try to talk to a twelve-year-old?"

"Not easy," I said.

"Yeah. But the best part is they haven't developed adult strategies for getting rid of boring people. You can keep a twelve-year-old talking for hours as long as you're willing to be the butt of jokes once they leave. I just kept asking her questions. About herself. About my daughter. And then I asked her if she was looking forward to school starting. You know what she said?"

"What?"

"She said she and her friends weren't going back to school. Guess why."

"Why?"

"Because Penny Winkler's dad was going to teach them to travel back in time so it was *always* summer."

I was definitely going to have to establish some rules of discussion with Penny.

"That's just goofy kid talk," I said.

"Ordinarily, I'd agree. But your visit— Your visit had a profound effect on me."

"I don't—"

"My family has been gone a month. No trace of them."

"And you think I had something to do with that?"

My question caught him off guard. His demeanor turned suddenly suspicious. "I hadn't thought of that," he said.

"The answer is no. To that *and* time travel."

"You knew your daughter was coming to my house before she arrived."

"I've explained that."

"I don't believe you."

"I can't do anything about that."

"I could pay you," he said.

"To do what?"

"Send me back. Or teach me," he said, his eyes avid.

"There's nothing to teach."

"But something— You did *something*."

"No." I waited for him to give up.

"I just want to go back to the day before she left," Burton said, his gaze far away. "I'd take the kids and the van and leave for a long weekend."

"Would that solve anything?"

"Maybe I'd be nicer to her, too."

"That's a start." I backed away, one of those adult strategies for extricating oneself from an awkward social situation.

"I see kids running up and down these shortcuts," he said.

"I've got to go."

"I can't entice you?"

"Your wife and kids left. That *happened.* It's wrong to mess with that, if you ask me."

"You wouldn't tune up your past to make a better present?" he asked. "*If* you could?"

"Absolutely not."

He sneered. "I don't believe you, but okay." He lifted his chin, indicating something behind me. "Who's that?"

Constance was standing in the doorway. A lack of focus in her expression made me wonder if she was walking in her sleep. Her hands were turned out and empty, but even from a distance I could see they were smudged with copier ink.

I ran to her, cursing myself.

"You won't mind if I try this on my own!" Burton called after me.

"Oh, Dash," Constance moaned when I reached her, turned her by the shoulders and marched her back inside. The three stories from 1908 were spread on the kitchen counter.

"They blame Dash!"

"I know. But—"

"My parents will be insane with grief!" She shook one of the copies at me. "Where did you find these?"

"At the library."

"So you know what happens!"

"No. These three stories were all I saw." Not the whole truth; but not a lie, either.

"He might still be in jail. I have to go back *now*!"

"Constance. Listen. Dash is— He's of another time."

"So am I!"

"I know. But you had the misfortune of losing your place."

"You're not making me feel better!" she fairly screamed.

"You can live with us. Penny has a million friends. It's not such a terrible time to be alive."

"I *have* friends," she said. "I'm not your responsibility."

"I feel like you are."

She arranged the copies in a pile. "I have to find out what happens to me," she said. "Take me to the library."

"That's not a good idea."

She put her hand over mine. "I can find out with your help. Or without it."

Constance was unmoved by the library's rich opulence, by the building's architectural line, by the room of humming computers, every last one in use. She only stopped short when she reached the first room full of books. Not one person was in it.

"We own three books," she said. "The Bible. *Family Stories to Be Read Aloud.* And *The Science of Apples.*"

"Doesn't the town have a library?"

"Yes. But my father says I do enough reading at the orphanage." She glanced at me, embarrassed and chagrined. "I want to find out what happened."

I showed her the cabinets of microfilm and how to load the reels onto the reader.

A crease of concentration and worry appeared in the space between her eyebrows when the first image came up on the screen from the August 16–31, 1908, reel.

"You're right," she said.

"I am?"

"Maybe I shouldn't know what happens."

I turned off the machine. I felt safer with the screen dark.

"You've made the right decision," I said. "You'll—"

"I haven't decided anything."

I waited. There was really no doubt what she would do.

"I want to know," she said with a firm nod of her chin.

"You're sure?"

"My mother and father are the kind of people who don't want to know the bad parts of life. They trust in God and hope for the best. I don't want to be like them," she said.

"It's a luxury—not knowing everything," I said.

"They've lived waiting to be hurt by what they were afraid of knowing."

"And now it has happened."

"It has?"

"You're gone."

She reached and turned on the machine. I fiddled with the focus. We scrolled slowly through the illuminated pages, Constance stopping me now and then to read a story, or to note an event whose immediacy for her, combined with its distance in the past, gave me chills.

"Emmeline Whitehead had her baby," she said, pointing to a small notice. "A boy." She turned to me. "We should check the records on him."

"He's in his nineties."

"He might have heard of me," she said, sounding faintly proud. "The legend of the vanished girl."

Constance reread the story about her from the August 20 paper, shuddered, and moved ahead. There was no mention of her over the next two days. Then we came to August 23, 1908.

A little weather bird atop the masthead announced that it was a blistering day in Hickory Hill. A story in the upper right-hand corner confirmed that Constance remained front-page news.

GUARD INCREASED ON JAILED APPLE PICKER

by E. Wayne Manger

Hickory Hill Sheriff Lloyd Horton added an extra deputy to the detail guarding orchardman Harold "Dash" Buckley in the town jail as a restless public weighed the conflicting histories attaching themselves to the young man detained in the disappearance of hometown beauty Constance Morceau.

Buckley has freely admitted to being the last person to see Constance alive and has steadfastly adhered to a story that is regarded far and wide as largely fabulous: mainly that the young woman vanished "into thin air" while running in the rain through her father's apple trees.

Sheriff Horton reports that young Buckley has cleaved to this story with a passion that "makes me think that he might be telling the truth; or at least believes what he is telling me is the truth."

It was in the background details of Buckley's life that doubt about his credibility surfaced. The mere rumors of these discrepancies attracted a sizable crowd of indigenes—mostly young men in possession of a certain lack of responsibility—to the square outside the jail. Even the trains that made their regular stops throughout the day disgorged knots of the curious on trips out from the city or provided a temporary viewing stand for the men, women, and children who nearly tipped the train cars as they packed the windows for a glimpse of Mr. Buckley or the hoosegow that held him.

Fissures began to appear in the suspect's narrative when an official of the A.C.E. School of Pharmacopoeia in Chicago, having read Buckley's claim that he was enrolled there, alerted this reporter and Sheriff Horton that no Harold Buckley was or ever had been a student at the school.

Further, a check of the references given by Mr. Buckley to Constance's father—Peter T. Morceau—upon applying for employment at the Morceau apple orchard revealed that Buckley had created his employment history out of whole cloth.

In fact, Sheriff Horton said, "There doesn't appear to be any record of Harold Buckley anywhere. It seems very clear to me that he has been less than forthright with the details of his past."

Constance turned toward me, something new in her eyes.

"He lied to me?" she said.

"Everyone fiddles with the details of who they are."

"I don't!"

"Well, you haven't had much time to muck it up."

"I can't believe he didn't tell me who he was," she said to the screen.

She spun the reel ahead, hunting for the next story.

"When I was a little girl I used to evaluate my chances of going to heaven," she said. "I was always able to reassure myself that I hadn't done anything so terrible that it would keep me out. Then I turned fourteen."

"What happened then?"

She sat back. "Nothing, really. But my thoughts changed. I became much harder on myself. I began to expect more of myself and less of other people. Mostly, though, I started lying to my parents. It was just easier."

"You won't go to hell for that."

"I've told some preposterously tall tales."

"To deceive them, or protect them?"

She thought a moment. "A little of both."

She spun us into the future. Her story was at the top of the front page on August 25.

We both gasped.

SHERIFF, SUSPECT KILLED BY MOB

by E. Wayne Manger

A mob of local cowards and out-of-town troublemakers—stoked by rumor and the infernal heat—last night burst into the Hickory Hill jail and took whatever unholy law they recognized into their own bloody hands.

After a brief but intense paroxysm of violence, two men lay dead and the community was led to ponder both its actions and inactions.

Sheriff Lloyd Horton, father, husband, friend and lawman, was overpowered in his efforts to protect Harold "Dash" Buckley and deliver him for trial in the Aug. 13 disappearance of local angel Constance Morceau.

Sheriff Horton suffered a fatal blow to the head with a length of pipe or stick of wood when he placed himself between the mob and his legal charge. The wielder of that murderous bludgeon remains at large, his identity unascertained in the swirl of events. A reward for that person's conviction is being pondered.

The sheriff's death took the starch out of his deputies, who proved unwilling to lay down their lives in protection of their prisoner, and the mob dragged the young Buckley from his jail cell. Clad only in trousers and undershirt and proclaiming his innocence in a terrified voice that carried into the night, Buckley was hauled bodily into the square and hanged from the century-old hickory tree that gave this sorry town its name.

No good citizen raised his or her voice in protest of the barbarity, although several hundred were present, witnessing the ugly scene by bonfire light and from the shadows.

The lynching of Mr. Buckley was just the latest page in a saga of such abiding unhappiness that its repercussions are not likely to free Hickory Hill's citizens from the prison of their consciences for generations to come.

The disappearance of Constance Morceau was not what set off the mob, however. Tragic as that was, the public had evinced patience in sorting out the mystery.

But that mystery took a despicable turn as the investigation into Buckley's past progressed. His claim that he was being educated at the A.C.E. School of Pharmacopoeia in Chicago was disputed by officials of the school. His previous work history likewise proved vulnerable to careful scrutiny.

The public grew restless as word spread of these apparent falsifications. An element of that public, fueled by an excess of unoccupied time, liquor's false courage, and a misguided apprehension of masculinity, began to press for a more direct course of action.

Sheriff Horton and his deputies were able to keep this element at bay until a private investigator named Earl Everett entered upon the scene.

Everett, employed primarily by Chicago clients, claimed to be in possession of proof that Buckley was in fact one Harold "Sweetie" Futrell, a denizen of big-city streets who slid through life on a thin grease composed of equal parts smooth talk, hot dice, and a confidence game known as Pie-Chart, the operation of which attracted the law enforcement officials of Cleveland, Pittsburgh, Youngstown, Ohio, Detroit, Goodland, Ind., and Chicago.

Futrell, the detective Everett alleged, was also deft at insinuating himself into the affections of young women through candied words and a talent for the latest dance steps.

Further, Everett alleged to possess proof that Futrell was one-eighth Negro.

Constance gasped, appeared about to faint, then leaped to her feet and raced from the library. By the time I got the reel put away and went after her, she was nowhere in sight.

NINE

Hilly Cutter, her wards safely delivered into Flo's care, was having a smoke by the perp walk when I got home.

"Who *are* these people?" she asked.

Eight were in sight just on the link between Clover and Chapman. Six were roughly Penny's age—three boys and three girls—sharing a posture of anxious enjoyment, like they were in the mood for something innocently dangerous, like skinny-dipping, or their first beer.

Standing apart from them was an elderly couple, the woman in sunhat and red Reeboks, the man a step or two behind, using a walker, even this four-point contact with the ground anxious and uncertain. They watched with bemused envy as the teens took their marks and ran with conviction and ungainliness from one end of the walk to the other. Each kid watched each other kid's flight. No one knew enough to be confident nothing would happen.

The old man and woman looked a little relieved, a trifle smug, when the kids pulled up panting and frustrated and stuck in the present.

"I don't know who they are," I said.

Hilly took a leisurely pull on her cigarette. The day was close and warm.

"You know your damsel is gone," she said.

"Who?"

" 'Who?' " she mimicked me. "Her foster dad called this morning. No sign of her last night. He didn't say so—it reflects poorly on them—but I suspect it's been more than just last night. We tell the fosters to call the minute anything *untoward* happens—but the more experienced ones will let things slide 'cause they know events usually shake out without dragging the state into it. Have you seen her?"

"I saw her today."

"Where?"

"The library."

"She try to sell you that line of time-travel foolishness?"

"She's very interested in the past."

"And her fosters can't break her of running the hot water cold and sitting on the throne for an hour at a time. But that doesn't add up to time travel."

"I didn't say it did."

A boy on a skateboard slalomed through, his head protected by a football helmet painted silver and accessorized with swept-back cardboard jet wings, complete with insignia and fuel tanks.

Hilly watched him, idly smoking.

The man with the walker had advanced six feet. His wife, partner, aide, mate could be seen visibly holding back to stay at his side, denying her desire to let loose and see what pell-mell motion might accomplish. Maybe her plan was to go into the past and choose a different guy. Or pick the same man but hide the cigarettes he sneaked throughout his diabetes, or water the gin that ate away his faculties.

"I will admit to one puzzle about her," Hilly said.

"What's that?"

"She doesn't appear to exist." She dug through a tote bag at her feet and came up with a file. "No birth certificate. No school records. No shots. No lost child report. No Social Security number."

"How far back did you check?"

Hilly blinked. "Girl's fifteen. I checked back fifteen years."

"Did you look for a death certificate?"

" 'Course not." She exhaled smoke. "Is there something you want to tell me?"

"No."

"Joshua, you are giving me the gooseflesh. I can't—are you saying? What *are* you saying?"

"If I see her I'll tell her to contact her foster family," I said.

"You tell her to contact *me*. I've got a stack of questions a mile high for that girl." She returned her attention to the walk. "Lord, it reminds me of the road to salvation out here."

The perp walk traffic had intensified, an actual line of people forming at the Clover Street end, awaiting clearance to proceed.

"Reminds me of my baptism," Hilly said. "Whole bunch of people with the glow on them. Like someone yonder's seen the virgin in the aluminum siding."

Flo would blow a BP cuff when she saw that mob. Worse, they would draw attention to Constance and me. A congested perp walk would not make an ideal runway through time.

A man pedaling a four-wheel contraption came from the Clover Street end. His quadracycle had an ice cream freezer box over the front axle. Smoke poured from it when he lifted the lid. He drew a crowd and blocked the way. An impatience that felt new sprang into my mind. He was in the way of what could possibly happen.

"I don't think you belong there," I called to him.

"Party pooper," Hilly said.

The vendor smiled at me, but dipped his hand into the smoking box like my suggestion could surely wait. After a minute he pedaled closer.

"You're him," he said. Business had constricted down to a single kid, frozen by the menu.

"Who?"

"You are, aren't you?" He kept his voice down, a step above a whisper, and the kid memorizing the selection paid him no mind.

"I thought I did it, too. Once," the vendor said. "I was *positive* I'd gone into the future—just by a little bit. Less than a minute, even. Not enough to do me any good. And then I remembered hundreds of people die every minute. I could've helped *them*."

"I don't see how."

He shrugged. "Yeah, I guess. What was it like for you?"

"Nothing happened to me."

"Don't *be* that way, man. You've got a gift. Look." He pointed up and down the perp walk, people running, walking, consulting watches, checking their pulses, laughing and waiting and wondering. "You've touched people. You're inspiring."

"Not me. Sorry."

The vendor lost patience with the undecided kid and snarled, "All I've got left is pineapple push-ups and acorn squash icies. So make up your mind or make tracks!"

The kid bolted.

"You made me do that," the vendor accused me. "I hate to see someone waste a gift. I get so mad when someone ignores what has been bestowed upon him."

"I'm lucky in love," I said. "That's my only gift."

"That's not a gift. That's just coincidence."

I stepped away from the fence. "Do you really sell acorn squash ice cream?"

He grimaced. "I *carry* it. Boss's wife's bright idea. Ain't sold one yet."

"What's next? Rutabaga?"

"Have you seen the girl?"

"What girl?"

He was so disappointed. "Don't do this, man. The girl from long ago. She's come to warn us."

"Warn us about the past? What good would that do?"

"She's been seen. I know people that have talked to her. She's totally ignorant of the now. TV. Movies. Advertising. The culture. The world at large. She's an innocent. You've got to ask yourself: Why is she here? What does she want with us?"

Hilly shepherded three children down the path.

"Is she in there?" the vendor asked.

I drew away. "No. There's no one—I don't know any girl from the past."

He opened the trapdoor on the freezer box, extracted a frozen concoction and tore away its wrapper, revealing what resembled a green hockey puck on a thin, wooden stick.

"Acorn squash icy," he offered me.

I licked it. It had a cold, heavy, vegetable taste, oily, not one hundred percent unpleasant, with a salty hint of melted butter. I took a small bite. The center of the puck was yellow.

"They don't have *that* where she came from." The vendor jabbed a finger at the icy.

I handed it back. "Score one for the past."

He made a point of finishing the thing, one reluctant nibble at a time. He did not move on until he was finished. I watched him from the window as he spat the seeds over the fence into our yard.

By midnight the perp walk traffic had cleared, and I sat with Flo out back in the warm, still air, side by side on chaise longues, sharing a strawberry daiquiri. Heat lightning broke to the north. Each silent puff of silvery light stopped our conversation, sporadic and uncomfortable though it was.

"I have good news and bad news on the MRI," she said.

"Okay."

"The good news is you don't have a tumor," she said. "You exhibit normal brain function."

"What's the bad news?"

"You don't have a tumor."

I wasn't certain if she was making a joke, but I laughed anyway. It wasn't out of relief, either. I had never considered for a moment that my going back fifteen minutes was the result of some chemical disturbance in my head, some delusion of bad wiring.

"What are you working on these days?" she asked in the checklist voice of a first date.

"Do you want to see?"

"Describe it to me."

She closed her eyes. Waiting. Waiting to be transported by my vision. Waiting to be reassured. Her glasses had worn a ditch in her temple that looked sore and tender. I hooked her hairs behind her ears.

"Don't change the subject," she said, without opening her eyes.

"I'm painting sticks," I said. "I have an abundance of sticks that came down in the storms. They're like a heavenly manna of work materials. So I'm saving you money there."

Her eyes flashed open, burned into me, then reclosed. She took a blind sip of daiquiri.

"The sticks remind me of people," I said. "Girls, to be honest. Not that they look like girls, but there's something in the sticks—in their shapes—that's familiar to me. So I've been taking a stick and painting it—and adding a head."

"A head?"

"A doll's head."

"I was—" she began. "How many have you finished?"

"None. Yet."

"I was expecting more."

"You were."

"Not more painted sticks. More of you."

"I could put on weight," I said, trying to make a joke out of it. She didn't even smile.

"You used to work as hard as I do."

"I felt guilty that I wasn't bringing in any money," I said. "I thought that if I at least put in as much time as you do, you wouldn't notice."

"I noticed," Flo said.

"That I didn't make any money?"

"That you worked hard. The money was never a big deal to me."

"But now it is?"

"No," she said.

A plume of heat lightning diverted our attention.

"Now I feel like you're hurting my business," she said. "Not just that you're not working as hard as you used to—but you're attracting attention I don't need. *We* don't need."

A commotion in the dark—like evidence, or a visual aid—ran down the perp walk. It was a line of kids hooting and waving sparklers over their heads, burning strings of light onto my vision.

"That," Flo said, "for example. Do you know that I am one of the last businesses in town allowed to operate in a residential area? Daddy got the zoning grandfathered in. But all the men he dealt with to get that are either dead or retired. That makes me—us—vulnerable."

"Has someone complained?"

"You're missing the point," she said. "I try to be a good neighbor. I'd like more parking, but I don't want to risk angering anyone."

"You're a slave to your location," I said. "Maybe you should move."

"I don't *want* to move. I like being able to roll out of bed and go to work. I like eating lunch with you. Having Penny close at hand."

She polished off the daiquiri, licking her top lip when she was done.

"My point is," she continued, "I don't want to give anyone reason to complain about me. I hold my breath every time Hilly and her state van pull up. They're beautiful kids—but they stick out here. And—"

"That reminds me," I said. "Turns out Constance's boyfriend was a fraction black. And *he* was lynched."

"Josh—what on Earth?"

"The good citizens of the former Hickory Hill strung him up for being part *Negro*."

She brought the glass to her lips, forgetting it was empty, or desiring the feel of warm glass between her teeth, ready to bite off a piece and spit it at me.

"It's in the paper," I said. "She's big news. A mob broke into the jail, killed the sheriff, then dragged out this kid who was one-eighth black and hanged him. Right in the square."

Flo rose to her feet without a word and went into the house. When I found her she was in the kitchen wiping her face with a wet towel. Her skin shined in the overhead light.

"This has to stop," she said, fighting to control a tremor in her voice. "Do you understand?"

"I can show you the stories. She's real."

"She's real, yes. But real *now*. Not from the past. We're not her future."

"She's seen her future," I said. "On this date in 1908 she's only missing. Her boyfriend is in jail—but he hasn't been lynched. *That's* her future."

Flo, with visible reluctance, asked, "How much time does she have?"

I couldn't help but smile.

"Don't!" she warned.

"You believe."

"No. I'm only asking. I feel like I'm keeping track of two parallel lives. Mine and my nutty husband's."

"Four days," I said. "He's lynched the night of the twenty-fourth."

"Okay," she nodded. "Before then, this girl will make her move for whatever it is she's after."

"You don't believe," I said.

"No, I don't. Have you asked at the library for a record of who's checked out that microfilm?"

"They don't keep track of that."

"How convenient."

"That doesn't prove anything."

"You watch. Within four days—more likely three—she'll reveal herself."

"I think she wants to go home before then."

"Well, keep your hand on your wallet."

A storm that blew up in the night stayed to the west, touching us only with a wind that woke me a significant distance from my wife's side. I couldn't reach her even with my arm outstretched. She found me in the morning in the yard. The wind had shaken down another lifetime's supply of sticks. Twisted, lean, expressive, they were usable or not. Potential stick figures or kindling. Those I couldn't picture with a head I caddied into a tall kraft paper bag. Flo waved to me from her office and went on with her day.

I worked in my studio for an hour but did not go deep enough to lose track of time. I painted a stick in the colors of a ball gown—deep blue, with an undercoating of jewels. The wood drank up the paint so completely that I might have been applying only the theory of the colors. I set the stick aside to dry before attempting a second coat.

Five heads were mounted like erasers on the ends of pencils. I'd combed out their hair and stood them up in a yarn-wrapped can Penny had made for me when she was six. They stared at me like quintuplets. I was about to select one when the throttled noise of an engine growled, roared, and then cut off almost directly outside my studio window.

It was Jock Itch on the perp walk, astride a police motorcycle, his legs spread for balance.

"We're looking for the girl," he said.

"I haven't seen her today."

"But you *did* see her?"

"Yesterday," I said. "Don't they have detectives to handle the important cases?"

"Let the record show that you got nasty first."

"What record?" I asked.

"You saw her yesterday on the path?" Itch said.

"At the library. We looked at old newspapers."

"You *talked* to her?"

"Sure."

"What about?"

Itch's attitude of found treasure made me wary. "Her family. Her boyfriend."

"Who's her boyfriend?" Itch asked.

"You don't know him."

"Come on, Wink. Does he go to Euclid High?"

I hesitated. Something wasn't right. "I don't think so," I said.

"Did you see her after the library?"

"No."

"Did you see anyone on the path last night?"

"I saw lots of people."

"Talk to any of them?"

"I don't—wait. An ice cream vendor."

"Seen Kurt around?"

"Kurt?" I said, thrown off by the turn in the questions.

"Your brother."

"I saw him—" I thought back. "Yesterday, too. Also at the library. Why?"

"Kurt's always on my list of people to keep track of when something bad happens."

"Something *bad* has happened?"

"A girl doesn't come home," Itch said. "That doesn't seem at least *potentially* bad to you?"

"Did you check with her foster family?"

"Foster family? Holly's mom went to school with us."

"Holly?"

"Holly Dearborn."

"*She's* missing?"

"Where you been, Wink? Yes. She didn't come home last night."

I clung to the fence for balance. I turned toward my house, almost for reassurance that the world was as I remembered it the last time I was paying attention. Flo watched from her office window.

"I haven't—" I began. "I take back—I was talking about a different girl. I haven't seen Holly in—" I tried to remember. "A couple days. She was on the walk. About where you are."

"Is that a threat?"

"What? No."

"You didn't see her last night?"

"No."

He slipped a color photo of Holly Dearborn from his breast pocket.

"She's a friend of my daughter's," I said.

"You don't remember her mom? Natalie Morton?" He made a hot-stuff motion over his heart with his hand.

"Who saw Holly last?"

Itch started the cycle, revved the engine. I screamed another question at him. He made a loud show of departing.

Flo came out of her office. A freshly stoked anger radiated from her. Jock Itch's coming and going was further evidence in the indictment she was building against me. Suddenly I was tired of not being believed.

"Holly Dearborn's missing."

Flo's anger drained away like that.

"She didn't come home last night," I said.

We both looked up at the second-floor window of Penny's room, the sunlight blocked by bamboo blinds.

"Is she up there?" I asked.

"A summer morning?" She checked her watch. "I'm guessing. Go check."

Flo returned to work. I went to Penny's room, where the door was closed. I tapped. No answer. I pressed quietly ahead. A warm aftermath of Love Spell suffused the air around Penny's gentle snoring. I had never been so relieved to see anyone in my life.

I sat just on the tip of her bed. That slight movement awoke her so abruptly that I wondered if her snoring had been an act. But if she had climbed into bed thirty seconds before I knocked that was okay with me, for the moment. I just wanted her there.

She stretched her arms and smacked her crusty lips. "Huh?"

"Holly didn't come home last night."

Penny came fully awake. "She—?"

"Did you see her?" I asked.

"Yeah."

She threw off her covers and climbed out of bed. She had on black-heart boxer shorts and a gray Bebe T-shirt. She crossed the room, out the door, down the hall into the bathroom, slamming and locking that door. I remained on the edge of her bed, not wanting to follow her, not wanting to be perceived by my daughter to be pressing too hard. Presently she was standing in her doorway, brushing her teeth, her bright, refreshed eyes hard upon me.

"Ah gah bunned," she said around her toothbrush, green-white foam overflowing her mouth.

"Yeah?" I said, not understanding her but not wanting to discourage her by requiring that she backtrack extensively.

Rather than explaining herself, she returned to the bathroom. I held my ground while she took a shower. The phone beside her bed rang and I answered it, but whoever it was hung up. The dead receiver—the sense of being assessed and rejected—bothered me. I thought of Constance, existing somewhere out of sight, without allies, and running out of time to save her boyfriend's life.

Penny returned in a long robe, her hair bundled up in a towel. She unwound the towel and raked her fingers through her hair.

"Who was with you last night?" I asked. "Besides you. And Holly."

"Regan," she said immediately. "Corey."

"Would they talk to me?"

Her eyes were momentarily stricken, a teen that feared being embarrassed by a lumbering parent.

"About what?"

"What if Holly is like Constance?"

She took in this possibility. "It couldn't happen," she said.

"It has. Before."

"I never believed. I still don't."

"So the last time you saw her she was with Regan and Corey," I said.

Penny blushed. "She left with Regan. I was with Corey."

I didn't pursue that. I only wanted to determine that Penny was not the last person to see Holly before she disappeared.

"I hope she went into the future," I said.

"Why?"

"Because in the past she could be anywhere."

TEN

Penny and I rode our bikes into the Dragon Hills early that afternoon. The neighborhood's stately, overarching trees kept out the withering sun, and I had the sensation of moving through a chamber maintained for the comfort of the preferred.

Regan Brownlee's family lived at 84 Escutcheon Drive, a blue Cape Cod house so long it curved to match the bend in the street. Five cars—one a police cruiser—were parked in front of a three-car garage.

I stopped across the street.

"What?" Penny said impatiently.

"Police."

She pointed off to her left. "Holly lives around the corner."

I couldn't see any corners, only shady sweeps, green curves, cool arcs leading out of sight. The right-angle rules of Euclid Heights didn't apply there. A brass horse weathervane made a quarter-turn on the peak of the Brownlees' roof. A storm door opened and a boy came out, hopped on a bike, and pedaled furiously away.

"Spencer," Penny informed me. "Her brother."

"Any other kids?"

"A baby girl. Regan was disgusted when her mom got pregnant."

"Does Regan have a boyfriend?"

"She gets Holly's throwaways."

"And Holly?"

"She wants Corey."

"Your Corey?"

"He isn't mine," she said curtly. "But, yeah."

This possible conflict between Penny and Holly frightened me. "She could try to mess with you," I said.

A fuss across the street diverted our attention. Three people exited the house—Regan, a woman, and a uniformed cop. The woman was coiffed and self-assured, done up in a blue blazer and canary yellow slacks. Regan was slightly taller than the woman, her mother, I assumed, or her Realtor. Before the cop finally departed she flashed him a cold smile of perfect teeth.

"Regan," Penny called, as the girl and the woman headed back toward the house.

Regan turned. The woman turned, too, and I saw the taut, anxious weariness in her bearing. They spoke, then the woman went on into the house and Regan came across the street to us.

"Hey," she muttered, staying within herself: blank expression, arms folded low across her belly, left foot turned out ninety degrees.

"Were you with Hol when she disappeared?" Penny asked.

A good first question, I thought. My first question.

"Wouldn't I have like disappeared, too, if I was?" Regan said.

"I don't know," I said. "Tell us what happened."

"We ate at six," Regan said. "My dad wasn't home, of course. Spence knocked over his milk, accidentally on purpose, and my mom made me clean it up. At seven I had a fight with her about doing the dishes."

"I mean about when Holly disappeared," I said.

Regan regarded me like I was a slow learner.

"This is context, *Dad,*" she said. "When I was fighting with my mom I thought about you"—she meant me—"and how it'd be so cool to be able to just like move back or forth. Back to a couple seconds before Spencer knocked over his milk. Or ahead to when the dishes were finished."

"That'd be a waste," I said. "Just do the dishes."

She scowled. I thought I'd lost her. It was oddly unnerving to be regarded by a teenager with something more than polite impatience.

"What then?" I said.

"At nine Holly called. She was with you"—a nod to Penny—"and Corey. My mom wanted me out of her hair 'cause my dad still wasn't home. I stayed on the phone with Holly. Then you. Then Corey. My mom got mad at me for that, too."

"I can understand that," I said.

"We *have* call-waiting."

"What time did you finally hook up with everyone?"

"What was it, Pen? Like ten?"

"About."

"Quarter after, maybe," Regan said. "Everyone was doing the walks."

"The walks?" I said.

"Yeah. Trying to travel through time."

"Did anyone else see Holly disappear?" I asked.

"I didn't actually *see* her disappear," Regan said. "Around midnight most everyone had gone home." She spoke directly to Penny. "You and Corey left then?"

"About then," Penny said.

"You better watch that boy," Regan said. "Holly is *so* after him."

"She can have him," Penny said airily. "If he wants her."

"So it was around midnight . . ." I prompted.

"You shouldn't be so quick to give him up," Regan said, still to Penny.

"I'm only saying . . . if he wants her, I'm not going to pop a stitch over it."

"So getting back to midnight on the walk," I said.

Regan returned her attention to me. "It was still like really hot, you know? For nighttime. And it was thundering, too."

"It was?"

"Oh yeah. Loud."

"And lightning?"

"Yes."

"Right above you?"

"No."

"Which direction from you?"

"I don't *know,*" Regan said petulantly.

"That way?" I pointed south.

She turned, getting her bearings. "It's hard in these curvy streets." She readjusted her bearings, and then pointed. "More that way."

"West. Okay. Then what?"

"We just started to walk home. She was in a really goofy mood." Regan locked on Penny. "She said she could tell she was getting to Corey. She said she wanted to find out what happened. So she took off running."

"Find out what happened?"

"Yeah. In the future. Isn't that what this is all about?"

"I keep hoping not," I said.

"But it's so cool!"

"Your friend has disappeared!"

She glared at me, like I'd squashed her mood. She pivoted and huffed back across the street. I went after her. Penny stayed where she was.

"You said she took off running," I said.

Regan kept going. I noticed for the first time her mother in the house's front window, a hand playing with something around her neck.

"Where were you when she started running?"

Regan's mom moved out of the window, toward the front door, as we came up the driveway. She might have intended to lend aid, or avoid being seen by her daughter. Regan stopped.

"She's coming back," she said. "I just know she's coming back."

"Why?"

"Because Holly wouldn't do something like travel through time without coming back and bragging about it."

"Tell me about her running."

"She just ran."

"On the path?"

"Yes."

"West?"

"Yeah."

"Between which streets?"

She thought a moment. "I don't know street names. We always take—what's the street that leads to the Hills?"

"Pincoffin."

"Yeah. She was heading that way. She was between Pincoffin and the street before it."

"Pine?"

"Okay."

"And that was the last you saw of her?"

"I was so mad. When I got to the end of the walk she was gone," Regan said. "And it was starting to rain."

"How hard?"

"It got me wet."

"Did you call for her? Yell her name?"

"I don't remember. I felt ditched."

"Has she ditched you before?"

Regan winced. "She's ditched everybody—at one time or another."

Her mother gauged our time at an end and called to her daughter through the screen door. Regan heeded. I took one last crack at her.

"Where is Holly, really?"

She regarded me oddly, a little disappointed, like she was surprised to discover she'd been wasting her time.

We followed Pincoffin out of the Dragon Hills, riding without a word until we reached the perp walk, the point where Holly Dearborn disappeared. People were hanging around: whispering kids, idlers disappointed there wasn't more to see, those hoping to follow Holly to wherever she had gone.

"I'm going downtown," I said.

"Okay."

"Come with me."

"I'm helping mom this afternoon."

"So you have to scrub up?" I teased.

"I don't have to scrub up to dust."

I laughed, but she didn't. I was afraid to let her out of my sight.

"Okay. Go. But stay off the perp walks," I said.

"Yes, father," she replied, mock demur.

I wanted to impart further instruction, but she didn't give me the chance, pedaling cheerfully up the forbidden path, weaving through a loose strand of the curious, a few who knew her and waved. A few who stared at me. Then she was out of sight.

I went directly to the library, to the microfilm readers, and there was Constance, her face sad and greenish gray from the light thrown off by the machine. A welter of reel boxes was at her elbow. She wasn't surprised to see me, just resentful at my having pulled her out of her world.

"No one's been arrested for Dash's murder," she reported.

"Another girl is missing."

She glanced at the machine screen, like my announcement was a story she had missed. "Now? Who?"

"Her name is Holly Dearborn. She's a friend of my daughter's."

"I know when my mother dies," Constance said, her eyes tearing.

"How?"

"I went to the cemetery where my grandparents are buried. Emil and Connie. She's there, too."

"When did she die?"

"When *does* she die, you mean. May sixth, 1920. And there's a small notice in the paper." She started crying for real, a silent dissolving, her face in her hands.

"Would it be so terrible, staying in this time?"

"Yes!" she said, close to a shriek.

"Even if you can't get back in time to save Dash?"

"My mother has only twelve years to live. I want those twelve years with her. *This* isn't my time."

"I think it's sort of encouraging—for you—that this other girl disappeared," I said. "Odd as that sounds."

"Another girl lost in time?"

"No. Just that it happened. There's something about those walks. I don't know why. Or *how*. But at least it's still possible. I'm just afraid you'll go back to 1808. Or 2008."

"No. My heart's in 1908. That's where I belong," she said. "That's where I will go."

"You have—"

She stopped me. "*That's* where I'm going."

"Do you feel differently about Dash?"

"Do you believe everything you read in newspapers?"

I excused myself and called home. The phone rang and rang. Not a bad thing in itself. Penny could easily be with Flo, being further indoctrinated in the powers and temptations of medicine. The machine came on.

"Just me," I said. "I wanted to be sure Pen got home okay. I'm at the library. Constance is here. I'll see you later. Love you." I hung up.

I was about to call Flo's office when I noticed Constance behind me.

"Who were you talking to?" I asked.

"My family."

"You didn't give them a chance to respond."

"It was an answering machine."

She stared blankly at me. "I want to go home," she said.

"Have you eaten?"

"Not since last night. Money is so much more important now."

"Come on."

We left the library and headed for my house, her walking and me riding my bike. At Collier Street I couldn't dissuade her from following it east. I was afraid of finding Kurt in front of our old house. He wasn't on the porch, or anywhere else in sight, and I hurried past, relieved.

But Constance stopped.

"Dash lived here," she said.

I came back to her. "Here?"

"Yes."

"I—my family—used to live here."

She didn't respond. In fact, she did not appear particularly surprised. I thought of Flo's prediction about Constance, and I wondered if the coincidence was the beginning of some plan falling into place.

"Did it feel sad to you?" she asked.

"It wasn't a—" I stopped. "The people in it weren't a happy bunch."

"Maybe the house made them unhappy."

"I don't believe in that. The animation of inanimate things."

"You traveled through time and you don't *believe* in something?"

"It only matters what *you* believe," I said. "I'm not going anywhere."

She returned to contemplating the house.

"I wonder if it's still there," she said.

"What?"

"Dash had a bag of coins he was saving." She glanced bashfully away. "He had plans for us." She grabbed my arm. "That's why I don't believe the stories about him."

"Does it matter at this point?"

"We were alone in the cellar," she said. "He had the bag in his hand and he was trying to impress me with how much he had saved. He thought he wasn't good enough for me. He hadn't even tried to kiss me."

Abruptly she went up the walk. I trailed helplessly. She rapped on the front door.

I reached around her and pressed the bell. She heard it inside the house and was amazed. She pushed it again, her ear pressed to the door.

"That's so pretty," she said, with the first smile I could remember from her. She pushed the button a third time. I winced, putting myself in the shoes of the impatiently summoned.

"*Finally,*" she said. "Something else to like about your time."

No one was answering. "Let's go," I said.

"Dash heard someone upstairs," she recalled. "He put the bag of money back in its hiding place. He didn't trust his landlord."

The door swung open just then and an old man, sour from interrupted sleep, confronted us.

"You!" he sputtered at me. "Damn you!"

A pill of pink blanket fuzz clung to a nose hair and popped in and out of his nostril with each breath.

But then his eyes fell on Constance and his demeanor changed entirely. He studied her with the utmost care and curiosity, not taking his eyes off her. His hand reached for her and she offered her own in return. I thought the handshake went on a little too long, but Constance didn't seem to mind.

When I tried to follow her into the house, the spell was broken. The old man put his hand on my chest.

"He's welcome, too, isn't he?" Constance said.

"Only if you're here." He leaned toward her. "You be mindful of your associates, girlie."

In the front hall, the light and texture were not what I remembered. But the smell was familiar. It was a mixture of odors I associated with my parents: cooked meat, disinfectant, full ashtrays. For a moment I wished Kurt were with us. He might never get another chance. He might realize the house he remembered was not the one we were standing in.

"Can we see in your cellar?" Constance asked.

The old man was helpless before her. " 'Course you can."

We went through the kitchen, all new, past a powder room I didn't recognize, then around a corner and down the stairs to the basement. The man switched on a light at the bottom. A pool table gleamed beneath a white drop ceiling. It took a moment to orient myself. My bed had been over there, and over there had been my desk where I should have been studying instead of drawing, and there the door to the steps that led up to the backyard.

Constance moved—almost floated—to a spot along the wall behind a new wet bar. She brushed her fingers doubtfully across the ceiling. The room was alien to me, too bright, so I couldn't imagine how it struck her, who might have used only a smoky lantern the last time she was down there.

She turned to me for help. I went behind the bar and pushed up one of the ceiling sections. It lifted from its track and I slid it over into the space above the panel next to it. The dark, familiar space I remembered was revealed. Constance shivered, then jumped up for a better look.

"What the hey!" the old man exclaimed.

I dragged over a bar stool and found a flashlight on the workbench in the opposite corner of the basement. I instructed Constance in its use. She knelt on the stool and shined the light into the space between two thick, age-dusted floor joists. She reached a hand in and I heard her scratch at something, then with a pop like a cork she extracted a small rectangle of wood, with a nail in it bent to hook a finger through.

The old man was not so amazed that he forgot his legal rights.

"We own this house!" he said to me. "I know you mean to cheat us but it's ours fair and square."

Constance wasn't listening. Her excited face gave way to dismay. She crouched on the stool to see deeper inside, the top half of her head going right up into the ceiling, a tight squeeze with the flashlight.

Her voice came down to us. "It's gone."

"What's gone?" the old man asked.

"Something I left here," Constance said. "He must've come back after I disappeared."

"You *are* a ghost!" The old man fell back.

"I'm not." She reached out but he refused her touch. In her other hand was the square of wood.

"I thought if I was stuck here I'd have a little money to live on," she said to me.

"Any money's mine!" the old man said.

"No money here," she said, her voice diminished by the ceiling's tight space. But she didn't come down, unwilling to give up on Dash, on her last link to him.

Something occurred to me.

"When you went to your mother's grave—"

"Wait," she said. "There's something—"

She extracted the hand holding the flashlight and passed it down to me. She threaded her arm back inside, reaching shoulder-deep into the hiding place.

"Whatever it is—*we* own it!" the old man said.

She brought out a folded square of paper, browned, water-spotted, brittle in the unfolding. She climbed down off the stool and opened the paper under the ceiling light. The ink was faded but still easily readable.

> *C. Where have you gone? When will you return?*
> *I'm going mad. I'm in terrible trouble.*
> *Tomorrow may be too late. D.*

"Mine." The old man grabbed for the paper. Constance jerked it out of his reach.

She slumped against the pool table, not sobbing as I had expected, but used up, her last reserves of energy and hope burned down to fumes.

I climbed onto the bar stool and replaced the wooden block, then slid the ceiling panel back into its suspension track.

"Thanks for showing us the house," I said to the old man.

"I showed *her* the house."

At the top of the basement stairs and into the kitchen I saw Constance rally. The paper was folded and out of sight. She stopped at the sink and drew a glass of tap water without asking. We watched her drink it down.

"This is the best thing about now," she said, smacking her lips.

In the front hall the old man stopped Constance from leaving. "When you came to the door," he said, "I recognized you."

"From where?" she asked.

He had to take a moment to catch his breath. He turned and pointed back into the kitchen, and beyond.

"A few years ago," he said.

My skin crawled. Constance got absolutely still.

The old man touched her arm with one finger, retesting her solidity.

"It *was* you. It was in the summertime," he said. "Night. A thunderstorm came up after all of us had gone to bed. I got up to close the windows and when I was done I remembered I'd opened a window in the basement, so I went down to close it. A big bolt of lightning hit and as I turned my eyes away there you were—clear as day—coming down the stairs. You smiled at me. I thought you were the prettiest ghost I'd ever seen."

ELEVEN

We were home before Constance spoke.

"Does that mean I die in that house?"

Three cars were parked in Flo's lot and Penny's bike was propped against the wall of the garage. Short of an actual sighting, this was sufficiently tangible evidence of her safe return.

"When he saw you—*if* he saw you—on the stairs, you hadn't gone into the future yet," I said. "So at the time he saw you—you *had* died in the past. But that's changed now."

"I'm older than he is," she said. "Can you believe it?"

"Maybe it was better that you came into the future," I said. "Maybe you *did* die in that house."

"No doubt I married Dash and died peacefully of old age in the bed we shared for fifty years," she said defiantly.

"No doubt," I said.

"But do people who die happy leave behind a ghost?"

I had to laugh. "I don't know the ground rules for becoming a ghost. I don't even believe in ghosts."

"But he saw me."

"He *says* he saw you. Maybe he did. I am totally without explanations. You should talk to Flo. She can give you a million reasons why none of this is happening." I remembered something from earlier. "When you were at your mother's grave—was your grave there, too?"

She was quiet a minute. Then she said, "My parents' were. Mine wasn't. It hadn't occurred to me until just now."

"I think that's good news," I said. "For your return, I mean. If you stayed vanished—your parents would bury you or their memory of you with them."

"My parents are alive."

"In 1908. Not now. The fact you aren't with them means—to me—that you got back, grew up, married, and are buried somewhere with your family."

"Or else haunting that old house," she said. "What am I going to do about money?"

"Can you travel through time carrying money?" I laughed. "Can you take it with you?"

"Why is that funny?"

"An old expression: You can't take it with you. Money to heaven."

"That doesn't answer my question."

"I think that you should have faith that you're going back—and so you don't need money in *this* life."

"I tried to go back," she said sheepishly.

I was shocked. "When?"

"Last night. During the storm."

"What happened?"

Her eyes filled with tears. "Nothing," she said. "I got wet."

I began to pace. "How did I miss this storm?"

"The air felt like it did when Dash and I were in the orchard," she said. "Like something was about to happen. So I hurried over there—to the place where I arrived. I ran myself ragged. And here I am. Still." She wiped her face with the heel of her hands.

"Did you see anyone else?"

Constance shook her head.

"Kids are on the perp walk day and night trying to travel through time," I said. "The girl who disappeared last night—she was trying, too."

"Maybe *she's* with Dash now," Constance said. She grasped the perp walk fence with both hands. "Where exactly was she? The missing girl?"

"West of here."

"Maybe they are very precise locations," she said. "And if you miss them by even a little—you miss them entirely."

"I think—"

I stopped because Constance had removed a Snickers bar from her pocket, unwrapped it, and begun to eat.

"Where'd you get *that*?"

"Downtown."

"How much was it?"

A devilish smile appeared. "I told you, money is so much more important now."

I didn't say any more about it. Her mouth was already full of candy.

"I thought I'd traveled in time just once," I said. "And I still do. But I'm convinced I've been involved in two time-travel incidents. Both times, though, I was at different points on the walk. The one time, east of here, I went back fifteen minutes. The other time—back the other direction—I was on my bike being chased by a dog. Then the dog vanished. I think it was the dog that traveled through time."

"Why?" she asked.

"When I reached home he was there," I said. "And he was afraid of me. Like he'd seen a ghost. Before, he was ready to eat me and my bike. If I'd gone into the past the dog would've chased me all over again. If I went into the future the dog couldn't be in front of me. I think the dog went into the future by maybe half a minute. And I caught up to him. The dog was frightened of me because he thought *I* was the one that vanished."

She pulled another Snickers bar from the pocket and tore into its wrapper.

"My mother doesn't allow me to have sweets. She says, 'You want a sweet? Eat an apple.' I'm *so* sick of apples."

"You have to put those back," I said.

"Why?"

"You have to buy two Snickers and replace the two you stole."

"I don't have any money," she cried.

"I'll buy them for you." I considered this a moment. "Better yet, you should earn the money. Then return the candy bars."

"But why?"

"Don't you want to get back?"

She didn't have to answer.

"I'll pay you to pick up sticks for an hour. That will cover the candy bars. Did you steal anything else?"

The hesitation before her "no" led me to believe otherwise.

"Tell me the truth."

She pouted. "Life is so much easier now."

"Can you remember everything you took?"

"To put it all back?"

"Yes."

"I'd be picking up sticks until doomsday."

"You're a crime wave from the past," I said. She didn't appreciate that. "It's important that you don't change significantly while you're in this time. That might be why you couldn't go back."

"Change significantly?"

"As important as you not altering the future—the future shouldn't alter you," I said. "Maybe deep down you don't want to go back."

"That's ridiculous." She scowled.

"How much shoplifting did you do back then?" I asked.

"None!"

"See?"

"See what?"

"You mentioned how much easier it is now. You're being corrupted."

"I'm not corrupt!"

"You're smoking, stealing, staying out all night."

She pondered this. "Taking the easy way," she said.

"Right. Although I don't think this time *is* any easier."

"My father would disagree," Constance said. "You get up late. Paint sticks. Wander around town."

I laughed. "It's hard work. Filling my time."

"Don't let someone who actually works for a living hear you say that."

"That's the essence of success," I said. "The least work for the most money. Time to spend as you wish. I could pick apples from morning to night for slave wages and be bone tired. What would that accomplish?"

"You'd have apples."

"Granted."

"My father loves his life," Constance said.

"But does he know anything different?"

"Not different like this, no."

"That's your biggest danger in going back," I said. "You'll know different. You'll run the risk of frustration, impatience. All those trips to the privy in winter."

"We *have* chamber pots," she said, though she shuddered.

Later, Penny came into my studio, a stethoscope around her neck and her fingertips stained violet.

"You arrived safely," I said.

"Yes, I avoided the dreaded time holes," she said derisively. "Then mom put me to work going through old files."

She held out her purplish fingers to me. She had slender, surgeon hands.

"She promised me clinical work," Penny complained. "Instead I get clerical."

"And you completed med school when?"

She ignored me, drifting to the studio window, through which she could see Constance picking up sticks.

"Who's that?" she asked.

"Constance."

"No. Who's that with her?"

Constance was talking over the fence to a man on the perp walk. I didn't know him. He was lanky, nearly skeletal, wearing a fringed black leather coat that was incongruous in the heat, a Dodgers cap, and baggy gray trousers. For a moment I was relieved that the fence was between them.

Suddenly the man walked away. He stopped shortly, turned, and spoke. I couldn't make out what he said, or Constance's reply. Then he moved on out of sight.

Penny and I went outside.

"He'd heard of me," Constance said.

"He wanted to go?"

She nodded. "He wanted a time when being homeless didn't make you a pariah. He'd heard stories of hobos getting food from people for a day's wood chopping. Or being allowed to sleep in a barn."

"Did you help him?"

"He couldn't meet my fee," she said.

"How much?" Penny asked.

"Twenty dollars. No guarantees." She looked at me, then snapped, "*What?*"

"I thought you were trying to become *less* corrupt?"

"It's just money," Constance said. "And if I'm hopelessly corrupt and not getting home—I'll *need* money."

"What if he had twenty dollars?" Penny asked. "What would you have done?"

Constance scraped the fence links with a stick. In an hour of work she had collected one small pile. Nothing in it reminded me of anyone.

An elderly couple, arm in arm, came into view. The man fanned his face; the woman blocked the sun with a hat the size of a wheel. They nodded genially to the three of us. When they were abreast of Constance, she said, "Are you searching for me?"

The couple stopped and turned with great care toward us.

"Should we be?" the woman asked politely.

"I'm the time traveler."

The man and woman stared. "Oh dear," she said.

"I can help you do the same."

The man chuckled. His fan was a Chinese restaurant menu folded into precision accordion pleats.

"Where would we go, mother?"

"Where would we go?" The woman seemed confused.

"Would we be this old in our new time?" the man asked.

"I think so," Constance said.

"Where's the fun in that?"

"You might see the future."

"We're getting there fast enough as it is."

"Do you remember when this area was an apple orchard?" Constance asked.

"When was that?"

"Around 1908."

"Goodness, I wasn't born until 1919," the man said, amused. "Do I look *that* ancient?"

"I was born in 1893."

"You're an inspiration to us all," the woman said, playing along. Then they moved away, even hurrying in their fashion, as though Constance's madness might be contagious.

"They couldn't run away fast enough," Constance said.

Penny giggled. I didn't say a word.

"I know the Cubs win the World Series in a couple months," Constance said to me. "And Wintergreen wins the Kentucky Derby next year. I can use that in *my* time. What good does it do me here?"

"You looked that up?" I asked.

"Yes."

"Just for the purpose of making money if you go back?"

"When! *When* I go back!"

"You're shoplifting. Gathering inside betting information," I said. "That's why you can't get back. You came through time as one person—Constance Morceau, never been kissed. You fit the keyhole. But you don't fit anymore."

Something like understanding came into her eyes. "I do feel different," she said.

"How?"

"Well," she said, "more modern. Freer. Like I can do anything. Like I left part of my conscience back in 1908."

"Your parents," Penny said.

Constance smiled. "I guess. Some days it's a good feeling, this freedom. Most of the time, though, it isn't."

"Did—does—your family go to church?"

"Yes. It's still there. I sang in the choir."

"Was it an important part of your life?"

"I pretended it was," she said. "I just liked to sing."

"That's encouraging," Penny said.

"What?"

"She lied to her parents—and still made it through."

"I didn't say she had to be perfect."

"I went to the church yesterday," Constance said. "They've hung portraits of all the ministers in the hall. The Reverend Crawford looks so forbidding. And so old. He stays until 1928. Then Lyle DePester takes over. He's *my* age. And *he* looks old and forbidding. Lyle—he set fires on All Hallows' Eve and tormented the orphans."

"He must've found religion along the way." I laughed.

"A woman is minister now."

"Maybe you could rejoin the choir," Penny said.

"Did Dash go to church?" I asked.

"He said he went in the city. I never saw evidence of it."

"How do you mean?"

"He was always available Sundays. He could be around at any hour of the day and still claim he was just back from church. I don't think he has to worry about passing through that innocence keyhole."

"What about you?" Penny swatted my shoulder. "You're only innocent enough to go back fifteen minutes?"

"Your mother has allowed me to stay innocent of a number of things," I said. "Financial concerns. Jobs. Getting along with unpleasant people."

"My father would have no use for you," Constance said.

I put my arm around Penny. "As long as I stayed planted in the here and now—my life was fine with your mother. It was only when I began traveling through time that she had problems with me."

In the heat of the afternoon I judged Constance's work sufficient to pay off her candy debt and accompanied her first to one store to purchase Snickers, then to another to give back those she had stolen.

"That's that," I said, squinting in the sidewalk glare. The day was infernally hot and the wrung-out blue of the sky bore no clouds that resembled the thunderheads I was pretty certain Constance needed to return to 1908.

"It's not," she said.

"Not what?"

She removed a familiar box from a pocket of her dress. It was a reel of microfilm. I thought it was from 1908, the chronicle of Dash's fate, but when Constance showed me the label it read *Nov. 1–15, 1918*.

"You didn't tell me about the war," she said.

I touched the date on the box. "It's all but over."

"Why didn't you tell me?"

"There's so much I didn't tell you."

"What if I rescue Dash only to have him die in some stupid war?"

"That's—I can't answer that."

"I can prevent the war," she said, gripping the box.

"Worry about Dash. Prevent him from being lynched. Preventing World War I, that's—"

"One?"

"Yes. There've been two."

"Two?"

"I'm afraid so."

"Well, I'll stop both of them," she said defiantly.

I took the microfilm box out of her hand. She gave it up without complaint.

"We have to return this," I said.

"I looked through a lot of the years between 1908 and then," she said, nodding at the box. She grabbed her shoulders like she was embracing herself. "In a way, I don't want to go back. I don't want to go through all that. Watch my friends and family go through it."

"I wish you'd asked me first."

"So you could hide it from me?"

"Well, yes," I admitted. "But for a purpose."

"So I'd be blind to the future when I went back?"

"There's something to be said for that. I think you'd call it hope."

"If a thousand people knew. We could stop it."

"Some events just have too much historical momentum. And there aren't a thousand of you."

"That's not an excuse for not trying," she said.

"If you could unknow it, would you?"

We had walked to the edge of downtown and I was anxious to get home.

"I wouldn't seek out ignorance," she said.

"Where are you going now?"

She shrugged. "I'm tired."

"Come to our house."

We reached the perp walk at Pincoffin Street. From where we stood I saw three separate groups of kids on the path, each—upon seeing us—going motionless and casual, caught in the act. When we passed the first group—four breathless, perspiring girls—they touched Constance like she was an apparition.

"It's you," one of them said.

Constance ignored them, kept walking.

"How'd you do it?" another girl asked.

Constance stopped. "I'll help you," she said. "For twenty dollars."

The four stared.

"Each," she added.

One girl, pretty and petite, with headphones around her neck, said, "Prove it."

"I can't," Constance said. She pointed at me. "But he'll tell you."

"What you do with your money is your own business," I said. Constance shot me a cold frown. "But I think she did travel through time."

"We want to go into the future," said one of the girls, her hair dyed cherry red and gathered into tufts that reminded me of little explosions.

"No guarantees," Constance said.

"You're from when?"

"Nineteen hundred and eight."

"Are you sure we'll come back?"

"No guarantees."

"Are you going back to 1908?"

"I want to," Constance said.

"But you aren't sure?" The girl shivered.

Two boys joined the group. One of them asked, "Can I go wherever Holly Dearborn is?"

No one laughed.

"Do you know Holly?" I asked.

"Yeah," someone said.

The girl with the headphones would not give up. "I only have—" She picked through a handful of ones and coins. "About eight dollars. Nine."

Constance shrugged. "It's twenty."

Her answer pleased me. She had some standards.

The boys had a ten and a one.

"We'll cover the rest," one of them said to the girl, "to see you disappear."

The girl smirked and snapped up the money.

"Shannon," one of her friends said worriedly. "You might get to the future and find out you're dead."

"Or really fat."

"God," Shannon said, "my final destination isn't determined by the losers around me when I go, right?"

"No guarantees," Constance repeated.

"Shan—" Her friend grabbed her arm. "She's basically saying she doesn't know anything about any of this."

"Like anyone knows anything."

"Have a few brews," a boy said. "It's the same thing."

"Do you drink?" Constance asked the girl.

"Not really," Shannon said. The boys hooted. "A little," she added.

"Have you been kissed?"

The boys whooped even louder.

"That is *so* none of your business," Shannon said.

"It seems to make a difference."

A boy said to Constance, "You've never been kissed?"

"No. But I was about to be."

"So if I've—" Shannon began.

"Say it!" a boy teased.

"If I've been *kissed*—I won't be able to travel through time?"

"It might be a problem."

"Then only dorks and social losers can time-travel," a boy complained.

"You want to go before me?" Shannon asked him. To Constance, she asked, "What do I do?"

"Wait for a thunderstorm," Constance said, "and run on these paths—as fast as you can."

"That's *it*?"

"That's all I did."

Shannon popped a hip and shot out her hand. "I want my money back."

"I told you: no guarantees. And you haven't even tried yet."

"Give me my money!"

Constance slipped past them. We moved across one block into the next, encountering a skateboarder, two girls on in-line skates, a boy riding a bike, and a boy on a pogo stick. Constance ignored them all, like they were too young to have money.

"I was thinking," she said as we came up on Clover Street. "If *you* went back in time fifteen minutes—did *all* time go back fifteen minutes?"

"You could make that argument. We're assuming—for the sake of saving Dash—that it's this time on this day in 1908. So going back an hour now would put it back an hour then."

"I could delay the lynching—"

"I wouldn't count on that."

She lost the hopeful spark in her bearing. We'd reached the house.

"I'm just looking for a silver lining if I don't get back all the way," she said.

"Go for it all at once."

"I *want* to. But if I go back a couple days, before I knew about the war—wars—maybe then my innocence would be untarnished enough at that point for me to make it all the way to 1908."

"You shouldn't count on that," I said. "This is a one-shot deal, as I see it. You have one cup of gas to burn. Don't waste it going back only two days."

"But losing what I know—that might make it easier to go the rest of the way."

"You could prevent the Great War."

"Well, which is it?" she demanded in a frustrated, frightened voice. "Do I know what I know and not get back? Or do I lose what I know and *maybe* get back—but be unaware of the war I might prevent?"

"Were you carrying the reel when you tried to go back last night?" I asked.

"Yes."

"Maybe that's it. Maybe you can't put the elements of time out of sequence. Think of the chaos a newspaper from 1918 would cause if it turned up in 1908."

"It's still up here," she said, tapping her head.

"That can't be helped," I said. "And most people aren't going to believe you anyway, I'm afraid. You'll be a young girl who disappeared who knows where, and reappeared to warn of something unimaginable."

We crossed Clover Street, went around the house and in through the patio door.

A vaguely familiar girl sat at the kitchen table, holding—clutching—with both hands a tall glass of ice water. She flicked a glance at me.

The door into Flo's office was open and a squalling baby was heard, but Flo stood her ground in the center of the kitchen, caught between the baby and her need to be present within her family.

Penny was there, too.

"Look who's back," Flo said. I thought she meant me.

Penny clarified the situation. "Dad. Constance. This is Holly Dearborn."

TWELVE

Everyone had the same first question for Holly. "Where have you been?"

She spoke into the glass, like a whisper down a well. "The future," she said.

Her answer caused such a general consternation in the room that the baby's cries ceased to penetrate my consciousness. I was most aware of Flo, irritated and impatient Flo, who blamed me for everything. She went to the door to her office and stood—hesitated—drawn to the reliability of the crying baby, then closed the door and returned to us.

Constance slipped into a chair, her eyes never leaving Holly.

"Have you been home?" Flo asked.

"It was more important that I see Penny first," Holly said.

"Why?" Penny asked warily.

"Because in the future—you're gone."

Flo gasped and crumpled against me.

"You—" she said. "You can't know that."

"I wish I didn't," Holly said.

"How far into the future?" I asked.

Holly shrugged. "Three days?"

"What's it like?" I asked.

"The same. Except Penny's gone."

"How did it happen?" Constance asked.

"She's just gone."

"I mean—how did you travel into the future?"

"I was just running," Holly said. "To get out of the rain. I was getting soaked and it was late and I wanted to go home. Regan was behind me. Then she wasn't. And the rain had stopped."

"What have we ever done to you?" Flo demanded.

"Mom," Penny said.

"What have we done to you that would make you want to hurt us with such nonsense?"

I put a hand on Flo's shoulder. I felt in her tensed muscles an electric desire to leap at this girl, tear her apart, be rid of her and the story she told. Or else do the same to me.

"What happens?" Penny asked.

Holly sipped her water, then wiped the glass across her forehead, leaving a shimmering streak. She shrugged, her eyes on Flo.

"You were just missing."

"Did you see me?" Constance asked.

Holly shook her head. She nodded to me. "I saw you," she said.

"You did?"

"Yes."

"When you got there?"

"No. Later. When the rain stopped I stopped running. I called to Regan. I walked back up the path to find her."

"But you didn't find her."

"No. In the morning I went to Corey's house. Regan's there. They're not the least surprised to see me. They only want to talk about Penny being gone."

"Is this all about a boy?" Flo asked.

Holly Dearborn started to get up. I couldn't let her leave just yet.

"What happens after you see Regan and Corey?"

Holly rattled her ice. "Not much. We filled each other in." She glanced at Penny. "Then Corey came on to me. But I left."

"He came on to you?" Penny said.

Flo touched her hand. "Don't, honey. It's just a way to hurt you. A very sick use of the rubbish your father has brought into our lives."

Holly folded her arms. "*Don't* believe me. I don't care."

"When did you see me?" I asked.

"I was coming back from Corey's. On the path—" She pointed at it. "And you"—she brought her finger around to me—"are sitting in your backyard. You're crying. Your shirt has blood on it. Then the police arrive."

"The police?" Flo said.

"How did you get back?" Constance asked. "To now?"

Holly pointed at me again. "He chases me," she said.

"Was it raining?" I asked.

"No. It's just like today."

Flo had heard enough and headed for her office door.

"It won't happen," I tried to reassure her. "Penny disappearing." Flo hesitated. "Holly's revealed the future," I said. "Now it can be changed."

Flo, uncomforted, left the room.

"Why do I chase you?" I asked Holly.

"The cop questions you about Penny. He suspects you."

"That's crazy," Penny said.

"Suspects me of what?"

"Well, your daughter *is* missing."

Penny didn't shrink from me, but I saw it in her eyes, the wondering.

"Don't worry," I said to her.

"But everything's come true so far!"

"*Nothing* has come true," I said.

"*She* has," Penny countered, meaning Constance. I couldn't explain Constance.

"*How* did you get back?" Constance pressed.

"He broke away from the cop and came after me," Holly said. She faced me, eyes alive with the experience. It *had* happened, at least in her mind. "You're running," she said to me. "So I run."

I waited, seeing it happen.

"The cop thinks you're trying to run away. You're totally nuts. Blaming me for Penny. The cop screams, 'Stop! Or I'll shoot!' "

"Shoot?" I said.

"Shoot," Holly repeated.

"None of this will happen," I said to Penny, to reassure both of us. "It's tainted time."

"It felt real," Holly said.

"It did happen. Now it won't."

"You're running . . ." Constance said.

Holly shrugged. "I'm running. He gets closer. The cop crashes his motorcycle—"

"What?"

"Yeah. He gets on a motorcycle to chase you. But he crashes."

"What *happens*?" Constance asked.

"There's a gunshot—but before I can turn to see, I'm back. To now."

"What did it feel like?" I asked, but hearing the gunshot.

"Like the first time. Running. I hate to run. Then *poof*."

"Who got shot?" Penny asked.

"Not me," Holly said.

"Daddy—"

"It won't happen," I said. "There are so many ways to make this not happen. None of this will happen."

"That must be it," Constance said, her face lighting up. "*Not* wanting it. When I came through the first time, the last thing in the world I was thinking about was traveling through time. Now it's *all* I think about."

"Same here," I said.

"And you"—she nodded at Holly—"returned because you were trying to outrun him, not travel through time."

"But how do you *not* think about time travel?" I asked.

Constance ate dinner with us under a beautiful sky. The oppressiveness of the day's heat had lifted, not quite to cool, and on any other evening it would have been welcome. We were together around the patio table, under a fringed umbrella, candles burning in blue cups.

Penny had hardly said a word since Holly's return. She had no appetite. Flo blamed me. I turned her wrist to check her watch. Constance noticed.

"Dash might be dead already," she said.

I examined the twilight. "They won't come for him until after dark," I said. "They're cowards."

"I'm supposed to just sit here until then?"

"Eat something," Flo said.

"Begging your pardon—but my mother is a better cook than you."

Flo turned up a corner of her mouth. "Penny made this," she said.

"Maybe my last meal," Penny said.

"Don't *say* that," Flo scolded.

Constance pushed away from the table and stood up. She had become part of the family in a very short time, with rights to stay or go, and a casual bearing that implied acceptance of us. She squeezed Penny's shoulder.

"I'm sorry," she said. She carried her dirty dishes into the house.

A minivan swung into Flo's parking lot and froze us in its headlights for a moment before the engine was turned off. A man and woman got out, then together—delicately—extracted a boy of about nine from the back seat. He was in a baseball uniform, gray with green letters. Solons. Something clumpy, pinkish, and sodden was pressed to his eye.

As I watched the three people approach up the walk Flo came into the picture and took command. I was proud of the way she lifted the parents' concerns and took them on herself. I saw the way the mom and dad eased back, grateful to have their son in better hands. The father eased back so completely that he didn't even accompany his wife and son into Flo's office.

I offered him a paper napkin—a corner dipped in water—to wipe blood from his fingers.

"Line drive off the old noggin," he explained. "The hot corner."

He dried his fingers on the seat of his pants. "Thanks," he said and dropped the tinged napkin among our dinner plates. "Pitch. Swing. Crack of the bat. He's down." He looked ashamed. "I didn't even see it."

"Flo will fix him right up."

"That's what the wife said."

"What's his name?"

"Derek. Weird thing is—he's a lefty. A southpaw third-sacker."

"Why is that weird?" Constance asked.

"Lefties don't play third."

"Why?"

"It's a tough throw," the father said. He assumed a fielder's stance. "Ground ball down the line—" He lunged to his right, sticking out an imaginary glove on his right hand. "Takes too long for a lefty to turn back and throw. Batter beats it out." He brushed his hands together. "But he wanted to try. And here we are."

"Why not go to the ER?" I asked.

He chewed his lower lip, like a man getting to the point he longed to avoid.

"No flexibility—financially—at the ER," he said. "The wife said Dr. Flo will carry a tab. Said she's old-fashioned that way."

"She'll have to be paid eventually."

"At the ER they don't know *eventually*."

With his cards on the table he no longer felt the need to charm me. After a minute of silence he went to wait in the minivan. The informative murmur of a baseball play-by-play man floated across the grass. As the twilight deepened the voice seemed to expand and take on detail as the world lost it. I found myself listening like a fan. The outcome of the game became important to me.

It was an hour before Flo's office door opened and Derek and his mother emerged, followed by Flo and Penny. Derek's mom held a bill—a flimsy sheet of yellow paper that she folded into threes, then sixes, then twelves, until it was so small and dense that one more fold might squeeze blood from it.

Derek sported a major-league shiner and a square, white bandage over the upper, outer corner of his eye.

"Four stitches," Flo said to me as mom and son hustled down the walk.

"Sammy's up!" I heard the father shout to the boy.

"She told me up front they couldn't pay," Flo said.

"*He* hinted at eventually."

"Well, she was more *never*."

"They were getting free medical care and still mom wouldn't let me put in any of the stitches," Penny said, twin stars of frustration blazing in her eyes.

"Pen . . . ," Flo said. "Those are the people who will sue me like that." She snapped her fingers. "They don't have money. And they want mine."

"You could've asked the mom to wait outside," Penny said.

"No, I couldn't."

Our attention was diverted by a dead-engine grind from the minivan. When we turned toward the sound it stopped like someone was embarrassed. After a long moment the cranking recommenced, the headlights throwing out a near-death flicker. When the dad gave up and turned off the key, the baseball game could still be heard.

He sent the kid over to us.

"My dad needs a jump."

"Sure," I said.

I backed our car out of the garage and parked near the minivan. The jumper cables were in the trunk. The announcer said, "That's the sixth run this inning."

"You'll have to turn off the radio," I told the dad. The mom stared straight ahead and her bandaged son stared at her.

Constance had come over. "What are you doing?"

"Dead battery."

"But what are you doing?"

"It's called a jump. My battery has power. His doesn't. I'm giving him some so he can start his van."

I attached the cable clips to the terminals.

"Positive to positive," I said. "Negative to ground."

When I turned she was gone, back into the house. I went around to the driver's side of the van.

"We're all hooked up," I said.

He reached for the key.

"Wait," I said. "Wait'll I rev my engine."

"Okay. Sorry." He was utterly crestfallen—crushed, broke, owing money, reliant on the pity of others, his son with slow reflexes.

I goosed the gas and gave him his cue and like that his engine started. I sat, satisfied, glad to help, letting the bounty of my life flow into the vehicle of the broken man. I daydreamed a little. I might even have closed my eyes.

A change in the pitch of the engine drew my attention. Constance was back. She had removed her boots and doused herself with water and plucked the cable clips off the minivan's battery. I reached for my key but I wasn't quick enough. She fastened the alligator teeth to her hips and for an instant I saw sparks snap into her before I got the engine shut off.

Constance was flat on her back in the grass. Singe marks smoked on her hips. Her half-closed eyes showed rolled whites. Flo knelt and put an ear to her chest, forgetting the stethoscope around her neck. She had her hands positioned on Constance's breastbone and was just leaning into the first compression when the girl groaned, coughed, and tried to get up.

When she saw us she was frantic.

"It's still *now*?" she said.

She examined each of our faces and shivered in her wet dress. She was steady enough on her feet, but a new determination, or desperation, was in her eyes. She grabbed for Flo's wrist to check her watch.

"Dash—" she said.

"Stay with us," Flo said.

Constance did a little twitchy dance right there, like she was trying to shake out an attack of skin needles, or a bone-deep itch.

"It's still in me," she said, excited and determined. "Maybe just enough."

I reached for her but she stepped clear. She took one step away and then stopped and came back.

"Penny," she said. She shook out her hands so hard I thought I saw sparks coming off them.

"What about her?" Flo asked.

"You'll find her if you know where to look."

"But—"

She broke away from us, hopped the fence, and took off running down the perp walk. Her stride looked old-fashioned, the way she held up her skirt with both hands, and how her wet hair bounced and her bare feet slapped the sidewalk. I wondered what she was thinking about. Hopefully not the process of getting to Dash—but Dash himself. It was dark—then and in 1908. She probably was thinking she was too late. But even turning up too late would teach 1908 a lesson. And there was the Great War to prevent.

I couldn't sleep that night, waiting for Constance to return, spooked by her warning about Penny. A cool, eerie quiet had settled over Euclid Heights. No one was on the perp walk, not teens wanting to travel through time, nor older couples happy to be taking the air. It was as if a spell had been lifted, something returned to its proper order.

Flo joined me on the patio at midnight.

"She got tired of her game," she said. "She figured out there was no money in us."

"Why give herself such a painful shock?"

"She needed a big exit."

"You said she could stay with us."

"So?"

"You believed."

"I didn't want to see her hurt herself any more."

"No. You *believed.*"

"Don't tell me what I did or did not believe."

"You thought—if she can't get back to where she belongs, she can stay with us."

"No. What I thought was: If she's so miserable in her life—*now,* wherever that life is—I would offer a gesture of our acceptance of her."

"If you say so."

"World War One still happened."

She was right. Nothing about that had changed, at least my memory of it, what I knew about it. Constance had gone back that night, but whatever she had done when she went back had happened more than ninety years ago.

I removed the 1918 microfilm reel from my pocket.

"In the morning I'm taking this back to the library," I said. "And I'm going to look at the 1908 reel."

Flo grew very still. "Can't you just leave it alone?"

"I want to know if she got back."

"It won't prove anything," Flo said. "Constance—or whoever she was—I'm sure read ahead. She knows *exactly* what happened to the missing girl she based her scam on."

I wouldn't have been surprised to find Constance there in the morning, maybe curled up with breakfast or a book, or taking one of her endless showers, nothing changed whatsoever. Flo's take on the situation made sense to me on a pragmatic level. Constance—if she was the actress con girl Flo suspected—would have an explanation for where she spent the night, why she couldn't get home to Dash, and what her future here in the future held.

But Constance did not appear.

I took the perp walk into town. At the library I converted a dollar into dimes and sat myself down in front of the microfilm reader. I spun through the newspapers of August 15–31, 1908. I blurred through the articles about the disappearance of Constance and the revelations about Dash Buckley. I slowed to read the story about his lynching. Nothing had changed. Constance hadn't returned in time to prevent that.

But something about the newspaper was different, at least as far as I could remember. Now, accompanying the story about the lynching, was an artist's rendering of the scene, showing Dash's body hanging limp from the tree, the watching crowd in sketchy detail, their faces a captured mix of jubilation, disgust, and remorse.

At the back edge of the crowd, at the very corner of the sketch—like someone coming late upon the scene—was Constance. Or it was a girl who looked exactly like her. Her face was panicky and bereft, her hair matted, her clothes wrinkled.

My heart caught in my throat, seeing her there too late. Knowing what she knew. Perfectly aware of the turns her life would take but unable to do anything about them.

She was on the front page the following day.

Constance returned. The tragedy of a young man wrongfully accused, wrongfully jailed, wrongfully judged and executed by a mob of his fellow citizens.

MYSTERY ATTENDS REAPPEARANCE OF MISSING BEAUTY

by E. Wayne Manger

The strange, sad story of Hickory Hill's star-crossed lovers—Constance Morceau and Harold "Dash" Buckley—took yet another serpentine twist yesterday with the reappearance of Miss Morceau, who had been missing and presumed dead since Aug. 13.

Miss Morceau, the daughter of Peter T. and Faith W. Morceau, had reportedly last been seen by Mr. Buckley running in the rain in her father's apple orchard. Subsequent searches for Constance proved unsuccessful, and Mr. Buckley was first questioned, then arrested, then charged, in her disappearance.

There followed allegations about elements of Mr. Buckley's family lineage that turned a curious public into a rampaging mob whose untoward actions had tragic consequences.

Breaking into the Hickory Hill jail, the mob overcame and fatally bludgeoned Sheriff Lloyd Horton and subsequently hauled Mr. Buckley bodily from his cell and hanged him with a homemade rag rope from the hickory tree in the town square.

Now—a day later—the tragedy has been compounded. Even as Mr. Buckley lay dying—proclaiming his innocence with his very last breath—Miss Morceau's period of being vanished was coming to an end. She reappeared only minutes after her beau was hanged, and even in the moments after her reappearance went unrecognized by the raving elements of the mob.

It was only later—much too late—that she made her presence known to acting Sheriff John Ketch in his jail office.

Ketch described Miss Morceau's explanation for her disappearance as "Frankly fabulous in the extreme . . . largely unsubstantiated by any evidence or adherence to the laws of physics and reality."

Miss Morceau has gone into seclusion at her family's house.

"We are delighted and relieved to have our baby girl home safe," her mother told this reporter in a brief, front-porch interview.

I read on to the end of the story. No mention of time travel, of knowing the future. No mention of a coming war. A Dr. Eddings was quoted implying that Constance had suffered some manner of blackout, of brain shock, of temporary derangement, caused perhaps by a blow to the head or a mental trauma, either of which was likely imparted by Harold Buckley.

Her face was drawn large across the page.

The next day's paper contained no story about Constance. I spooled through to the end of the reel. There was no mention of her that I could find.

On a hunch, I threaded the reel for May 1–15, 1909, into the machine, and advanced through the days until reaching the paper of Tuesday, May 4. I skimmed the paper's coverage of Wintergreen's victory in the Kentucky Derby, not interested in the race, but seeking something in the stories that came in the days that followed. I reached the end of the reel without finding what I sought, but at the end of the May 16–31 reel, in the edition of Sunday, May 30, my hunch paid off.

BEACON SCRIBE DEPARTS ON GLOBE-HOPPING JOURNEY

Intrepid Beacon correspondent Edward Wayne Manger will be missed by his colleagues as he embarks on a voyage that will see his Saratoga trunk stamped at New York, London, Paris, Berlin, Tehran, Tokio, Shanghai, and countless exotic locales in between.

The article went on at some length about what a swell fellow Manger was, recounting his love of practical jokes (he was fond of mailing fake fan letters to his fellow reporters) and his stated vow that he would one day chip off a piece of the Great Wall of China and carry it with him to his grave. Nowhere in the story, however, was it explained how he amassed the money to pay for such an expensive journey.

By then it was getting along toward lunchtime. I bought a blueberry muffin and a bottle of apple juice from a vendor on the sidewalk in front of the library. While I ate, sitting on a bench in the shade, I saw a girl nearby using a pay phone. She was vaguely familiar. The vendor was, too. I wondered if those feelings were the result of Constance's return to 1908. She might have caused just enough of a ripple to change my life that fraction of a moment.

When the girl got off the phone I called home. The machine picked up.

"It's me. I'm at the library. I'll be home in a couple hours. Love you."

I considered reading through 1909 and into 1910 (E. Wayne Manger had promised to file dispatches from the road) but decided that would be a waste of time. It was not likely that he would reveal in print that he had accumulated his traveling stake betting on Wintergreen in the Derby or the Cubs in the 1908 World Series because a girl had returned from the future and told him to do so.

Instead I threaded in the Nov. 1–15, 1918, reel that Constance had been carrying. She definitely hadn't stopped the war. The rolls of dead and injured filled a page with agate type. Photographs of local dead and wounded were grouped in a daily feature called "Homegrown Heroes." The headlines trumpeted Allied victories and the tone of the news was grimly hopeful of peace.

Then it was November 11—Armistice Day—and the war to end all wars was at an end. I pushed on into the postwar future. I was deep into the back pages of the November 14 paper when the film broke. The sudden screen of gray-green light jarred me back to my own time. I took the reel and the take-up reel to the desk.

"This broke," I said.

"Oh dear," the librarian said, rising. She was a short, shapely blonde, with her sleeves rolled up. She held the two broken ends of the film together.

"Odd," she said. "This has been cut."

We returned to the machine. She fed one end of the film under the magnifier lens until the page jumped up on the screen.

"The edges are too clean for a break," she said. "And they don't match up."

She touched a finger to the screen. "This is page forty-one," she said. She fed in the other half of the strip. "See? This is forty-three. Page forty-two has been cut out."

The librarian expertly spliced the two ends of the strip together, and I proceeded uneventfully to the end of the reel.

That missing page nagged at me, though. Any future examiner of the reel would likely not notice that a page was gone. It was as if the events reported on that page had never happened. I wondered if that had been the intent of the person who cut it out.

And had that person been Constance?

I went home thinking I might stumble upon her, hoping I would, because now that she was gone I felt somehow alone and uncertain of what came next.

Only Flo was there.

"Did you get my message?" I asked.

"Yes. Have you seen Penny?"

"I left pretty early."

"Was she here when you left?"

"I didn't check."

"Her bed isn't made. But then she never makes her bed."

"Are you saying she didn't sleep here last night?"

"Did you see her last night?"

"Yes. She kissed me good-night. It was right after you went to bed."

"Did you check on her later?" Flo asked.

I couldn't remember. Worse, a whole world of unobserved possibilities opened up in my mind. And what if I were called to account for them?

"I don't think so."

"You were up most of the night," Flo said, and it sounded like an accusation.

"So?"

"You should have been on alert."

I kept mixing in my mind the image of Constance's last run down the perp walk with Penny's liquid presence.

The bell in Flo's office sounded. She stood in front of me. I wondered if she was thinking about Holly Dearborn.

"Find her," she said.

I made a careful inspection of every room in the house, hoping—but not with any conviction—that Penny was curled somewhere private with a book or her pillow and blanket, cocooned in her headphones, her life progressing as it had up to that point.

But I didn't put any credence in that vision. First, Penny didn't like to read. Second, it was not like her to be out of the family stream for any length of time. And, finally, I didn't want to hope too much, for fear of how I'd feel when the hope proved groundless.

So trusting that Penny was safe I went on to the next step of my search, hoping that my daughter's whereabouts would be one of the mysteries I solved.

THIRTEEN

The Beacon Building was a four-story stone dungeon on Violet Street, a block off the square, and I could picture E. Wayne Manger hustling from his desk to the jail, his hat flying, his shirttail out, thanking his lucky stars that such a juicy story had fallen practically on the newspaper's front stoop.

A man named Fustus was in charge of the archives, on the fourth floor, and he presided over his dust-free and humidity-controlled kingdom with a personality both unwelcoming and suspicious.

"You want to view the paper from when?" he asked peevishly.

"First two weeks of November, 1918."

A pica pole, scissors, six sharpened No. 2 pencils, and four red grease pencils peeled to identical lengths were laid straight as rails on his desktop.

"I can't let you touch papers that old," he said. "The oils from your fingers—"

"You have originals from back then?"

"We have ninety-nine percent of originals back to 1930. Ninety-two percent to the '20s. Nearly seventy-five percent of the aughts and teens."

"Microfilm would be fine."

"I'm using our only reader, as you can see."

The machine hummed behind him.

"I really only need one page of one day."

He huffed, the simplicity of my request underbidding his resistance.

"*What* page of *what* day?"

"November fourteenth, 1918. Page forty-two."

He disappeared into the racks and stacks. I was tempted to rearrange the identical items on his desk, so only I would know he was operating in a disordered world. But that reminded me of Penny—not missing so much as misplaced—and promoting chaos anywhere was not something I felt confident enough to risk.

Fustus returned with a reel of microfilm, threaded it into the machine, and whirred through the days. He did not slow down to check the date until he came to his first complete stop.

"Page forty-two. November 14, 1918," he announced.

"Could you print it out, please?"

"Copies are a dollar."

I wasn't about to argue. He could have charged me ten. Twenty. I needed to see that page, see what Constance felt compelled to excise from the past, her future. I paid Fustus in dimes. He hit the Print button.

I carried the page, fluttering damp and redolent of ink, down the stairs and out into the sunlight, taking a seat on a sidewalk bench. My eyes flashed up and down the page's contents: an ad for five tons of White Oak smokeless egg coal, $25; brief stories about a stolen horse, a molasses shortage, a businessman's suicide. In the upper right-hand corner was a long list of names in tiny print, under a slightly larger, darker heading:

INFLUENZA VICTIMS

Abercrombie, Millicent K. *adult*

Adler, Daniel *adult*

Brebeuf, Thomas *orphan child*

Craker, Rachel *orphan child*

Dillard, Fredrik *adult*
Erickson, Agatha *adult*
Farmer, Lucas *beloved child*

and so on, scrolling under my fingertip until almost halfway down the list I came to:

Manger, Constance M. *adult*

My finger stopped there. My heart, too. Constance M. Out of the entire page it was the first word I'd read that struck any chord with me.

For a moment I thought I'd have to return to the fourth floor, to Fustus, but then I remembered that this was the only missing page, that time resumed uninterrupted at the library. I hurried back there.

I found what I sought, what I was pretty positive I would find, in the microfilm record for November 16, 1918:

CONSTANCE M. MANGER, WIFE OF BUSINESS TYCOON

Constance M. Manger, nee Morceau, 25, devoted wife of Edward Wayne Manger, founder and president of EWM Co., succumbed Nov. 13 to the Spanish influenza.

Mrs. Manger was a loving wife and mother who endured a brief spell in the public eye when she disappeared for a period of several days in 1908—an evanescence which was never fully explained but which precipitated the lynching death of one Harold Buckley, who was Mrs. Manger's swain at the time of her temporary vanishing.

Mrs. Manger made the acquaintance of her future husband when Mr. Manger, a onetime reporter, wrote about her disappearance for this publication. She said in an interview at the time of their betrothal in 1913, "I feel in the strongest terms that fate set me on my strange journey for the sole purpose of meeting, falling in love, and spending the rest of my life with Mr. Manger."

A bulletin from EWM Co.'s corporate offices expressed "bottomless disconsolation" at the passing of Mrs. Manger. Employees will receive a half-day off with pay to attend funeral services, which are pending.

Mr. Manger frequently credited his wife for the success of his company. EWM Co. especially profited during the Great War when the firm had on hand warehouses filled to the roof beams with gauze bandages of all widths and absorbencies, which the governments of the U.S. and several European countries purchased for top dollar.

I read to the end of the story, which included a smattering of club activities befitting Constance's role as a businessman's wife, and more lavish praise for her husband. The last line caught my eye:

Mrs. Manger is also survived by her beloved son, E. Wayne Jr., and her father and mother, Peter T. and Faith W. Morceau.

I printed out the page and carried it gently home. It had dried by the time I pushed through the back door into the kitchen.

Flo was there with a document of her own in hand. She threw it at me like a backhanded knife toss.

"I'm being kicked out!" she said, her anger barely in check.

The message bore a village letterhead. I skimmed its contents. It mentioned a hearing on her status as a business in a residential area. It didn't seem entirely hopeless to me, but I trusted Flo's interpretation.

"They're changing my zoning." She snatched the sheet from me and began to reread it.

"I found this," I said, spreading the two copies on the table. "She's dead."

Flo went still. "Who's dead?"

"Constance." I pointed. "See. She dies—died—of the flu in 1918."

Flo stared at me in disbelief. "I'm being zoned out of existence—and you persist in this delusion!"

"It's not—"

"I won't be able to subsidize your silly art career!"

"Flo, don't. I know you don't mean to say that."

"Oh, but I do!" She stormed toward her office door.

"Any sign of Penny?"

She stopped, turned, and shook her head.

"I'll keep looking," I said.

"Have you talked to her friends?"

"No."

"Why not?"

"Constance had a son," I said.

Flo buried her face in her hands.

"She married the reporter who covered her disappearance. Her son would be in his eighties."

"Stop it!" Flo hissed, tamping down her voice—but not her anger—for the benefit of any remaining patients. "I don't want to hear another word about that."

I found the copy of the story reporting Dash Buckley's lynching, spread it on the table, and pointed out the girl at the edge of the mob.

"See? That's her."

Flo approached me.

"She got back," I said. "But not in time to save Dash."

"This?" Flo said, pointing. *"This smudge?"*

"It looks just like her."

Flo leaned in close. "It's—what? A few lines of pencil. It's barely a representation of a girl—let alone a specific girl," she said.

"That's *her*!" The more I studied it, the more I was convinced. "She got back. Met and fell in love with this reporter, and died ten years later."

Flo cupped a hand against my cheek, fond and pitying.

"I'm sorry for what I said. You know I think you're very talented."

"No," I said. "You're right. I've never loved it. I've never worked a minute that I wasn't looking forward to the minute I could stop."

"Everyone is like that," Flo said. "To one degree or another."

"But this," I said, rattling the copy. "You don't believe in it—but it's the most real thing that's ever happened to me."

It was evidently a slow afternoon at EWM Co., the lobby so quiet you could hear a bandage unroll, and the security guard so eager for company that he hailed me the instant I stepped through the revolving door.

Behind his desk was a relief map of the world, beneath a furling plaster banner that declared **EWM: EXCELLENCE WHERE IT MATTERS.** A scattering of red lights burned in distant posts, but outnumbering those lights were empty bulb sockets.

"Welcome. Welcome to EWM Company," the security guard said cheerfully, turning a guest book on a swivel. "Whom do you wish to see?"

I took a chance. "Is E. Wayne Manger Jr. in?"

"Goodness, no. Junior died in '64."

"When did his father die?"

"A year later. Junior was a good man. A sad man. Lost his mother when he was four," the guard said. "They used to say the Boys—that's what we called Senior and Junior—were never the same after she died. Nor us, for that matter."

"How do you mean?"

"Of course, I only know what's been passed down. But I've been here since '62. I knew them both. They both liked a fresh carnation for their lapel every morning. I was in charge of buying them. The carnations they're wearing in the grave—I bought them. Strange to think of those flowers down there now—that carnation smell."

The guard's attention wandered. His last words drifted in the dust on a sunbeam coming in through high windows.

"How's business?" I asked.

"We soldier on," the guard said, sitting up straight and flexing the lapels of his coat.

"Did Junior have any children?"

"A daughter. Would you like to meet her?"

"She's here?"

"She's the boss."

I was allowed to walk unescorted through a doorway off the lobby and then through a warren of cubicles that gave off a low hum of activity. At the end of the hallway I came to another door, this one of fine-grained, polished wood, with beveled panes and milky-blue teardrops of glass set in it. The door squeaked when I pushed it open.

Constance rose to greet me from behind her desk.

Or, rather, a modern version of a grown-up Constance; Constance filtered through two generations but leaving so much of herself behind that it took my breath away.

"I was told you were on your way," the woman said.

"I wanted to speak to E. Wayne Manger Jr.'s daughter."

Of course I knew it was she. I just wanted to verify it. She came around the desk, holding out her hand. I shook it.

"We pronounce it Mang-er. Hard G. I'm Connie Manger Winslow. How may I help you?"

"You look just like your grandmother," I said. I don't know why I said it. I had nowhere else to go with my visit. I'd been convinced long ago.

"My grandmother?"

"Constance Morceau Manger."

She studied me intently, for a long, long moment, during which she went back behind her desk, adopting the savvy businesswoman's cool distance. I wondered all over again what I was doing there.

"You can't be much older than me," she said.

"Did your father ever talk to you about her? Your grandmother?"

"He barely remembered her. But—of course—I heard all the stories. How she and Grandpa met. The scandal. Grandpa crediting her for starting the company."

"Did he say how?"

"She predicted World War One. And a horse race."

"Did he saw *how* she predicted those things?"

She glanced away, and then back at me. "Yes," she said.

"Did your grandfather believe her?"

"By the time I was old enough to talk to him about it—the legend of grandma—it had taken on the weight of a biblical story. Grandpa had long since stopped examining the details. He believed her enough to get as much money together as he could to bet on that horse."

"Wintergreen."

"And the Cubs. And he believed enough to stockpile a product every war is going to need. And after grandma died, grandpa proved to be a pretty lackluster businessman. Uninspired, you might say."

"How about you?"

"We're in a little bit of a downturn. But the company has grown since I took over."

"No. I meant do you believe what happened to your grandmother?"

"Parts."

"Which parts?"

"The parts that I can touch. The real parts."

"She was at my house," I said.

Tears came into her eyes. "Grandma?" she said.

"You cry easily. You got that from her."

"What do you mean she was at your house?"

"She was here for about a week. We all got pretty attached to her."

"How old was she?"

"Fifteen."

"That is of course the part of the story I had the most trouble with," she said. "Even by 1908 there were signs in Europe that war was coming. Predicting a war is a pretty safe bet. And people pick winning racehorses every day."

"She was here," I said. "I wish there was some way I could prove it to you."

"So . . . you're saying I could have been walking down the street last week and bumped into my grandmother—when she was fifteen."

I had to laugh.

"You appreciate how insane that sounds," she said.

"My whole life has been like that since she showed up."

For a moment she looked disappointed at missing something important, something once in a lifetime.

"If she comes back—promise me you'll bring her by."

"I don't think she'll be back."

"Why?"

"A hunch. She didn't like it here—now. Except for the indoor plumbing. She missed her mom and dad. And she wanted to save her boyfriend."

"But she didn't."

"That's part of the legend, too?"

She came around the desk and crossed the room. I went with her. A set of double doors built flush with the wall opened on a ceiling-high mirror framed with fluorescent lights, which flickered to life. To the left hung a collage, and I recognized it immediately as a shrine of sorts to the legend of Connie's grandmother.

"Grandpa made this," she said.

Pressed behind the glass were clippings of Constance Morceau's disappearance and reappearance—but not the drawing of the lynched Dash Buckley. There were also fanned winning tickets from the 1909 Kentucky Derby, one signed by jockey Vincent Powers, a pressed rose, and another clipping declaring the Cubs winners of the '08 World Series.

In one corner was the wedding announcement for E. Wayne Manger and Constance Morceau. Another corner held the receipt of EWM Co.'s first order—one million feet each of three-inch, six-inch, and twelve-inch gauze—from the government of France.

"Grandpa went on a round-the-world trip to make business contacts," Connie said.

"Years before the war," I reminded her.

In another corner was the obituary for Constance Morceau Manger that I had read that day. Preserved under glass, the clipping was almost as white as the day it was cut from the paper.

"May I take it down?" I asked.

She reached beyond me. "It's loose."

She lifted it off the hooks and placed it in my hands. One of the Derby tickets slid to the bottom of the frame.

"I keep telling myself I should get it redone," she said. "But I kind of like it this way. I always feel like grandpa's breath is caught inside—and if I opened it . . ."

I turned the frame again, to read through the glare from the mirror light, and in turning it nicked the corner of the frame against the folded door. A dark scrap of material fell into view from behind Constance's obituary.

Connie pressed in behind me. "What's that?"

I knew what it was. It was proof.

"A piece of microfilm," I said.

The piece was too small and dark to read without a magnifier and backlight, but I was certain that if I removed it from the frame and took it to the library it would fit perfectly into that gap—that page—that Constance had cut from the newspaper of November 14, 1918.

Connie's eyes were wide. "Did they have microfilm back then?"

"I don't think so."

"Then how did it get there?"

I barely heard her. A question nagged at me, maddeningly elusive, like a fact or a scrap of information that I knew I possessed, but was unable to call forth. I tried to draw out the question by working around it.

"Are you certain your grandfather made this collage?"

"That's the story I was told."

"That's a piece of microfilm your grandmother took back with her," I said.

"Took back," Connie repeated.

I sketched for Connie the time I'd spent with her grandmother in the library, how I'd taught her to operate the microfilm reader.

"That's where she learned her boyfriend's fate," I said. "Why she was so desperate to get back."

"So how did she do it?" Connie asked, a natural question, but one out of sequence with my thoughts.

"Wait. She was stuck here. She felt trapped. She was drawn to the information on those rolls of film. Who wouldn't be? To be able to read the future. I warned her that information would be dangerous if—when—she got back to 1908. But she couldn't stop. Frankly, I think she didn't have anything else to do. This wasn't her time. She had no reason to be here."

"But how—?"

I held up my hand. "She took one of those reels from the library. The first two weeks of November—1918."

"The war?"

I pushed on. Something drew closer.

"She already knew about the war. But she wanted to take that reel back with her. I'm not sure why," I said. "Proof? As a bargaining chip? It would be worth a fortune. But it didn't work. I told her I thought the knowledge she was accumulating about her future was making it difficult for her to go back. And trying to take that reel would be like dragging an anchor through the eye of a needle."

"This is so hard to believe," Connie said.

I didn't care. "I returned the reel to the library. This was after she'd returned to 1908. A page had been cut out of the film reel." I tapped the glass over the collage. "That page," I said.

"What's on it?"

"A list of flu victims."

"Flu?"

"The Spanish influenza. The pandemic."

"And she was on the list?"

"Yes. Constance M. Manger."

And there it was.

"How did she know her name would be Constance *Manger*?" I asked.

Connie didn't answer. She rehung the collage. Watching her, I was reminded of Flo's doubts about Constance, and here was Connie like a grown-up version of the girl from the past.

"Do you have kids?" I asked

"Yes."

"A daughter?"

"Yes. And two sons."

"Does she look like you?"

"People say she does."

"She'd be Constance's great-granddaughter."

"What's your point?"

"My wife thinks this is all a scam—that Constance was a girl from now, from the present."

"My daughter is eight years old," she said. "She's a schemer—but they're an eight-year-old's schemes."

I nodded, distracted. I wanted to get out of there, to pursue the question that filled every available inch of my thoughts.

"But—how did she do it?" Connie asked.

"To be honest—I don't know."

"You can't just leave me like that."

"I believe it is both as simple and as complicated as hitting a particular spot at a particular moment at a particular speed. And a doorway opens."

"Great. That tells me nothing."

"You couldn't do it," I said to discourage her. "You'd want it too much."

"Want it? God, no. Leave my kids behind?"

"That's what frightens me the most. Lost in the past or the future—unable to get back."

"Have you done it?"

I smiled. "I went back fifteen minutes."

"That's all?"

"It doesn't sound like much. But it changed my life."

FOURTEEN

I returned home by the usual route, doing nothing to either increase or decrease my chances of arriving safely. A part of me expected Constance to be waiting—and I wondered how much of that was a result of recently being in the company of her granddaughter.

A troop of state wards had descended on Flo's office. Their chatter and energy gave the place a liveliness that was in contrast to the cold watchfulness of my wife.

"She hasn't come home," she hissed at me from the office door, her patients forgotten behind her.

Irrational helplessness coursed through me. I took a moment to reorder myself in the situation, not to feel better about Penny being gone, but in order for me to be able to do something about it. I checked the afternoon light: several hours before darkness was an issue, not long before Penny would have been gone most of the day.

"I called the police," she said.

That seemed to give credence to Holly's prediction—but it was the next natural step.

"What did they say?"

"Give her time. She hasn't been gone long enough."

"Good advice. Don't worry."

"Did you talk to her friends?"

"I met Constance's granddaughter."

Flo was no longer listening to me. "Go see Corey," she said and shut the door.

I took the perp walk carefully to Holt Street, and then turned north. Corey lived a couple blocks past the Burton house. He answered when I rang the bell.

He stayed behind the screen door. "Hey, Mr. Winkler."

"Have you seen Penny?"

"Not today."

"When did you last see her?"

"Last night."

His mother materialized out of the shadows. "Corey has nothing more to say," she told me.

"What time last night?" I asked.

"Late."

"After midnight?"

"Corey—" his mother warned. To me, she said, "I'm sure you'll find her without our help."

"Mom, it's okay," Corey said. "She was on her way home," he said to me. "The last time I saw her."

"Was it after midnight?"

"Yeah."

"Was she running?"

"Corey—" his mother said.

The kid glanced at her. "We'd had a fight," he said to me.

"What about?"

"Boy-girl stuff," he said.

"Your idea or hers?"

He hesitated. "Hers."

I was surprised. "Really?"

His mother had taken a step back into the shadows. The effect was of someone releasing herself of responsibility for a situation.

"She wanted to swim," he said. "Naked."

I was startled, but moved ahead. "Where?"

"We have an in-ground pool in back," his mother said.

They showed me. It was small and oval, with leaves pivoting slowly on the surface.

"What happened?" I asked.

"She was wired." He glanced at me. "She'd snuck out of the house. It was hot. She wanted to go swimming."

"Did you?"

"*I* didn't."

"But Penny did?"

"Not swim, exactly. She just jumped in and jumped out." He considered something for a moment. "I think she was disappointed in me."

"And she was naked?"

Corey swallowed, nodded, like he feared I might hit him for what he had seen. And he was right, I realized.

"It was no big deal," he said.

"What happened then?" his mother asked.

"I still wouldn't do it."

"Geez, kid," I said, wanting to make him feel bad, "a naked girl asks you to go swimming—*go*!"

"I'm proud of you," his mother said, with a frosty glance at me. "Somebody had to show some common sense."

"Then what happened?"

"She jumped out and left."

"Was she wet?"

He nodded.

"Was she running?"

"Sort of hopping and running and crying and trying to get dressed," Corey said, "sort of all at the same time."

I believed the kid. He seemed decent enough—but mostly young and frightened.

"Your daughter will be back," his mother assured me, able to be magnanimous now that her son's story had held up.

But her son wasn't finished. "She accused me—" he began.

His mother's face lost its sunny smirk of relief and she actually grabbed Corey's arm and tried to pull him out of range of me.

"Accused you of what?" I asked.

"Of cheating on her. In the future."

His mother's grip tightened. "Corey," she warned.

I reached for him and my fingers bounced off the screen door.

"Tell me."

He made a point of pulling free of his mother's grasp and stepped out onto the front porch.

"She said that in the future—after she's gone—I'd hit on Holly Dearborn."

"She said that? 'After I'm gone'?"

"Yeah."

"Where did she say she was going?"

"Just gone. She said she knew the future. It was kinda creepy."

"Is *that* when she took off all her clothes?" his mother asked.

At dusk, the house empty, I called the police and was put on hold. Piano music began to play in my ear. While I waited I unpinned the 1918 influenza victims list from the bulletin board. I read down the list to:

Manger, Constance M. *adult*

And then down from there:

Miller, Ophelia *adult*
Nellison, Thomas *adult*
Olston, John *beloved child*
Praeger, Arthur *orphan child*
Pzerter, Katherine *adult*
Quinn, Daniel *adult*
Tully, Millicent *adult*
Vincent, William *orphan child*
Voss, E.J. *beloved child*
Winberger, James *adult*

Winkler, Penelope *orphan child*
Wisteria, Vitrine *adult*
Wooster, Blanche *adult*
Young, Muriel *adult*
Zook, Kenneth *adult*

The name didn't stop me the first time through. I might have made an unconscious decision not to notice it. Maybe I didn't connect with the designation of orphan child. But there was no avoiding it on the second pass.

Winkler, Penelope *orphan child*

Was this why Constance had tried to hide the page from me? Did she know Penny was lost and alone in 1918, an orphan dying of the influenza more than eighty years from where she was supposed to be?

The piano music shut off. A man said, "Euclid Heights Police Department." I hung up.

I carried the list of names through the darkening house. I found Flo in the attic, up a fold-down ladder, searching in that infernally hot, high space for something I couldn't imagine.

"I think I know where she is," I said. I had to bend over under the roof beams, sweat already sliding off me.

Sweat and dust made Flo appear sculpted out of delicate, pale mud. She crossed to me in three steps.

"Where?"

"I *think*."

"*Where?*"

I crackled the flu list at her. Like a promise, it got her to follow me down the attic ladder into the hall, where cool air bathed me and gave me confidence. It was already too dark to read and I didn't want to do this too close to Penny's room. So I lured Flo farther down.

In the kitchen's bright light, with no sign of Penny—just me and a sheet of paper—Flo's faint hope flagged.

"Did you call the police?"

"I started to. Look." I spread the paper on the table, put my finger next to Penny's name.

Flo bent close to read it. I saw, as she stood back up, the usual skepticism, this time accompanied by a sort of ultimate impatience.

"What *now*?" she asked forlornly.

I jabbed at the name. "That's her," I said.

Flo pressed her hands to her temples. "Oh, Lord," she moaned. "Oh, Josh."

"It's her!"

"You're saying my little girl is dead—in 1918?"

"Technically it says influenza *victims*."

"They aren't going to print the names of people who are only sick," she said.

"I was trying to spare you."

"Why start now?"

"This is the page Constance cut out of the microfilm reel," I said. "I think she saw Penny's name."

"Her name is on it, too."

"How would she know she'd be Constance *Manger*?"

Flo had no answer for that.

If Constance was right—that she was confident of returning to 1908 because that was where she belonged—then what was it about the year 1918 that drew Penny to it?

"Penny is missing. Let's assume," I said. "I talked to Corey. Penny snuck out last night. She was with him. They had a fight."

"Arrest Corey," Flo said.

"He said she wanted to swim naked with him."

"Penny wouldn't—"

"She took off her clothes and jumped into their pool. Then she ran away. This paper is from November fourteenth, 1918. But it's August there now like it's August here. We have time to get her back. Before she gets sick."

Flo just stared at me as I spun out my explanation. A tear ran down her cheek. She was utterly alone. I knew how she felt.

"Call the police," she said.

"They'll just get in the way."

"In the way?" she sputtered. "In the way of what?"

"Constance got back," I said.

Flo did not remove her pitying, hopeless gaze from me.

"If Constance can get back there," I said. "Penny can get back here."

The police came without calling. A detective and Jock Itch appeared in the yard. The detective was about half Itch's size, and fifteen years younger, their pairing reminding me of a big goof required to keep a resentful eye on his kid brother.

"Did you call the police earlier this evening?" the detective asked. "Mr. Winkler?"

"I changed my mind."

"Why did you call?" Itch asked.

"Why was I put on hold?"

"You didn't call nine one one."

"That shouldn't make a difference," I said. "I was on hold for ten minutes."

The detective checked his notepad. "Actually, it was forty-eight seconds."

Jock Itch smirked. "Seemed longer, huh?"

"Why *did* you call, sir?"

"Do you follow up with all the people who change their minds?"

"Do you know a female juvenile named Constance Morceau?"

"Yes."

"Ms. Morceau is a state ward. A state employee—one Hilda Cutter—reported her missing—and can place the girl in your presence. Your name on *that* file—combined with your name on the hang-up—was a winner."

"My wife called even earlier about my daughter being gone," I said. "Why didn't you call her?"

The detective checked his notes. "We have no cross-indexing of her call and your situation."

"So it's not an infallible system," I said.

"Is she still missing?" the detective asked.

"Yes."

"Could she be with Ms. Morceau?"

"Possibly."

"Mr. Winkler," the detective said, "your name came up a third time—in the Holly Dearborn case."

"She's not missing anymore."

"But she said she talked to you."

"Yes."

"Even before she went home."

"She told me Penny would be missing."

"Who's Penny?" the detective asked.

"My daughter."

"And Holly Dearborn predicted she would be missing?" the detective asked.

"She *knew.*"

"How did she know?"

"She went into the future."

I watched their reactions as I said this. The detective, for the first time, had heard something worth noting and was writing furiously. Itch just gaped at me.

"What else did she see in the future?" the detective finally asked with phony solicitude.

"Nothing."

"She didn't tell you what happened to your daughter?"

"Only that she'd be missing."

The detective studied his notes while he asked, "Do you believe her?"

"Yes."

"You believe she traveled through time into the future."

"Yes."

"Have you traveled through time yourself?"

"Yes."

Itch actually winced, as if stricken with a sudden compassion for me after a lifetime of bullying.

"Regularly?" the detective asked.

I felt pleased—sane—to be able to say, "No. Just once."

"Did you see the future?"

"I went fifteen minutes into the past."

Now Jock Itch laughed uproariously.

"Winker! I'd at least go back and see something famous like—"

"Could you do it again?" the detective interrupted.

I shook my head. At that moment, Flo came out of the house.

"According to her—I didn't do it even once."

"Detective Hamblin," the detective said, offering his hand.

She shook it. She didn't appear to recognize Itch.

"You're here to help find my daughter?"

"Do you have any idea where she might be?" Detective Hamblin asked.

"No. None." She glanced at me. For a moment we were a team again, getting through things together. It was a state of existence I hadn't missed at all in the preceding days, but now that it was back—even briefly—I ached at its rarity.

Then Flo said, "*He* thinks she's gone back to 1918."

He. The way she said it broke my heart. He. The man she couldn't count on any longer.

"Flo," I said, helplessly.

"Nineteen eighteen?" Detective Hamblin said to me.

"Yes," Flo continued like a hostile witness. "Where she died of the flu."

"*Will* die," I stressed. "In November."

"You're saying she'll die *this* November?" Itch asked.

"November of 1918."

"You're sure of this?" the detective asked.

"No."

It was disconcerting to have my wife be the most skeptical of the three. Even dunderheaded Jock Itch's eyes showed more open-minded curiosity than Flo's.

"Then why do you *think* she's in 1918?" the detective asked.

I led them into the house and showed them Penny's name among the influenza victims.

"Penelope Winkler. That's her."

The detective was plainly unconvinced.

"She isn't an orphan," he said.

"Not *now*. But in 1918 she has no parents. And there"—I pointed to Constance's name on the list—"is Constance Morceau."

"Constance M. Manger?"

"Yes. She went back. Got married. And died in 1918."

Detective Hamblin moved to the door. "Mr. Winkler," he said, "we need to talk to you at greater length."

"Right now?"

"Tomorrow morning would be better. I'll send Officer Ketch for you."

"Not necessary," I said.

"All right. But be there at ten A.M."

After they had gone, Flo took a seat at the kitchen table, but tentatively, like she was only holding it for someone else.

"Bring a lawyer," she said.

"I'll be okay."

"You're the best thing they've come up with—a man who admits knowing where two missing girls are." She shook her head in disbelief. "*And* he says they're lost in time. The cops are fluffing the pillow in your jail cell right now."

"Bringing a lawyer would indicate I had something to hide," I said.

"I think you do," she said angrily. "And I wish you'd done a better job of it."

FIFTEEN

Come morning, being in no hurry to stop in at the police trailer, I made my way to the house Constance had pointed out across from the library. I pressed my hand to the old orphanage gate's bricks, wondering if I would feel some of the loneliness of the place, the children's sadness soaked into the stone. But nothing reached me. Just bricks, warm and rough to the touch. And this gave me hope that Penny had not spent enough time there for her spirit to inhabit the place.

At ten o'clock, the hour I was expected by the police, I waited for the Euclid Heights Historical Society to open its doors. Henry Hinsdale remained in charge, but showed no sign of recognizing me, maybe because I was traveling alone. He was surprised that I knew my way down to the files, that I even suspected their existence.

"Do you have records from the old orphanage?" I asked.

He said, "Yes," but reluctantly.

"May I see them?"

"Those are very personal."

He reached for something in his hip pocket; I hoped it was a key. But he removed his billfold—thin and limp as a sock and worn white at the corners—and from it took out and carefully unfolded a sheet of paper.

"This is mine," he said. He centered it under the lamplight. It was the carbon receipt of an official document, and at the top was the heading.

EUCLID HEIGHTS CHILDREN'S HOME

Below it was the name "Hinsdale, Henry," and the date of his admittance, February 1, 1930.

"You lived there?"

"Six long years," he said, grim but proud. "Until they closed the place. I was supposed to be transferred with the rest of them—but I was seventeen, I'd done some typing for the office, and I knew how things worked."

He was not quite smiling, but his eyes were alive with the past.

"I got myself lost in the shuffle. In all the hubbub of moving, I just walked away. I ceased to exist. Hell, I was an orphan."

"What'd you do then?"

"Got a job. Then another job. Then the Marines. Then I met my wife. Had four kids. Eleven grandkids. Not one of them an orphan." He laughed full out. "And I've kept this with me every step of the way." He returned the document to his wallet.

"What was it like? The orphanage."

"Not bad. Just a business. No frills," he said. "The funniest thing—the other day my youngest daughter called me, said her car was broke down and she needed me to pick up my granddaughter Kyra from day care. The second I walked in that place I started sobbing. It was the smell. Smelled exactly like the orphanage. A little poop. A little pee. Tears. Sweat. Disinfectant. And added to all that the smell of a business. Profiting off kids. Kids everywhere—but nobody really loving them. I took Kyra home and offered to keep her with me during the day but my daughter said no. That's another story."

"What happened to your parents?" I asked.

"Died," he said. He did not elaborate, only unlocked the door and led the way down the stairs to the file room. Then he unlocked the door at the foot of the stairs.

"Go to the opposite corner and turn right," he said.

He was surprised I knew about propping open the door with a shoe, and then he handed over a flashlight. I tried not to think about the documents I was passing—Constance's death certificate, and Penny's, too, maybe—and decided that if I didn't see them they didn't exist.

I found the orphanage files and went immediately to the *w*'s. Each orphan's history was contained in a manila folder, the name on a raised tab in the upper right-hand corner.

"Winkler, P." was there, and when I slid out the file its thinness and apparent scarcity of information both comforted and alarmed me. She hadn't been an orphan for long. But also, if she died young, there was no further data to accumulate.

In fact, the file contained only a single sheet. It was the same form Henry Hinsdale had shown me.

It began with Penny's—or Penelope's—admission to the orphanage on 8/26/18. That day, she was five feet five inches tall and weighed 119 pounds. Her mental state was recorded as "DSPN." Despondent? Despairing?

The remainder of the sheet was devoted to a series of paragraphs written in longhand:

> Orphan girl was admitted EHCH 8/26/18 by sheriff, who reported finding OG unresponsive and hysterical and wandering east side of downtown area. No record of mother or father.
>
> OG frequently belligerent and consistently delusional. Claims both parents are alive. Statements and contentions indicate mental disbalance.
>
> OG shows quick mind. Devilish. Has no interest in organized activities. Is of considerable help in Inf. and with younger children. Avid reader.
>
> Delusions about future events ongoing and detailed.
>
> Reported to Inf: 10/2 w/cough and fever.
>
> Released 10/6.

Diagnosed SI 11/2.
Perished 11/12/18.

At the bottom were scrawled the initials JTK.

My hands shook, reading such a condensed and dispassionate recounting of my daughter's fate. I reread it, imagining her sick, frightened, and alone. But I also pictured her avidly reading and being devilish. A pistol. Beloved by the other orphans; entertaining them with her vivid predictions about the future. She would be hell on the adults, exclaiming with absolute conviction that she didn't need to know the lessons of the day.

I folded the sheet and put it in my pocket, returned the empty file folder, and closed the drawer. Henry Hinsdale was waiting for me upstairs.

"Find it?" he asked.

"Yes," I said. "Thanks."

"My pleasure," Henry said. "You know, after you've been an orphan—you'll never be lonely again."

I considered—but not for long—stopping at the police trailer on my way home. I was unsure how to proceed on most fronts, but I was absolutely certain that a long period of interrogation by people who suspected me in the disappearance of two girls was not a smart use of my time.

Flo was seeing patients. I was so convinced of Penny's existence in 1918 that I did not even check her room to see if she might have returned. Nor did I feel the panicky compulsion to search in the present that a father of an ordinary missing child would.

I knew where my daughter was. I had it in writing.

What was becoming increasingly obvious was that I would have to go to her—bring her back. This struck me as both completely reasonable and utterly terrifying. Penny was lost in 1918. I had no desire to be lost there, too. Nor did I wish to be lost in some even more arbitrary year. If I could control things I would simply go to that moment when Penny climbed naked out of Corey's pool. I'd help her dress, put my arm around her, and walk her carefully home.

But I wasn't in control of anything. I could only try—and trust that I would arrive where and when I most wanted and needed to be.

And finally I had no choice. I knew where Penny was, and I knew I would never get her back if I waited until I had a shred of understanding, let alone control of the situation.

I found the book I wanted on the shelves of my studio and inside the book I found the information I needed. I took a red felt-tip pen and began to write. I got lost in the process. Time flew by. I didn't hear Flo come in.

When I glanced up, she was crying.

"Oh, God," she said, turning to flee.

I ran for her and grabbed her. What a sight I must have been, maybe her personification of the last straw. She fought to get free.

"I'm going after her," I said.

Flo went quiet in my arms. I wondered if she would protest my plan, express her fear of losing both her husband and her daughter in the past. No. She stepped free of me.

"How?" she asked, willing to be convinced.

"I don't know." I smiled. "The usual way."

She pointed at me, at what I'd been writing. "And this?"

"I have to take something back . . . something useful."

"And if you don't make it?"

"I'll try again. Look." I showed her Penelope Winkler's orphanage form. "We have a little time. She doesn't get sick until November."

Flo took the document and read it, a hand on her forehead. She got to the end and checked the other side for more.

"It's not her," she said in a flat, hopeless voice.

"Of course—"

"No! She's not an avid reader now. Why would she be an avid reader then?"

"Nothing else to do?"

"She'd make friends."

I threw up my hands. "It's her name, Flo! Her height and weight."

"It's not her! It can't be her!"

"Don't you see? This is good. We know where she is. She's safe—

for the time being. Would you rather she was lost here—in the present—where we have no idea where she is, who she's with, how to reach her?"

"If she's in the present, there's hope she'll return. If she's in 1918 . . ." Her voice trailed away, gave up.

"Trust me," I said. "It will work."

"Did you talk to the police?"

"No."

"They called to ask where you were."

I sat back down, returned to my project. Flo watched with a sort of appalled fascination.

"Are you even going to talk to them?" she finally asked.

"Eventually."

She waited a moment. "Josh?"

I stopped working. I held my finger on a line in the book.

"Are you hiding something?" she asked in the gentlest voice she had used with me in weeks.

"I'm sitting here in my underwear. What could I be hiding?"

"Is there a reason you don't want to talk to the police?"

"If I go there, I can't do this. Or anything else. And if I go there like this—they'll definitely find a reason to hold me."

"Put on some pants. Then go."

I shook my head, went back to work. "I told them everything I know yesterday."

"So you're refusing to talk to them at all?"

"For the time being."

It all made perfect sense to me. Flo watched me for another minute and then her call button beeped and she returned to her office. I finished what I was doing and put on jeans and a long-sleeve white shirt. The sky was cloudless, but an encouraging humidity weighted the air. It could have been the forerunning wet kiss of a summer thunderstorm. It gave me hope, anyway.

I headed back downtown. I was on the lookout for Kurt. It felt important that I see him before I left. He was not outside 1112 East Collier Street. This was something of a relief, a hint that he might be easing the grip on his obsession, but once I had walked into the heart of downtown I felt pursued. I couldn't forget that the police wanted to talk to me.

I found Kurt on Greencloth Street, on a sidewalk bench, facing away from traffic, his head lolled back to take in the sun, his eyes closed.

"Hey," I said, nudging his laceless sneaker with my toe.

He jerked up, guiltily, as if I had caught him doing something he shouldn't.

"I'm going away for a while," I said.

He rubbed a hand over his eyes, his mouth.

"Go see Flo if you need anything."

He didn't really nod, but his fidgeting moved his head in such a way that he might have been nodding.

"You know the house."

"One one one—"

"No. South Clover Street. Two one eight."

I sat on the bench next to him and removed the laces from my work boots, then knelt in front of him and laced them into his sneakers. His feet gave off such a stench that I had to hold my breath at the end.

"Blood," Kurt said.

I didn't follow. "What?"

He pointed at me. "Blood."

Before I could answer I heard a motorcycle engine goosed on the next block over.

"Flo will help," I said to Kurt.

I jumped up, checked the traffic on Greencloth, and then darted across, feeling pursued, feeling on the edge of losing my boots with each step.

At the corner of Collier and Pincoffin I thought I saw a police car up ahead. I turned south, down Pincoffin, to the perp walk. I didn't hesitate at its mouth. What was the point of caution? I knew what happened. I started to jog up the path, leaves brushing my shoulders, trying to keep my boots on and my mind free of any desire or ambition for a specific goal. Penny popped into my thoughts. It was a memory from when she was on her first bike, just learning to ride.

I came to Pine Street.

I was teaching her to ride on the grass so that when she fell she would have a softer landing. But she didn't make any real progress until Flo took her into the street, where the pavement was made for travel. After that, she was gone. She rode to the end of the block and out of sight. Flo and I blinked at each other, afraid of what we had set in motion. A minute later Penny was back, coming up behind us, having circled the block. She was beaming as she went around again.

"Where are you going?" I'd called to her.

"I don't know," she said.

I was running full tilt and carrying my boots when I reached the perp walk alongside our house. I was winded and sweating, my shirt plastered to my back.

I went inside and drew a glass of water, then returned to the yard and collapsed in the chaise longue. Curls of red ink, thin as hairs, bled through my shirt. Sweat burned in my eyes. More ink came through my sleeves.

My attention was thus elsewhere when Holly Dearborn appeared. She was on the perp walk, bewildered, wearing the clothes she'd had on when she came to tell me about this very visit.

"Hi," she said.

As I recalled, I was supposed to be crying. I was worried, but not tearful. Holly's appearance—on cue—had restored my confidence. I felt like a scientist whose oddball theory was proved true.

"Do you know where Penny is?" she asked.

Holly waited for me to answer. I waited for Jock Itch.

"She's missing," I said.

Holly nodded. "This is *so* weird. Do you know what's going on?"

"I think so. You told me about this moment," I said. "You'll be going back in a few minutes."

"Back?" she said.

I lifted my shirt, showed her the red words and numbers written upside down on my stomach.

"You told me I was bleeding. This isn't blood," I said.

She just stared at me like I was completely nuts.

A motorcycle rumble thundered in front of the house. I decided not to tell her about the police. Or about chasing her. A culmination of events was approaching. If I didn't play it right I would fail at my primary objective.

"Hear that?" I asked.

Before Holly could answer Jock Itch rolled down the perp walk, smiling, coming to get me. He cut the engine.

"We expected you at ten," he said.

"She knows where Penny is!" I grabbed Holly by the arm.

She was surprised—maybe even a little shocked—but not ready to run.

"You're the only suspect we got, Winker," Itch said, smug, laconic.

"Ask her! She knows where she is!"

I jerked Holly's arm, pulled her off balance toward me, hoping to get her running in the opposite direction out of sheer repugnance.

"Arrest *her*!" I shouted.

Holly finally turned and ran. She looked at me and at Itch and she ran. She was a strong, fast runner and in no time she was out of the yard, across Clover, and down the next perp walk link.

I took off after her.

"Winkler!"

The motorcycle engine kicked over behind me, its roar obscuring any further warnings from Itch.

When I entered the mouth of the perp walk Holly was almost out the other end. Running, I had a moment's appreciation of how lush and peaceful the walks were in summertime, one of those little idiosyncratic details that give a town its unique character.

Itch had his motorcycle turned around and was leisurely in pursuit, crossing Clover, entering the shadows of the walk. He was removing his sunglasses and hooking them in his pocket and so got too close to the fence along the path and snagged the knob of his handlebars. He went down with a heavy crunch of glass and metal. In the sudden silence of the stalled engine I heard him curse, then roar, *"Wing-kler!"*

I didn't stop. I was running full out and had to imagine his wide-set stance, his enraged face, his two-handed pistol grip.

"Stop! Or I'll shoot!"

The warning sounded insincere, like he had just remembered a bothersome rule.

I was coming to the end of the path. Up ahead, a car traveling north on Tinker Street passed across the opening. Beyond, Holly was increasing her lead.

A crack sounded behind me. An electric pop, like a camera flash, froze my shadow in front of me. I ran through it.

I didn't stop running until I almost ran over Penny.

She was at the end of the walk, barefoot—like me—bent over and pulling arrowhead burrs off her skirt. She glanced up when she heard me and for a moment we were both surprised, like people who had thought they were alone.

Then she flew into my arms.

"Oh, daddy!" she sobbed.

I rubbed her back, held her up, savored the solidity of her, as happy as any father who recovered his missing daughter, but who also had other things on his mind.

The road beyond was dirt. The perp walk was unpaved, too, barely more than a groove worn through the woods.

Penny finally pulled free of me.

"Let's go back," she said urgently. "Right now!" She wiped her face with the heel of her hand.

"It isn't that simple," I said.

I stepped into the road. Toward town, I saw scattered houses plunked down amid wide fields of corn and sunflowers and prairie grass, all of it parched from lack of rain. The sky looked endless and I realized why: fewer houses and younger, smaller trees opened up the horizon.

Penny took my hand. "At least I'm not an orphan anymore," she said.

I put my hand on her forehead. "You feel okay?"

She drew back. "I feel fine. Why?"

"Just checking."

Her face paled. "You know something, don't you?"

"I know it doesn't matter now."

"What doesn't?"

"Your future isn't here anymore." I took her by the hand toward town. "Come on. I want to see 1918."

SIXTEEN

The town's grid pattern was already in place. It only awaited filling in. I could see across the land to the west that the streets lay roughly where they would be in the years to come. Dust smoked up between my toes with each step. I felt at once more vulnerable and more alive.

"Where are your shoes?" Penny asked.

"Long story."

"I wish you could've brought me some clothes." She plucked at the white blouse she wore, stuck a finger into the pinching collar.

"Where *are* your clothes?"

"Does Corey miss me?"

"I think so."

"Is he with Holly yet?"

"I don't know. Have you seen Constance?"

"She wanted to put me up. Her husband said no."

"Is she okay?"

Penny glanced at me. "What happens to *her*?"

I shook my head. "We should go see her."

"She's got a kid. And money. All her doing—but her husband gives her no credit."

We came to an east-west cross street. "Collier," I said. I knew exactly where we were.

"Your old house is here," Penny said.

Collier Street was wider than it would turn out to be, almost three lanes wide. Houses became more frequent as we approached downtown. Most of them were made of wood, some quite substantial. A faint whiff of privy passed on the breeze. The thing I couldn't get over was the openness, the long views, and the quiet. We passed one house where a woman was in the side yard hanging wash, and I could hear the snap as she shook out a wet sheet, then the wooden clatter in her apron as she dug out clothespins, putting the extras in her mouth. She saw us and waved. The squeak of the pulley was clear as a bird as she drew the clothesline toward her.

"Their cars sound like they're going to fall apart any second," Penny complained. "And *nothing* is air-conditioned. My room is an oven!"

"I'm here to bring you back."

"You said it was dangerous to mess around with time."

"I'm not going to let you stay in 1918. I'll risk that."

"Constance is disappointed she couldn't stop World War One."

"Some things are too big."

"But it made her rich. She disappoints me, actually."

"Why?"

"She's turned into such a *mom*."

Up ahead, like a mirage, or a ghost, a plodding gray horse clopped through the intersection, pulling a wagon whose tall, red-slat side read **BOOTH**. The driver flicked his hat brim at us, and his whistled tune was as beautiful to me as the squeak of the clothesline pulley.

"I think I want to stay here a few days," I said.

"You've *got* to be joking."

"No. It's wonderful."

"It won't be so wonderful if we're both stuck here forever."

"Look at the colors," I said. "I see pictures from the past and they're all in black-and-white, or sepia, or shades of gray. You forget it wasn't like that."

The house at 1112 East Collier Street was the first one we reached that was built of brick. It was unnumbered, but it was the first thing I'd seen that was built to last. It was also smaller than it eventually would be, lacking a garage, and the family room addition that would be put on in the years just before my parents bought it. Dash Buckley's letter to Constance was folded carefully away in the basement, I knew.

A popping, sputtering, trucklike vehicle came toward us down Collier. It had a black metal demicab and a rear bed with low sidewalls, and a man in goggles and leather gauntlets at the wheel.

Penny muttered, "Damn," and moved behind me as this truck approached. As it passed she shifted her position to try to keep me between her and the truck.

But the driver wasn't fooled. He glanced our way, and then braked sharply. The cloud of dust the truck had simultaneously been raising and outrunning caught up with it and I heard the driver cough.

"Damn!" Penny said again as the truck backed toward us.

"What?" I said.

"It's Mr. Ketch. From the orphanage."

"Ketch?" I said, disbelieving.

He stopped alongside us, set the brake, but didn't turn off the motor. Lifting his goggles, he revealed an undusty space in a corresponding shape.

"I see you found our reluctant resident," he said to me.

He did, indeed, resemble Jock Itch. Thick arms, devious eyes, low forehead topping a wide, flat face. He thrust out a hand.

"John Ketch, sir," he said. I shook the hand of Itch's grandfather. "I own the children's home. I can't place you, however, sir."

"I've come to get my daughter," I said.

A flash of confusion—then wariness—crossed his features and as quickly passed.

"Your daughter?" he said amiably.

"Penny—Penelope Winkler." I touched her arm.

Ketch scratched his chin. "Knowing her name doesn't make you her father, sir," he said. "You have legal documentation, of course."

I felt at my hip pocket, but only for show. I knew I wasn't carrying ID. "I left my wallet in my other pants."

"And did you also leave your shoes on your other feet?"

He bumped open the truck door and stepped out. He might have been an inch or two shorter than Itch, but he was imposing nevertheless, broad and thick, a man on his own turf, a man accustomed to getting his way.

He grasped Penny's upper arm with a gauntleted hand and when I reached for her he turned out his jacket and flashed a gold star that was so big it looked fake. A kid's badge.

"I'm also the sheriff," he said.

He spun Penny around and pushed her ahead of him into the truck.

"I'm paid a dollar a day for every orphan in my care," he said. "So for me to give up a dollar a day, sir, I'm going to require more than your say-so."

Penny went willingly enough, resigned, as if orphanhood was a state of mind she already was getting used to. This worried me. I had come into a time with its own rules and ways, its own inevitabilities. My daughter was already ensnared. A dollar a day.

Ketch cracked his knuckles, reset his goggles, and released the brake. Penny turned in her seat and watched me plaintively as they drove away.

I backtracked to the perp walk I'd arrived on. Seeing the Collier Street house had raised a question in my mind. I proceeded carefully up the path, swatting through the dusty green overhang of leaves that pressed both sides of the track.

I reached Tinker Street. On the other side of its rutted width was a small patch of corn, sunflowers, tomatoes, and cabbage. Bugs buzzed and ticked in the heat. A scarecrow sported a reverend's collar and a White Sox cap. They would be the Black Sox after the next summer's season. A fresh thrill at being present surged through me.

The path resumed across Tinker, skirting a shed with a definite westward lean, its walls flocked green with moss. I was certain it could be pushed over in a heap with my fingertip. The perp walk was barely a path anymore. Head-high ferns encroached. I counted a hundred paces, walking east, then another hundred, trailblazing by then, and still no sign of Clover Street. My home road did not exist. Neither did my house, my wife, or my life. I only had my daughter, held captive in an orphanage.

It was so disorienting that I had to stop. The thing was, our house on Clover Street should have been there. The original section, built by the paranoid bachelor—Mr. Portmanteau—who insulated his walls with glass, had gone up in 1910, I clearly remembered, and yet now, in 1918, it did not exist.

A bee hit me in the head. I brushed the spot above my brow and it was like a fog lifting. I turned in a circle.

Apple trees stretched away in every direction.

I was in Constance's orchard. The trees marched away in gnarled ranks. One of them would survive to be the tree in my yard. The bees that flew around me might be the ancestors of the bee that had bounced off Constance's cheek. Which tree had she been standing under when the storm broke and she began to run, away from Dash Buckley, toward an unimaginable future? Had she been seeking the shelter of that mossy shed?

Her father's orchard was supposed to be gone by now. Sold off for houses, one of them mine. We had seen the maps, the careful grid of her future, and I had warned her that it wasn't a wise idea to know what was going to happen. She had used what she knew about the world's future to save her family's financial present. It didn't matter whether she had used a horse race bet or convinced her father to invest in her husband's bandage company. It was done.

Before setting off in search of Constance's house, I went past the orphanage. The lot that would contain the library was now the site of a boarding house, with a wide porch running around three sides of the ground floor, where two men played cards and two women watched me, fanning themselves. Their examination didn't falter for an instant as I walked past. I was, after all, a barefoot stranger with traces of blood on his shirt. The two card players were younger than I was, apparently healthy and capable of working, yet frittering away the hot afternoon. Maybe they were artists.

The Euclid Heights Children's Home took up an entire block. It was built of whitewashed wood, the windows and doors upstairs and down trimmed in red paint. The twin brick posts of the gate were more substantial than the building itself, and I placed my hand on the exact corner of the gate that would survive into my lifetime.

Children, happy—to judge by their shrieks and their energy—had worn the play area bare of grass. Every swing and seesaw was in use. A game of chase was in progress on the fire stairs up to the second floor, where an older girl watered a trough of flowers.

Ketch's truck was parked in the front driveway. I saw no sign of Penny. I imagined her inside dispensing her knowledge of the future among parentless children, like a bounteous compensation for having to go through life without a mother or father. Then as I watched, she came out on the front porch with a rug and a metal beater. She didn't even glance at me as she flailed away, the cloud of dirt she raised casting into doubt my identification of her.

Constance's house was on the edge of the land that would become the Dragon Hills, presently occupied by a dense weave of forest so forbidding that I expected some elemental creature—a panther or a pioneer—to emerge. Her house was deep green, like something carved from the next-door woods. The backyard ran deep and narrow into a garden. Beyond that was the privy Constance hated so.

As I stood on the road her front door opened and a group of young men and women emerged, excited and chattering, some through gauze masks. They formed a loose confederation of farewell on the porch, paying compliments to a woman framed in the doorway shadows, then went off in all four directions, one woman even lifting the hem of her skirt and intrepidly entering the forest down a thread of path I hadn't noticed.

The woman in the house shut the door when they were gone. I went up onto the porch and knocked.

Ten years on, Constance had grown beautiful, serene in her maturity and motherhood. A little boy gripped her leg like a bear cub on a tree. She knew me right away.

"Oh, Lord," she said, putting a hand over her eyes and laughing ruefully. "I knew this day would come."

She darted her head out then to see where her young visitors had gone. Only one remained in sight, a young man with a bad limp, struggling toward town.

"You'd be the equivalent of the Second Coming if *they* saw you," she said.

She didn't invite me in, but came out onto the porch, transporting the clinging child without a thought. No offer of refreshment, either. Yet she didn't seem to resent my presence, not even bothering to raise the mask tied around her neck.

"Who are they?" I asked.

"Aficionados of my past experience."

"You talk about what happened?"

She nodded. "And what will."

"Constance—"

"And they pay me," she said defiantly.

"E. Wayne didn't make enough on the war?"

Her tired eyes flashed at me. "You know about him?"

"Yes. His business. Your legend."

She sat down on one of two facing porch divans and I sat opposite her.

"Look at you," she said. "The barefoot time traveler."

The child had woven himself into the folds of her skirt.

"Who's this?" I asked.

Her face suddenly was aglow, which was somehow a relief to me. "This is Edward," she said. She made an effort to extricate the boy from his place of safety among the folds of his mother's clothes. I studied him, the father of Connie at the EWM Co. building. I was knocked off balance each time I gave much thought to where I was and what I was doing.

"He's been sick," she said, coiling her fingers through the little boy's hair. She regarded him with a sad smile. "He's not the best hand with money," she said, returning to the subject of her husband. "He thinks I should've remembered more about the future."

She leaned down so her face was next to the boy's.

"Father gets angry with mother, doesn't he?" she said in a singsong, baby voice.

A cloud of apprehension, startling in its sophistication, swept over the boy's face.

"I might be able to help," I said.

She appeared to make a conscious decision not to respond. "I saw Penny. Living in that awful place."

"I've come to take her back."

"Back," she said wistfully. "I'd go back in a second—if I didn't have this little guy. And if my parents weren't alive."

"Speaking of your parents. I noticed the orchard is still there."

She nodded, as if acknowledging an obvious point.

"It's supposed to be gone by now."

"I gave my father a little help," Constance said.

"Constance—"

"What did you expect?" she asked sharply. "That I'd let their life be sold out from under them?"

I had no argument for that, only a sense of unwanted momentum and complications getting away from me.

"They believed you?" I asked.

"They were happy to see me. I got back just as they were cutting down Dash."

Her eyes overflowed then. The little boy had separated almost entirely and stood watching his mother, tears of his own—of doubt and fear—in his eyes.

"I saw you in the newspaper," I said. "On the edge of the crowd."

"I caused quite a sensation," she said, wiping her eyes with a hankie drawn from her sleeve. She reached for the boy. "Oh, don't cry, little sir!" He plunged back into her skirt and she embraced him.

"No one believed me, of course," she said. "I was just a love-struck girl who'd made a tragic, selfish bid for attention. Eddie came round to interview me. At least he listened to me. He said he wanted to write a story for the paper—but he never did."

"Why did you marry him?"

"That's none of your business," she flashed at me.

I shrugged. "What do you talk about to those people I saw?"

"They're young. Their minds haven't entirely closed," she said. "I provide some sort of reassurance. The young man with the limp was a soldier. He was wounded training in Kansas. He didn't even get to see Europe. He wants to know it was worth it, losing a part of himself."

"Did you tell them when it ends?"

Constance nodded.

"Do they believe you?"

"I don't care. That's the source of my authenticity. I don't try to convince them."

"But you charge them money."

"Of course. Why do this then?"

I couldn't think of any other reason, but then I didn't really know this woman. I knew slightly the girl she had been, but as a wife and mother and seer she was a stranger to me.

"Do you still have the piece of microfilm?" I asked.

She was startled, remembering. Then she smiled.

"You figured it out," she said.

"It's what sent me here," I said. "I wouldn't have found Penny without it."

"I thought about telling you, warning you," she said. "But I was afraid if I did I would change something and somehow ruin *my* chances of getting back. So I cut that one page out of the reel. Like a clue for you to track down."

"You took a big chance with *my* family," I said.

She was unapologetic. "I'd do the same thing all over again, too."

"Did you know you were—are—on the same list?"

She clutched the boy tighter to her, watching me in disbelief. I could see I was as strange to her as she was to me. I also was a seer whose veracity was in question.

"I am?" I saw her come to another decision. She raised a hand, palm out to me. "I don't want to know," she said.

"But this is something you *should* know," I said. "For your family."

"I know when my mother and father die—that's enough for me."

"What about him?" I nodded at the boy.

Her eyes refilled with tears. The child burned a hateful glance into me. I kept making his mother cry.

"Maybe it will open me up to more pain in the future," she said. "Pain I'm not meant to feel."

An otherworldly jangle of bells sounded inside the house. Constance excused herself. The boy stayed behind, leaning against the divan arm, one foot atop the other, curiously, murderously, watching me. Constance returned grim-faced.

"That was him," she said to me. "He heard you were in town."

Had Ketch told him? Was I viewed as a threat? It would be easy enough to lock me away, helpless in jail while autumn and the armistice came, and Constance and Penny took sick and died.

"When I told him you were here now, he asked me to ask you if you brought results," she said.

"What did you tell him?"

"That I'd ask you. And I have."

I unbuttoned my shirt. Dates and names were printed upside down on my torso.

Constance made a conscious effort to turn away.

"I'm not going to help him," she said. "He's used everything I ever told him for himself. Anything he attempts on his own blows up in his face. And then he blames *me*. Other men do all right without getting the answers before the questions are even known."

I rebuttoned my shirt. "What about your son?"

She rubbed his head and he leaned lovingly into the pressure from her hand.

"It would make him more like his father," she said. "No. He can make his own fortune by dint of his talents and hard work."

I didn't try to change her mind.

"You should go," she said. "He might rush home to see you. He won't believe that you came empty-handed."

"Tell him I brought just one. Omaha. In 1935."

"What happens there?"

"He'll know when the time comes. Tell him I said, 'All three.' "

She shook my hand. The Constance I'd seen on the perp walk not so long ago—but far in the future—was entirely gone.

"That's a long time for him to wait," she said. She flashed a crafty smile. "It'll be good for him."

She was glad to be rid of me, I think. She and her son went inside the house and the boy appeared immediately at the window and watched me with unadulterated loathing for the few minutes I remained on the porch, standing barefoot and dusty with nothing to do, nowhere to go, but glad to be present.

Then I heard a gunshot in the Dragon Hills woods, followed in quick succession by another. I heard two more shots when I reached the mouth of the path the woman had taken after leaving Constance's house. The path curled south and west, passing out of sight among greenery and sunlight. Another two shots went off, very close by, and something about their paired domesticity convinced me it was safe to investigate them.

The packed-dirt path was cool under my feet, intersected now and then by other paths going off out of sight. The effect was of a latent busyness in the forest that only awaited the clearing of the trees before it flowered. The path I was on kept to a southwest direction, but with the meandering ease of a thrown line.

As I rounded a long bend, the smell of burned gunpowder itched my sinuses, and I sneezed. Farther on I reached a sunstruck clearing. A woman at the far edge aimed a shotgun at me. Three men watched her, one kneeling over some sort of mechanical contraption, and I don't think they saw me, because the contraption flung a clay pigeon into the air straight toward me and the woman tracked it and fired a moment after I dove to the ground. A second pigeon was sent aloft in conjunction with the disintegration of the first. The woman blasted the second disc neatly into four pieces.

"You there," one man called out.

I lifted my head above the grass. They waved me across.

A picnic was laid out on a fallen tree, with linen, china, a bottle of wine, and shotguns spread along the trunk. The woman reloaded, smiling at me, then two more pigeons flew away and the woman blasted both.

"She's chums with *that* gun," one man said, and the others chuckled.

"You were too far away to warrant a dive for cover," the woman said to me.

"Aggie bags the men she aims for," another of the men said, prompting another shared laugh.

They offered me their wine, which I refused. Unfortunately all their food was gone. They didn't ask my name and didn't introduce themselves. The woman did all the shooting, while the men smoked, talked, and admired her.

The man operating the trap had folded a napkin into a kneeling pad. "Blast," he muttered. He'd dropped a pigeon and it had broken in two. He picked up one curved, pointed piece and drew back to throw it into the woods. My eyes locked on the shard and an instant of recognition overwhelmed me: *saber-toothed tiger tooth.*

I knew exactly where I stood.

"Cobb's quitting to go to war," one of the men said.

"I purchased some stamps on his say-so," another answered.

"Convenient of him to go just as it's about to end," the woman said. She shot two more pigeons out of the sky. For several seconds the air and light around us were jumpy with the disruption of the double blasts. I watched her carefully. Was she the girl I'd seen departing Constance's house? The last of the wine went around. No one wore masks.

"Are you worried about catching the flu?" I asked.

They looked at me like they had forgotten I was there.

"It *is* only August," one man said. He blew a mournful note across the mouth of the empty bottle. "It's a beautiful summer day. Not flu season."

"What have you heard?" the woman asked.

"I see people in masks," I said.

"Worrywarts," a man said. "I'm planning to spend the season in sunny southern California. Eating nothing but oranges and drinking nothing but the local wine. If the bug finds me there I'll tip my hat to it and die happy."

"My mother talks about the great grippe epidemic of '90 and '91," the woman said. "It started spreading the year before. Paris in November. London in December. New York by the first of the year."

"And she survived to produce you," the man reassured her. He raised a hand above the woman's head. "Gentlemen, I give you the worrywart."

He took the shotgun from her, loaded it, and nodded to the trap operator. A clay pigeon floated out, the gun discharged, the pigeon dropped untouched into the safety of the high grass. The second bird met a similar fate.

"The fall killed them—no doubt," the woman said.

"Where's that dog that retrieves untouched birds when you need him?" another man asked.

"They'll mate and next summer this glade will be overrun."

The bad shot was a good sport, though. He broke open the gun and returned it to the woman.

"As with anything," he said, "I could master this skill if I put my concentration to it. I choose not to."

"What skills *have* you chosen to master?" one of his friends asked.

The woman had stepped next to me. "What have you heard?" she asked again, in a lower voice.

One of the men heard her. "*Agatha,* you're not sick *now.* Enjoy *now.*"

"There is some concern at the children's home," I said.

"They're orphans. Who'd care?" a man said.

"Wilson—" another began.

He was cut off. "Wilson has no concerns but to get us clear of the war," a man said. "He has no interest in orphans with sniffles."

"It ends in November," the woman said, her eyes downcast, as if afraid how this good news bulletin from the future would be received.

"Of course it does," one man said patronizingly.

"November eleventh—to be exact."

The men who hooted her down seemed nonetheless unsure of the footing for their mockery.

"How do you know that?" I asked.

"Agatha is a follower of Mrs. Manger," the man said. "Our local Cassandra."

I examined the woman. She brushed her eyes over me, checking out my reaction but not expecting anything.

"I don't understand," I said.

"She claims to know the future," the man said derisively. "Worse, she claims to have actually *lived* in the future."

"And you believe her?" I asked the woman.

"Yes. I *do* believe her."

She watched me expectantly, but I kept my mouth shut. There was no point in my being the Second Coming. Events would transpire as before. On November 11, Constance—with only hours to live—would be proved correct. The woman's faith in her would be redeemed.

"I'm Josh Winkler," I said.

"Agatha Erickson." We shook hands.

The name rang a bell so far back in my memory that I wasn't certain I heard it.

"Can we continue with our summer idyll?" the man who had missed both shots asked jealously.

"You're exactly right," Agatha said. "I *do* feel idle." The spell was broken. Agatha even shook her head to clear it. "I won't waste another day with you layabouts."

The outing lost its spirit when she was gone. The men grumbled, then fell silent, nursing headaches, lacking wine, food, and purpose.

I repeated her name: *Agatha Erickson.*

Where had I seen it before? If it was from that era, the only way it could be familiar to me was if it had been on the influenza list. I wished I had warned her to keep her distance from Constance.

SEVENTEEN

The quiet of 1918 Euclid Heights deepened as evening came on. Ketch's truck was not at the orphanage. I saw no sign of Penny. The side yard was empty of children.

It occurred to me that I had nothing left to do there. Or then. Beyond retrieving my daughter I had no place in 1918. No responsibilities. No one who cared about me. I missed Flo for the first time in years. I missed Penny, too, for not having her close at hand, and for the threatened loss of her.

Other than that, I was bored. I walked south from the orphanage, past a row of substantial houses, past a park, then a butcher, a laundry, a store selling notions, a millinery, a collar and cuffs store, all closed, and an apothecary, which was still open. A sign perpendicular to the wall displayed a blue circle with an orange silhouette of a glass and straw. Beneath was the word **COLD**. I was suddenly quite thirsty.

I took a stool at a long, mahogany counter, its surface polished and nicked. Beyond it was a wall of glassed-in shelves packed with medicines. Nitrogen mustard. Tincture of cantharides. Laudanum. Alum cakes. A man in a white shirt and apron came from out of the aisles behind me and circled around behind the counter. He lifted a mask in place over his mouth as he approached. His eyes above it were deep-set and weary.

"Help you?"

"I'd like a cold drink."

"Flavor?"

"What have you got?"

The man sighed. "Apple. Apricot. Alligator pear. Checkerberry. Dewberry. Hagberry. Huckleberry. Whortleberry. Cherry. Citrus. Grape. Guanabana. Lemon-lime. Peach. And persimmon."

I blinked, amazed. "I'll take a cold apple juice."

He turned away, muttering, "Could have stopped me."

"Do you really have all those flavors?"

"I don't say 'em to keep my memory sharp."

He slid a metal coaster in front of me, placed a tall, full glass atop the coaster. The apple juice had a deep golden color, a frothy head, and a long silver spoon topped with a tiny crest that matched the sign out front.

"Five cents."

The flaw in my reality dawned on me. I had no money. I should have asked Constance for a few dollars. The apothecarist sensed this in my hesitation and pulled the glass of juice back to his side of the counter.

"You a betting man?" I asked.

"Not with my store's money—or merchandise—I ain't."

"You give me the juice—plus a roast beef sandwich and a piece of that peach pie—and I'll give you the winner of next year's Kentucky Derby."

He gaped at me like I was the looniest bug he'd seen in years.

"I weren't born yesterday," he said.

"When *were* you born?" I just wanted to hear him say the year.

"Eighteen sixty-one."

"You know Constance Mor—Manger?"

" 'Course."

"We're old friends."

“That supposed to be a recommendation?”

“Come the Derby, if I’m wrong, she’ll cover my bill. But I’m not wrong.”

“A little full of yourself for these parts, ain’t you?”

His mask made me feel I was passing the time of day with a surgeon. Yet his voice was absolutely clear, as if the cloth over his mouth was the latest step in evolution, and perfectly acceptable.

“How many have the flu in town?”

He backed away from me, as if the word itself was contagious.

“Don’t know that anyone *has* it just yet,” he said. “But they *will*—when the weather gets cold and wet. I’m one of them folks don’t want to be caught wishing they’d put their masks on a day earlier. You ask me—it’s a last-gasp trick of the Hun.”

The store’s door opened and a woman and girl entered. The girl was such a perfect miniature of the woman in carriage and dress that I missed Flo and Penny all over again. The apothecarist went to help them. I overheard his murmured, familiar address in the aisles.

He left the glass of apple juice on the counter. I pulled it across to me and sipped. It was delicious. I finished it in one long gulp.

With the apothecarist occupied with the woman and the girl an aisle over, I found a bin containing inch-thick pads of drawing paper, and next to that a rack of pens, nibs, and bottles of ink. I selected what I needed. I lifted my shirt and found the name I wanted. Back at the counter I unstoppered the bottle of ink and dipped the pen in. The scratch and feel on the paper was rough, grabby, yet oddly satisfying. I scrawled SIR BARTON, tore the page free, and left it on the counter.

I had never been an artist who worried much about the light. My work didn’t rely on it. But now that it was getting away from me—just as I was aware that what I was witnessing was fleeting—I was in a panic to make some use of it. I went in search of something to draw and found myself in front of one thing I knew would be there when I returned. The house on Collier Street. And having arrived, I realized immediately that I could draw it in my own time, at my leisure. I also was nervous about who might come out the front door.

I gravitated then toward the land our house would one day occupy.

I made a quick sketch of the mossy shed, immediately didn't care for it, and ripped it out of the pad. A question of disposal presented itself: Should I be leaving traces of myself in this time?

I lodged the sketch in the back of the pad and continued up the path. In Constance's orchard I sat with my back to a tree and sketched the area where I guessed my house should be, only stopping when ants began to run inside my shirt. I stood, shook them out, headed deeper into the orchard. The size of the place surprised me. The trees marched east into the deepening shadows. Their number and robust condition irritated me; they were supposed to be gone.

A dog—barking and slobbering and overreacting—came charging after me, like I had slipped his guard and he was trying to win back lost ground. I stood still until his spring wound down. Just as the dog was getting quiet, a man in a hat and suspenders appeared in the gap between the rows. The dog reignited, showing off for the boss.

"Duke!" the man snarled. The dog shut up.

The man was tall and weathered, at the end of a long day. He came up to me without hesitation, banging his dusty hat against his leg and wiping his face with a red kerchief.

"Can I help you?" he asked, civil, but not friendly. Up close, in his eyes and the timbre of his voice, I thought I saw and heard Constance.

"I know your daughter," I said.

"Are you one of those people?"

"Sir?"

"She doesn't live here anymore."

"I know."

He returned his hat to his head. Duke twitched, yipped, the hat on the head maybe a signal of something commencing.

"She has a family in town," he said.

"I just saw her. All grown-up."

"Yep."

I waited for him to say something more, but he was finished.

"She told me your orchard was in danger of being sold."

His civil manner hardened. "Not for a long time now. Those problems are behind us."

"It must be a relief to have her back."

He shut one eye to scrutinize me. "Just who *are* you?"

"I'm from—" I hesitated; it was easy to sound crazy when opening a conversation about being eighty some years removed from the time where you belonged. But a shift in the man's expression—an easing of the suspicious set of his mouth and eyes—indicated he was not unfamiliar with what I was about to say.

"Constance told you where she had gone?" I asked.

"Yes," her father said, glancing away, his eyes narrowing.

"You didn't believe her?"

"She's my little girl. I took her side, of course. But, no, I didn't believe her."

"But you believed what she said about the Derby."

"I listened, sure. Girl comes back from who knows where with the name of a horse—it was my job as her father to listen."

"And bet."

He gave the dog a kick. "Get!" Duke skulked away. "I know a little something about horses, mister. I handicapped that field and I came to the conclusion that Wintergreen was the best horse. Just coincidence that I agreed with what Con said was going to happen."

"Did you bet everything you had?"

He chuckled. "And then some. But you had to. The horse was the favorite. You had to put up a lot to get a lot."

"I haven't met her husband," I said.

His face clouded. "Not my cup of tea."

"Did you invest in his company?"

"I won't put my fate in that man's hands," he said. "I invested in what Con brought to it. It's all her doing anyway."

"She was right about the war, too."

He chewed his lower lip. "I wish she could've foreseen my kid brother getting it over there," he said.

The man's life was scattered around my memory like a train wreck: his brother in the war, his wife in two years, his daughter in November.

"I'm sorry," I said.

He shrugged. "He was a cuss. Always had to have an adventure.

Always thought he was missing out on something. He was my best hand, though. Can't seem to keep up with the place without him." He sized me up. "You looking for work?"

"Thanks, no. I'm going to get my daughter and go home."

"Suit yourself. Where's home?"

I jerked my thumb over my shoulder. "Back there," I said, striving for vagueness.

He glanced behind himself. "Do you know what happens to me?" he asked.

"Not specifically, no."

"Constance?"

"I make a point of not learning about the future," I lied.

"But you *do*. Horse races. The Cubs."

"That's just money. It's not someone's fate."

"It could be."

I nodded. He was right. But I didn't want to stay on the subject, fearful of what might slip out if I continued talking. I noticed he hadn't asked about his wife. Maybe Constance had filled him in on her fate.

He pointed behind me. "Your house is over there?"

"It will be."

"When's it built?"

I spared him further. "You know—I'm not sure. It's a big house on a big lot. My wife paid for it."

"Your wife."

"She's a pediatrician."

"What's that?"

"A kids' doctor. Her office is in our house."

"So *she* hasn't even been born yet."

"Her *mother* hasn't been born yet," I said.

"Well—what if your wife's mother's father lost a wagonload of money on a horse race and that night he and your wife's grandma was supposed to make your wife's mother but they didn't because your wife's grandma was mad about the money and didn't feel lovey-dovey? No wife's mother. No wife? And you could have fixed that if only you had given out the right information."

"That's why I don't want to spend any more time in 1918 than I have to."

He thrust out a hand. I shook it.

"Fair enough," he said. "I'll go to my grave not having a soul believe this or my daughter—but I'll know what I heard. Good day to you."

"I was just thinking—"

"What?"

"Did you bet on the Cubs in 1908?"

He grimaced. "Not as much as I should have."

"In the World Series," I said, "put your money on the White Sox."

"This year?"

"No." I raised a hand. "No. *Next* year. The 1919 season. Put your money on the White Sox."

"I could use the money *now*. Who's going to win this year?"

"I only know about next year."

"The White Sox."

"Yes."

"You're positive?"

"Bet the farm."

I walked back west, toward downtown, my feet sore, dust on my tongue, my heart heavy with my predicament and what I'd just set in motion. I was eager to get out of town, out of 1918.

At Tinker Street the perp walk resumed, and already I was accustomed to its worn-path feel between my toes. I met a man coming the other way. He was dressed in a threadbare suit, leather boots with long cracks along the outside edges, and a pencil behind his ear. He was counting his paces, his mouth moving, and, on the off chance I might be tempted to engage him in conversation, he raised a finger to silence me as he went past. I was left with no choice but to follow. At the end of the path, at Tinker Street, he stopped, took the pencil from behind his ear and a notebook from inside his coat, and jotted down some numbers.

"Do you know the hour, sir?" he asked.

I held out my hands. "Sorry."

"The light says post seven. I sold my watch for half its value—and the loss of it has far outlived the money," he said. "I'm forever forgetting where I am. It's the oddest sensation—lacking correct time actually causes me to lose track of *where* I am."

"Euclid Heights, Illinois, six zero zero zero one." I threw in the ZIP code out of habit, and I saw its oddness register on the man's face.

"Did you say zero one? Don't tell me it's 1901 again!"

"No," I said. "That was something—"

"Because I remember 1901. I had my life ahead of me. I had the love of a good woman." He winked. "And my wife was fond of me, too. Why, sir, I was mayor of this benighted burg!"

"Mayor McDeedle!" I said.

He put one hand on his belly and gave me a one-sixteenth bow. "At your service, sir," he said. "A former constituent?"

"Sorry, no," I said. "I wasn't here then."

He glanced around. "It's changed. For the worse, in my informed opinion. And they should never have changed the town's name. A new name doesn't change anything. Cutting down the hickory tree and selling it for firewood doesn't change what happened. Bad things go on. You can't help that. I'm here to tell you, sir, that the key is to not *do* the bad thing in the first place. Better advice to ignore I've never heard. Everyone wants to know—*has got to know*—what the bad thing will feel like. Will the cataclysm be worth the pleasure? Man is made to take the wrong turn. It's nature. Even doing the right thing is often proved the wrong course. But there's no hiding from it, once it's been done. Take my case, for example. I've never hidden what I did. I didn't change my name, I didn't leave town. You know my story. I'm a penniless wretch wandering the streets of the town I once ruled, scorned by my fellow Euclideans, but I don't turn away from my actions. Life is consequence. I wish I had my family back—my children, anyway. And I miss most piquantly the sweet attentions of my dear Jacqueline. But mostly I miss my watch. And the satisfactions of honest work. And being of service to my fellow man. My watch rooted me in the here and now. If I could just reclaim that timepiece I honestly believe I could rebuild my life."

He stopped, blinked, and refocused a confused smile on me.

"Mayor?" I said.

"My apologies, sir. A moment of light-headedness," he said. "Do you experience those? A sensation of being somewhere and returning abruptly to an altogether different location?"

"Something like that," I said.

"Where was I?"

"Here."

"No, no. What was I talking about?"

"Your watch."

"Of course. I recall. Hiding from the consequence of one's actions. Well, sir, it can't be done." He pointed beyond me, into the orchard. "I got it into my head to see Jacqueline's house again—although she's long gone. She moved to the city—where her honor is not besmirched—and took a husband. I'm grateful to you for blocking my progress eastward, sir, for our interlude has cleared my head of the nostalgic fantasies that bewebbed my better judgment. It would be sheer self-flagellation to stand outside that house where I once was so eagerly welcomed. Thank you, sir, for setting me on the proper path."

He reached for and furiously pumped my hand.

"Could I impose upon you for a dollar?" he asked.

"I'm afraid I'm as tapped out as you are, Mayor."

"Ah, a fellow traveler on life's rockier shores," he said. "My best wishes to you, sir. Our respective fortunes are bound to turn."

"Why were you counting your paces?"

"It's the surveyor in me. My equipment was lost in my transition from mayor, husband, and father to what you see before you—but I find myself falling back on the most basic form of measurement. My stride. It's all I have left. And—surprisingly—quite sufficient to my needs."

Then he continued on in the direction he had been walking.

With nightfall came an end to my wandering, my observing. I'd done more than a dozen quick sketches—a palm reader's door, a milk can maker's billboard, a horse being shod—and hadn't really cared for any of them. The pages slipped one after the other into the back of the pad felt like an encumbrance I was imposing upon myself, a weight I would have to drop before I could return home.

But my curiosity remained wide open. It was only the darkness that stopped me. And having stopped, I was reminded that I hadn't eaten in more than eighty years. My stomach growled so loudly it hushed the crickets. I watched shadows move in the orphanage's windows. Penny was in there somewhere. Was she making friends? Was she a freak of foreshadowing? Could she get me some food?

The orphanage's double front doors were locked down. I had better luck around back. The kitchen crew was just leaving, two lean boys and a short, wide woman, each of them carrying a bag of garbage in one hand and a smaller paper sack in the other. The boys deposited the garbage in a large wooden bin and then hurried away without a word.

The woman stopped to listen to me. She had a white kerchief covering her head and a face mask that she lifted into place as I stepped up.

"My daughter is in there," I said.

"Girls in there is nobody's daughters," she said.

"It's a long story."

"You a war bum?"

"No."

"No shame in it."

"Can I get something to eat?"

"Kitchen and stores is all locked up. Sheriff got the keys," she said.

"Just some bread?"

"Sheriff lock up the *crumbs,*" she said.

I pushed my luck. "What about that?" I nodded to the small sack she held against her hip.

"This is my kids' supper," she said. "Sheriff don't pay us much—but he lets us take a little something home."

A chugging car pulled up in the street and beeped its horn. She waved back.

She regarded me, like testing a weight or the soul inside her. Then she reached into the sack and removed a small, wrapped, greasy bundle.

"My kids gonna eat rice tonight cuzza you," she said, passing the bundle to me.

"Thank you," I said.

"Water in the rain barrel there," she said. "Sheriff locks up the pump, too. You got a place to stay?"

"I'll manage."

The smell of the meat in the bundle made me ravenously impatient for her to be gone.

"Suit yourself," she said.

The delicious smell came from a small pork chop, still warm, still with a skin of tomato paste and an onion slice attached. I ate it down to the bone in less than a minute. I gnawed the bone off and on through the night, stowing it in my shirt pocket between chewings. I made a cup with my hand and ladled rainwater out of the barrel, which was not quite half full, the water a little crunchy with bug husks and twigs, but delicious nonetheless. I felt full, sleepy, for about a half hour.

I returned to the bench across from the orphanage. The moon rose and set and not a single person, car, horse, or dog went by. A quiet as complete as I ever wanted to experience settled over the town. The humming in my ears was all that remained of the future I had left behind.

EIGHTEEN

My first thought when I awoke at dawn: This is how my brother lives. Stiff, sore, damp, curled around my stolen art supplies, the food from the night before only a sticky aftertaste of onion in my mouth. I went back for a drink of water and while I stood running my tongue over my teeth the car from the night before returned the orphanage cook.

"You put in a long day," I said.

She pulled her mask into place. "Home away from home," she said.

"Thank you for the food."

"No need."

"Are you a gambler?" I asked.

My question caught her by surprise, froze her with one hand on the doorknob.

"Who wants to know?"

"Remember Sir Barton in next year's Kentucky Derby."

"Now just who are you?"

"Don't forget. Sir Barton."

She shooed me away. "You go on now, Sir Barton. You're scaring me."

I passed her two yawning assistants as they arrived for work. I had a moment's longing for Flo, who kept me free from days of being on some job's short leash, a prisoner of someone else's agenda.

I could hear the orphanage awaken from my spot on the bench. It sounded like my house, some mornings. I folded open my drawing pad, got some ink on my pen. Pulling up my shirt I got a whiff of myself.

The red names and dates on my torso had worn faint, they had been through so much. I wrote "1919 SIR BARTON" on the paper, reinked the pen, then "1920 PAUL JONES," then "1921 BEHAVE YOURSELF," and on and on. When I finished with my torso I unbuckled my belt and lowered my pants enough to transfer the remaining results from my thighs to the paper. The last line I had written was "1961 CARRY BACK."

I couldn't remember why I had stopped there. Maybe I'd liked the sound—the promise—of that name.

In a little less than an hour I had created a document that unnerved me with its power. It was my doing, too. The consequences of that single sheet of paper would be mine to deal with. For a moment I thought of Constance's father, up early to work among his doomed trees, his imagination tormented with the dangers of a sure thing.

I rose and went to get my daughter.

I saw her from the front hallway of the orphanage, but she didn't see me. She was at the end of the hall, in a line of children waiting to enter the dining room. She was braiding the long hair of a younger girl in front of her. The girl was talking, and as the line moved forward they moved together with it, Penny's hands bound up and busy in the girl's hair, her eyes rapt with concentration.

She viewed my approach as an intrusion.

"What are you doing here?" she asked.

"I came to get you."

Her hands continued to braid the girl's hair. The girl asked Penny, "Who's this?"

"My father," Penny said.

The girl's eyes went wide. "Your *father*?"

"Yes," I said. "I want to take Penny home."

The girl curtsied so deeply she almost pulled her hair free of Penny's hands.

"I'm Bette Andresen," she said.

"Pleased to meet you."

Bette turned her head enough to bring Penny into the conversation. "Are you going with him?" she asked worriedly.

"Of course she is," I said.

"No, Bette, I'm not," Penny said, steering the younger girl through the dining room door, where she couldn't see the go-away look Penny threw me.

Sheriff Ketch was behind his desk in his office at the opposite end of the hall. He barely glanced up when I knocked.

"No jobs," he growled, his big head dropping dismissively at the sight of me.

"I've come for my daughter."

He paused, turned a ledger page, before regarding me. It was eerie how much he was a template for Jock Itch, his bulk, his smugness, his slow, self-satisfied movements.

"You've had a rough night, sir," he observed.

"I've had better."

"I can smell the dew on you from here."

"Penelope Winkler is my daughter."

Ketch formed a steeple with his fingertips and pursed his lips.

"Now, I'd venture to say every child here would tell me if he or she had a mother or a father," he said. "Some *do* have one or the other. But they don't want the child. Now if one had a parent who *wanted* them—I'd hear about that, I'll venture. And I haven't."

"She's in line for breakfast."

"Eggs and tea today," he said, just—I was convinced—to stab my hunger's imagination.

"Bring her here and ask her."

"Oh, I know what she would say. She's old enough to *want* to get out of here. She will say anything you've coached her to say. And then you'll peddle her virtue on the streets of Chicago."

"No—"

"I say she's safer in *my* care."

"At a dollar a day."

He smiled, ran his fingers lightly down a column of numbers. "Now that you mention it."

"Put us side by side. We look alike."

"Hardly proof."

"You look just like your grandson."

He hesitated, blinked, sputtered. "I . . . I have no grandson, sir. I have no son." His smugness slipped for an instant. "Hell, I don't even have a wife."

I stepped toward him. "But you will. A wife. A son. A grandson."

He regarded me balefully, suspiciously. "So *you* say," he growled.

"You know Constance Manger," I said.

"Our most notorious citizen. I was at hand when her boyfriend killed Sheriff Horton."

"I thought they didn't know who killed him."

Ketch shrugged. "In the confusion—no one could say. But that boy was the *reason* for the confusion—and therefore to blame."

"Constance is a friend of mine," I said. "We met eighty years from now."

Ketch came around from behind his desk. He stood so close I smelled his breakfast eggs.

"What is your game, sir?"

"I just want my daughter back."

"I detect a con. An effort to bilk me out of both money and a young orphan girl."

"No—"

"I can't say I know your means—but I know the desired end. And I will not be party to it!" he bellowed.

A salival mist of outrage bathed my face. I stepped back.

"Have you spoken to Constance?" I asked.

He lifted his chin. "We do not travel in the same circles."

"But you know the details of her story."

He nodded. "A finer man than Sheriff Horton did not exist."

"Do you remember that night?" I asked.

"Like it was yesterday." He returned to his chair. "Please leave now."

"May I speak to my daughter?" I asked desperately.

"Since you have no daughter here—I don't see how you can speak to her."

"Just for a moment?"

"Are you thick, sir? Haven't I made my position clear? You're not welcome. Your continued presence—I must warn you—has me of a mind to take you into custody."

"Ask Edward Manger about his wife," I said. "Her experiences."

Ketch sighed. "I *have* talked to him—at some length. He interviewed me after the lynching. And after I became sheriff. He regaled me with fanciful tales about his new bride and her alleged travels. And let me add, sir, if you didn't know already, that Edward Manger has a passion for strong drink that is only exceeded by his pathetic need for attention."

"She knew about the war. And the 1909 Derby."

Ketch's eyes burned into me. "She *knew* one winner. Even mediocre horse players possess *that* sort of clairvoyance every day."

"She was busy getting back here."

"Getting back?"

"She was more worried about preventing Dash Buckley's lynching than memorizing horse race winners."

"I have a full schedule, sir," Ketch said, waving me toward the door. "Perhaps a man of your small accomplishments and responsibility can't appreciate—"

"Sir Barton," I said.

"Pardon?"

"Sir Barton wins next year's Derby."

"And what good does that do me now?"

"Paul Jones wins in 1920."

Ketch's eyes got momentarily round, and then returned to their hooded watchfulness. "You are marvelous, sir, at throwing out results that cannot be immediately verified."

"Check it out."

"How?"

"See that those horses exist."

Ketch stroked his chin. "Come back this evening. After supper. I need to make some enquiries."

"Behave Yourself wins in 1921."

"I don't believe the winner of the 1921 Kentucky Derby has even been born yet."

"I want my daughter."

He released me into the long, empty hallway. I followed it to the dining room's open double doors, drawn by the roar of children. They were eating at long tables, talking and laughing and shoveling in great, yellow mounds of scrambled eggs and slurping from enormous mugs of tea. And that was all. No toast, no fruit, no juice. Ketch had described the menu in its entirety: eggs and tea.

Penny was in the far corner. The girl whose hair she had braided, Bette Andresen, sat on one side of her; a woman in a prim blue uniform and white mask sat on the other. She was addressing Penny with some conviction, but the mask over her mouth gave her an unsettling aspect, like she was malformed and desperate to communicate.

Ketch's crab hand on my elbow pulled me away.

"Until this evening, sir," he said, leading me to, then pushing me out of, the orphanage's front door.

What remained with me in the street was the smell and sight of those eggs and that tea and a painful ache in my belly. I stood transfixed by my desire for food and my complete lack of any way of acquiring it, and also by the sheer weirdness of a beautiful day unfolding in 1918.

A milk truck's ground gears startled a horse a block down, and the rider had to fight a moment for control of his mount. The shied horse in turn caused two children to giggle as they walked hand in hand with a regal, behatted woman, who shushed them. She avoided my eye as she hurried her charges past me. I was a bum, hungry and unwashed, barefoot to boot. But the children sneaked glances at me. They were curious and happy, a boy and a girl. I gave them a wave, from the hip, as they went by. They might be alive in my time, closing in on ninety, milky and translucent with age. Would they remember me? Doubtlessly not. But I appreciated their brief attention now. They proved I existed.

I walked toward the center of town, pulled by the empty space in my stomach. Smells cascading out the doors and windows of houses and offices nearly staggered me. Baking bread. Frying bacon. Milk. Sliced apples. Eggs and toast. Something with cinnamon. Coffee. And I didn't even drink coffee.

The most delicious combination of smells pulled me up a box canyon alley to a window emitting a cloud of steam. A screen door opened and a woman in a long skirt and apron emerged. Sweat had pasted her hair to her temples and her large, dark, exhausted eyes gave me a steely glare of suspicion. She toted a wooden bucket of something that she poured out onto the alley stones.

Through the screen door I saw a naked skin-and-bones boy of about eight standing in a metal tub, shivering with a towel around his shoulders, his eyes disengaged and unhappy. A pan of corn bread cooled on a stove. Onions cooked somewhere nearby.

"What do you want?" the woman asked sharply, stepping back into her kitchen, the bucket bouncing against her knee.

"I'm hungry," I said.

"Work for your food," she said. She began to briskly rub down the boy in the tub. "Here there is ample opportunity for work—then you eat."

"Do you need work done?"

"Not *here*. In America."

"You must need *something* done."

"My husband is handy." Her eyes were flinty and smug.

I held out my sketch pad. "I could draw a picture of the boy. For some corn bread? Some onion soup?"

She laughed, harsh and truncated. She said something to the boy in a language I didn't understand and the boy tried to smile, but his heart wasn't in it. She scooped her hand into the boy's bathwater and held it out to me, but at arm's length, keeping her distance.

"Here is your onion soup," she said.

My eyes burned, it smelled so delicious. Bits of onion floated in the cup of her hand.

"Onions keep away the influenza," she stated.

She sounded so certain, but her eyes betrayed her doubt and fear. She plucked a loop of string from around her neck. At the end of it hung a small muslin pouch—and a cross.

"For me, too," she said and waved me away. "Now go. Work for food."

The closed end of the alley contained a fenced-in area, beyond which I could see the leafy dome of a small tree. An unlatched gate was open a few inches. Inside was a small patio with a table the circumference of a waiter's tray, two wire-back chairs shaded by the tree, and a screen door opening into a dark, quiet room. The only sounds were my pounding heart and growling stomach.

On the table was a plate of toast, a small jar of jam, and a glass of orange juice. A bee buzzed the meal like a sentry. I stepped into the small enclosure. Coming closer, I smelled raspberry. A leaf fell from the tree. I slid my drawing pad inside my shirt.

A knife was laid across the rim of the plate. The smell of melting butter bathed my face as I bent over it. I took up the knife and gouged a large divot of jam and spread it on the bread, the scrape of the knife on the toast incriminatingly loud. I shouldn't have taken extra seconds to cover the bread to all four corners—and I wasted more time smoothing out a wave in the jam I spread on the second slice. I picked up the plate and when it reached head height I tilted it so one piece of toast slid over the rim. I caught its edge in my mouth. The bread was fresh, with a delicately crunchy crust, and the jam had a sweetness I had never tasted before. I was taking a second bite when the screen door opened out and a large man in greasy coveralls emerged, wiping his hands on a clean rag.

"My breakfast!"

I had toast clamped in my teeth, another piece on the plate, the plate held with both hands in front of my mouth. The man didn't look like he'd miss the two pieces of toast, whereas I now regarded them as something akin to sacred objects.

I finished the first slice with one gulping bite, then took the second piece in my teeth and flipped the plate to the man, hoping to occupy him with saving his crockery while I got away. I would have escaped easily, too, had the woman not chosen that moment to empty the boy's onion bath into the alley. I went down hard on the slippery stones, knocked a chewed piece of bread from my mouth, soaked the back of my shirt in onion water, and was delivered effortlessly into the hands of the man whose toast I had stolen.

On the bright side, I was fed in jail.

After eating, I slept remarkably well on the narrow cot in my basement cell. I was the only man in custody through the long afternoon. The view up through the barred window was of the town square, and I wondered if it was the last view that had greeted Dash Buckley. When I awoke I was hungry again. The deputy upstairs refused me a snack, supper being at six.

"I need to speak to Sheriff Ketch," I said.

"He comes in after supper."

"Can I have my drawing supplies back?"

"You could stab someone with that nib."

"Nobody's here."

He left without further argument.

Ketch visited at eight o'clock sharp. He was enjoying a postmeal cigar. He brought a slat-back chair and sat with his boots up on the cross bar of my cell.

He studied the report of my incarceration. "Stealing toast?"

"I was hungry."

He grunted, barely listening. "You're in good shape for a man born in '51," he said.

"Nineteen fifty-one."

He blew out a cloud of smoke. "Nineteen fifty-one," he repeated. "Thirty-three years from now."

"Yes," I said. Had he checked my drawing pad? Had he found and confiscated the sheet of winners?

"I made enquiries into your Sir Barton."

"And?"

"I also spoke to the girl you claim is your daughter."

"What did she say?"

"What I expected." He waved his cigar so a small barrel of ash went flying. "You have your stories in line."

"We really just want—"

"She is quite good with the children. The sick ones love her. I am thinking she might save me the expense of a real nurse."

I turned away, fighting panic. "What did your enquiries into Sir Barton turn up?" I asked.

"That's very interesting. The first man I contacted knew of the horse. But nothing about the other two. So I telegraphed an acquaintance in Louisville and received this reply."

He held out a slip of paper. I read, *Sir Barton young and strong. Paul Jones just young. No Behave Yourself. Ask why?*

"What should be my response?" Ketch asked coyly.

"You could reward him for his help," I said.

"And lower the odds? No. Besides, he's not a gambling man."

"This isn't a gamble."

"According to you."

"Sir Barton is as sure a thing as you will ever get."

"Sir Barton? I already *have* Sir Barton. And two others."

"I have more. I have them all," I said.

"All the winners?"

"Let me out."

Ketch didn't give it even a moment's thought. "Do you know the name of the woman I am to marry?"

"I'm afraid not."

"Is she handsome?"

"I don't know that, either."

"It would simplify the courtship so."

"Let me out. Give me my daughter. I'll make you the richest man in town."

He dropped his feet from the cell bars. "It's a small town," he said. He stamped his boots a couple times, like he was marching. "My feet fell asleep."

He stood and did a clumsy little dance.

"Owens didn't press charges," he said.

"Who's that?"

"The mechanic whose toast you stole. He's too nice for his own good."

"Then I'm free to go."

He nodded, but made no move to unlock the cell door. I stood very still, completely at his mercy.

"Is this the cell Dash Buckley was in?" I asked.

Ketch scratched his chin, spat out a shred of tobacco.

"What sort of man is my grandson?" he asked.

"A lawman. Like yourself."

"And my son?"

"The same."

"Geez, Louise," he muttered. "Three generations of Ketches and all we can think to do is lock up people?"

"You're like a dynasty," I said.

"Is the orphanage still there?"

"No," I said, not exactly sure why I was being so forthright, but knowing no reason not to be.

"Why?"

"I don't know. It just isn't."

"I don't suppose they have cured the condition of being an orphan, sir."

"No."

"Why don't I go to your time and—"

"You belong here," I said.

"You're here. You don't *belong* here."

"I only came to get my daughter."

He wasn't listening. "I could find out what happened to the orphanage. I could find out who I'm supposed to marry."

"It isn't that simple."

"If the orphanage goes under—I can't live on my sheriff's salary."

"Let me out. Give me back my daughter," I said. "You'll never have to worry about money again."

He watched me carefully, rolling the wet end of his cigar in his pursed lips. He made no move for his keys.

"How do you do it?" he asked.

"I can't explain it."

"Can't? Or won't?"

"I don't know how I do it. I don't even know where I'll end up."

"Where?"

"I mean when," I said. "What if you ended up in my time and couldn't get back?"

"I'd move in with my grandson," Ketch said confidently.

"He wouldn't exist."

He digested this. "I have to have a son first?"

"Exactly. You jump ahead like that—you start changing the future."

"How can I live knowing this?" he asked, stricken.

"You get used to it."

"Every young lady I see, I'll think: Is she the one? And what's the fun of betting if you win every time?" he asked forlornly.

"It's only one race a year. One sure thing. The rest of your life will be a mystery."

"Do you know when I die?" he asked.

I shook my head.

"Do you know when *you* die?"

"No. I don't want to know."

"If you find out—about me. I don't want to know, either."

"Can you let me out now?"

"Where's the list?" he asked.

We studied each other through the bars.

"Please let me out," I said.

"First the list."

"I'd really like to get out of here first," I said.

"Maybe I'll leave you in there until next May. To see if Sir Barton really *does* win."

"He will."

"But if he doesn't?"

"I may still be in town. If he loses, you can lock me back up."

"You'll be gone," he said. "I can tell."

"But you have no legal right to hold me," I said.

"True. But people let me do pretty much whatever I deem fit in this town," he said. He brought out a ring of keys. "The list gets you out of jail. But the girl stays with me."

"She's my daughter!"

His eyes went dead and cruel, so much like Jock Itch's eyes that I almost believed he had come back through time to lord his power over me.

"She's an orphan," he said in a low growl. "I have the paperwork to prove it."

I decided to cut my losses. "Okay," I said.

He unlocked the cell door and swung it open.

"No more regular meals," he teased.

"The food isn't that good," I said.

"Where's the list?"

It was where I'd left it, folded in the back of the sketch pad. Ketch ran his eyes down the rows of names and dates.

"Do they stop having the race after 1961?"

"No. I just stopped writing."

"Well, hell. What am I supposed to do after 1961?"

I shrugged. We'd come to the top of the stairs. The jail's front door was straight ahead. I wanted out of there in the worst way.

"How old will you be in '61?" I asked.

"Seventy-six," he said, after a moment's calculation.

"You should have plenty of money by then."

"Plus my sheriff's pension."

"Right."

"And my family to care for me."

"No doubt," I said.

NINETEEN

Out on the square I felt more homeless than ever. An oppressive, humid overcast had settled in. A number of people took evening walks, the women fanning themselves, the men erect and proud of bearing. A few wore face masks. All of them, when pausing to greet their neighbors, maintained a safe distance. I was stunned all over again: afoot on a hot August evening in 1918.

I was also a pariah in their midst—barefoot and stinking of onions—and they gave me a wide berth. In hopes of being mistaken for an artist, I opened my pad and readied a pen. I tried to draw from memory the cell I'd just been freed from. After ten minutes I gave up. The light was just about gone and I failed to capture the cramped hopelessness that had visited me there.

The night stretched before me devoid of comfort or answers. I had given away the one thing of value I possessed—and Penny still was an orphan.

Footsteps from the south drew my attention as I sat on the bench across from the orphanage. A man came toward me out of the shadows, walking with determination, and as he came closer—as I came to *his* attention—he slowed and finally stopped in front of me.

"Mr. Winkler?" he asked.

I hid my surprise fairly well, I thought. "Yes?"

He held out a hand and I shook it. "Edward Manger, sir."

He was a handsome man, sturdy and self-assured, dressed in a suit and tie that I would have thought too warm for the evening.

"Sheriff Ketch told me I might find you here," he said. He sat down beside me. "May I offer you a bath, a bed, and a meal for the night?" he asked graciously. "My wife speaks ever so highly of your help in her travels."

"Thanks, but no. I'm leaving."

"Is that so? Leaving."

"I'm getting my daughter and returning home."

"Is that your plan—or just your desperate hope?"

I smiled briefly. "A little of both."

Ketch drove his rattling truck out of the orphanage and away. He did not deign to glance at Manger or me. The bed of his truck was covered with a flapping tarp.

I had a thought. "You were there the night Dash Buckley died."

"Of course."

"Did anyone think to step forward?"

"And stay the hand of the mob, you mean?"

"Something like that."

He drew himself up. "As a member of the press, it wasn't my place."

"It just seems like it could have been prevented," I said.

"You mean like the Great War?" he asked sardonically. "We didn't possess your talent for the future. We didn't know we'd still be living with our actions ten years on." He leaned closer to me. "Mr. Winkler, Constance indicated you brought future race winners with you."

"She refused to take them," I said.

Manger sighed, deflated. He tugged at his tie until it came undone. "My wife is a great believer in the hard road," he said. "*I'm* decidedly not."

"She dies of the flu in November."

He rocked back, a reaction of shock that did not sync up with the glint of relief that flickered in his eyes.

"Does she know?"

"She didn't want to hear it."

"You're sure she dies?"

I nodded. "So you'd better take out some life insurance."

He gave me a cool smile. "I admit I am not much attached to her," he said. "I am not much attached to anything in this town. But I wish her no harm."

"Make the boy the beneficiary," I said. "Show me the policy and I'll give you the next ten Derby winners."

"But you're leaving," he said.

"Then you'd better hurry."

He did not move. "I can't impose upon you for your trust?"

"I'm afraid not," I said.

Still he didn't move.

"There is no way I can obtain such a document at this hour," he said, "so I will continue to take the evening air with you—Mr. Winkler—in hopes of winning your good feeling of me in some other way."

Several minutes then elapsed without either of us speaking a word.

"Would it be worth the next ten winners for you to have the details of that evening?" he asked finally.

"Details about what?"

"Local color. My beloved wife, for instance."

"What about her?"

He held out a hand. "The winners?"

When I didn't respond, he withdrew his hand.

"I don't need to know anything about her," I said.

"Did you know she got back in time to save the unfortunate Mr. Buckley?"

"She was—I saw a drawing. She's there on the edge of the crowd. Like she just arrived."

"On the edge of the crowd, yes," Manger said. "But Dash was still alive. They were still trying to get his neck in the rope. She stood and watched with the rest of them."

"How do you know that?"

"I'm a professional observer. She was the sole reason for the story. She won't admit it—but she was troubled by those reports Buckley was fractionally a Negro."

"That doesn't sound like her."

"You don't know her," he said. When I didn't respond, he asked, "Isn't that worth something?"

"In 1935—bet Omaha."

"Yes, she told me that one. But that's *forever* from now."

"Best I can do," I said.

He glanced carefully around. "What if I told you who killed Sheriff Horton?"

I shrugged, but a cold certainty gripped me. "Who?"

"You'd best not speak his name in Hickory Hill. Or Euclid Heights."

"You could say anything about anybody. Where's your proof?"

"Who benefited when Horton died?"

"That's not proof."

"I talked to most of the people on the square that night," Manger said. "No one remembers seeing Sheriff Horton."

"It was a mob. Who could reliably remember anything?"

"Everyone knew and respected Horton. And nobody—no matter how drunk or falsely courageous—would have crossed him. A mob outside his jail and he's not on the scene? Unthinkable. Yet no one saw him. It was only after Dash was brought outside and that horrid business begun—*then* Horton's body turns up on the jail floor. His head bashed in. No arrests. Barely an investigation. Who benefited?"

I started to speak but he quickly raised a hand.

"The trees have perfect hearing, sir. Something else to ponder. Why was it so easy for the mob to get Buckley that night? Why wasn't the jail locked, bolted, and shuttered? Yet they practically *strolled* in."

"Write it," I said.

Manger winced. "I'm not a reporter. Who put me in touch with the man who cast doubt on Buckley's past? On his race?"

"You didn't find him on your own?"

"I told you—I wasn't a reporter. I took what came to me."

"Did you check it out?"

He cleared his throat. "I was pressed for time."

"So, no, you didn't."

"He understood his fellow man," Manger said. "He knew how to play on their basest emotions. Then he led the crusade to change the name of the town. He tore it down—and rebuilt it with him in charge."

"He has the winners now, too," I said.

Manger was incredulous. "*What?*"

"I gave them to him to buy my way out of jail."

"What winners?"

The desperation in his tone made me hesitate. "His grandson drowns a boy," I said. "And he almost drowns my brother."

Manger didn't care about that. "*What winners?*"

He had my sleeve in his fist. I made a point of pulling it free. "Some Derby winners," I said, standing.

"How many?"

"They won't keep your wife from dying."

"I have to keep living, though. And our son. Tell me for him."

"Next year—the winner is Sir Barton."

"Sir Barton," he repeated to himself, digging through his pockets for something to write with. "And 1920?" he asked avidly.

"Paul Jones."

He grabbed my sketch pad and pen from my hands, scratched the two names on the paper with a dry nib.

"Nineteen twenty-one?"

I took back the pad. "I don't remember." I tore out the sheet that contained the two names and gave it to him.

" 'I Don't Remember' isn't a horse, I assume."

"No, it isn't."

"How many does *he* have?"

I held out my hand. "My pen, please," I said.

"He'll ruin this town," Manger warned.

"It turns out okay," I said.

I expected to be stopped as I went into the orphanage through the back door. A racket of cleanup came from the kitchen, but no one appeared and no one saw me. I didn't hesitate when I reached the main hall, but swung around a newel post and raced upstairs into an eerie quiet. I didn't know the time, but it couldn't have been much later than nine o'clock, and certainly the children couldn't already be asleep. Yet I heard no giggling, no talking, no laughter, hardly any sound at all.

The first door I opened made an awful squeak. I entered a good-size room that contained six narrow cots, each one covered with a taut white sheet and crisply folded blanket—and each one empty. I found variations of the same thing in every upstairs room I checked—empty beds, perfectly made. I went back downstairs.

In the hallway, one of the kitchen aides—heading outside with a garbage pail—saw me. His head lifted in the barest recognition, but his eyes were frightened—of me or for me, I couldn't be sure.

I skirted Ketch's office, even though I'd seen him driving away in his truck, and glanced into the infirmary. The woman I had seen Penny talking to in the dining room was seated on a three-wheel stool next to one of the beds, her back to me, gently daubing the face of a girl about my daughter's age.

For an instant my heart seized up. Then the girl moved her head slightly and the way the light caught her I knew at once it wasn't Penny. Five other beds contained children, all of them asleep, none younger than ten. The nurse turned when a board groaned beneath my feet.

"Penny?" I whispered.

"She's talking to the others."

I thanked her and started to leave.

"Are you truly her father?"

"Yes."

She rolled away from the child in the bed, the stool wheels making little thumps as they crossed the gaps between the floorboards. She stood and walked past me into the hall.

"We had a death tonight," she said in a low voice.

"Was it the flu?"

"I'm not sure. I don't think so. But it was our first death since last winter. Penny is a great comfort to the others."

I nodded, not knowing what to say.

"With her reassurances about the future."

"She shouldn't be talking to them about that."

"They find comfort in knowing the world goes on. With the war and the influenza—it sometimes feels like we're on the edge of the end of mankind."

She smiled, a round-face woman, very tired, with the damp cloth twisted in her hands. "And the inventions!" she said. "It sounds like a marvelous, luxurious time!"

"And you believe her?" I asked.

"I don't *not* believe her. She reminds me of my aunt who visited us when I was a little girl. She'd been to China. India. Persia. She told us these wonderful stories. I'll never see India or China. And I won't see the year 2000. But I believe they exist."

"She has a very vivid imagination."

The woman was disappointed in me. "You're saying it's not true? The things she says?"

"Of course," I said. "She's always looking for attention. I haven't been a very good father. Why else would she pretend to be an orphan?"

The woman stepped away from me. She touched the cloth to her forehead, then her neck, as if fighting a fever of her own.

"It *is* actually a relief," she said. "To know that. Or—rather—to *not* know what's coming."

"I've warned her that it can only lead to trouble," I said.

When I opened the dining room's double doors I had the distinct impression that time had stopped. Motionless children were turned to examine me, and Penny was at the head of them. She was very composed, sitting on a chair, legs crossed at the knee, regarding me without surprise.

"Yes?" she said.

"Time to go."

I expected a fight, some form of resistance, but Penny stood and came directly to me. Every child watched her. At the door she addressed them.

"I'll see you all in the morning. Get ready for bed. Wash your hands like I showed you."

It was out front, on the lawn in the darkness, that she made her stand.

"They need me here," she said. "I'm not going back."

A raindrop struck my cheek.

"But your mother—"

"Tell her—" She hesitated. "I don't know. Tell her she'd do the same thing. I'll come back when I'm finished here."

"The other day you couldn't wait to go back."

"I know."

It occurred to me that she was already lost to me. She had changed in some irreversible, fundamental way in the time we had been there.

"You'll know where I am," she said. "Where to find me."

"You're going to die," I said.

"So are you."

"You're going to die in November. Of the flu."

"Don't say that." She shivered.

"It's in the paper. Your name. The date. The reason."

"You're just trying to scare me."

"Yes. But it's still true."

She wiped her eyes. A raindrop hit the part in her hair.

"I'm going to die in the future, too," she said.

"But maybe not until 2050. Or 2075. But now—in 1918—you die in November."

"I might bring it back with me."

"That's why we have to leave now. Before you catch it."

A sputtering engine announced Ketch's return.

"He took away Katie Waters," Penny said.

"Who's that?"

"She died tonight."

Ketch exited the truck, kicking shut the door with knee-high rubber boots.

"She's another reason I can't leave," Penny said. "They would be doubly devastated to lose me, too."

Ketch—scowling—nodded to us as he went past. He didn't look sad, merely impatient. It bothered me somehow that he made no attempt to talk Penny into remaining, as if the possibility of her doing otherwise was unthinkable.

"He's upset about her," Penny said.

"He's upset because he's out a dollar a day."

"No."

We heard his voice through a window, a harsh, imperious voice informing the cook that he was back, and ordering a pot of coffee brought to his office.

A gust of cool wind blew across my face, filtered through the orphanage windows, and somewhere beyond that, thunder sounded.

Penny heard it, too.

"You'd better get going," she said. She touched my hand, gave me a sad, teasing smile. "Time-traveling weather."

"Your mother will never forgive me if I come back without you."

"These kids need me."

The arriving rain made a rattle high in the trees, and I got a cold drop in the eye when I turned my head up to the noise. It didn't hurt, but I doubled over with a hand to my eye. Part of that was to make Penny worry about me, worry that I couldn't get back without her help.

But she wasn't fooled. "You'll live," she said.

"Please come with me."

She shook her head. Not a shred of doubt.

"Walk to the path with me, at least."

She hesitated, expecting a trap. "I'll get an umbrella."

She was inside for a minute, and while she was gone a couple lightning bolts went wasted. I moved up onto the porch, out of the rain under a drumming tin overhang.

Penny came out with an umbrella, pushing it open. Before we were off the orphanage grounds Ketch came running after us.

"I'll arrest you for kidnapping her," he shouted.

I ran out from under the umbrella, into the rain, hoping that Penny might be caught up in the excitement and realize that between me and home and Ketch and death there was no choice.

But she didn't run. So I came back.

Ketch had a gun drawn when he reached us. Just like his grandson.

"Put that away," Penny said.

Her voice was so direct and authoritative that he obeyed at once.

"I'm just walking him home," she said.

"You're coming back?" Ketch asked.

"She dies in November," I said. "Of the flu."

This news caught Ketch short. Rain poured off the brim of his hat. "Is that true?" he asked Penny.

"How should I know?"

"You're with him." Ketch waved at me. "He knows things. I thought—"

"Tell her to come back with me," I said. "Tell her she's just a dollar a day to you."

"But she's not."

"You'll bury her like all the other orphans," I said.

"I don't want you to die," Ketch said to Penny. "I don't want you to die because of me. Go." He walked back inside.

Penny watched him until he was out of sight. I waited for her to make up her mind. Our clothes were already wet. I feared she was catching the fatal chill even as I tried to get her home. And then Penny sneezed. The expulsion and recoil got her moving.

We went across town without speaking, through a wet darkness that chilled me with its totality. I was afraid any word from me would stall the momentum I felt I had with Penny. Every time she sneezed it felt like proof that her return was the best course.

A crack of lightning illuminated for an instant the wet, green walls of the shed alongside the perp walk. It was a landmark I hadn't realized I'd been watching for. I went to it, to the door, and thumbed open the latch.

"What are you doing?" she asked.

I held out the sketch pad. "I can't bring this back with me," I said. "I was going to put it in here."

She reached out. "I'll hold on to it."

I grimaced. I thought I had had her.

She flipped through my sketches, though she couldn't see much. "Stick to sticks," she said.

We both laughed and my heart broke.

"You can't insult me—then leave."

"*You're* leaving."

She closed the pad and handed it back. I slipped it through the shed door, leaning it on a shelf just inside.

"Come get me in a month, Daddy," she said. That lack of commitment to her decision gave me hope.

"What if I can't get back?" I asked.

"These kids need . . . I don't know. I don't know what I want."

Lightning struck so close Penny jumped.

"You used to be scared to death of this weather," I said.

"I still am," she said. She wiped her nose with the back of her hand. "Are you *positive* I die in November?"

I nodded. She glanced behind, closed the umbrella and leaned it against the shed. "Okay," she said.

"Come on," I said, grabbing her hand. I tried to be confident but it wasn't easy. I had no faith in what came next. I could only do what I had done before.

I ran down the path.

The rain and the wind and the slapping leaves soaked us and made Penny squeal in a sort of surprised disorientation. We reached the end of that segment of the path, thoroughly soaked, still firmly in 1918. Across the muddy road, the scarecrow in the White Sox cap hung ghostly in a lightning flash.

Halfway down the next link, we came upon a crying child.

It was a little boy, maybe five years old, dressed in a nightshirt. He was both sobbing uncontrollably and staring around like he was not just lost but newly removed in his sleep to another world.

In that little boy I saw the loss of my daughter.

She knelt in front of him, putting a hand on his shoulder, then the crown of his head, trying to both control her breathing and comfort the boy.

"You go," she said to me.

"I can't—"

"He's like us," she said. "Isn't he?"

"Maybe," I said, though I was positive he was.

"He'll need someone to take care of him then."

I had no argument for that. "After you get him settled—" I began.

"I'll try."

"Maybe I'll stay a couple more days," I said.

"No." Rainwater dripped from her chin and eyelashes. She kissed me goodbye. "Go."

"Before November," I said. "You get sick in November."

She was sorting out this information when a bolt of lightning struck a tree not ten feet from us. In the explosion of white sparks and wood splinters I saw two-thirds of the trunk cleaved from the rooted third. This majority of the tree hung suspended for an instant in the flash burned on my eyes, and then it began to fall. Penny grabbed the boy's hand and pulled him away, back toward the Euclid Heights Children's Home, and I had a moment's fear that they would run together into yet another time, when I would have to begin searching for them all over again.

I ran in the direction of the tree's fall, which was the direction I'd been running in all along. The tree was large, about sixty feet tall, and the segment that was falling included the very highest branches. Running out from under it I was aware of the darkness beyond the white lightning burn that was fading on my vision. I was aware of the rain and my pounding heart and the presence of the falling tree above me.

I felt like I could run forever.

I wondered if I would feel the outermost fringe of wet leaves just before I was crushed. I wondered if Penny would come back and search for me beneath the fallen tree.

But by then I was at the end of the perp walk, the road in front of me was paved, and the stars were out. The ambient hum was back, quite pronounced. Someone had lined both sides of the path with small, white ground lights. They reminded me of an airport runway.

Breathless, dripping, I waited for Penny. She might have missed me at the last instant, might have stepped around the fallen tree and come running after me, toward the spot where I had disappeared. I waited a little longer.

But she had her own life to live.

TWENTY

As much as I dreaded telling Flo about Penny staying behind in 1918, I was anxious to tell her how much I had missed her. It was still only August, I'd say. We had time to rescue our daughter. Time to go back. Time to try again. But for the time being I wanted a shower, dry clothes, food, and my wife.

I crossed Clover Street and stopped in front of our house. Disorientation washed over me like a wave of nausea. I turned one complete circle, and in every degree of the circle I noticed tiny discrepancies in what I remembered, and then I faced my house again.

My studio space was gone, replaced with a traditional, face-forward garage, its door closed.

I double-checked the address. Yes. Two one eight Clover.

I went down the perp walk. Flo's office wing was gone. The brick path that led to the parking area and the garage was gone. The parking area and garage were gone, too.

I closed my eyes and took a deep breath. Rational explanations were in short supply. Near as I could figure, I had returned to a time prior to the year we'd added Flo's offices. Maybe Penny remaining in 1918—my reluctance to leave her there—had put some sort of drag on my return, prevented me from getting all the way back.

But that didn't explain the apple tree.

A single, twisted, stubborn old apple tree had been growing in the backyard when we bought the house. It still bore fruit, the Realtor had said, telling us a sales tale about the tree being the last one remaining from some long-gone orchard.

But now there were two trees, side by side, dropping apples onto the path.

A light went on in an upstairs room. Penny's room. I entertained the faintest hope.

The light went out. I watched for life downstairs, a light going on, any sort of movement. But there was nothing. No one came looking for me. No one called my name.

I struggled to not fall apart. I decided that I had returned to an even earlier time than I had originally thought. It must have been a time before the second tree was cut down, before Penny was born, maybe even before I married Flo. An ache of unimaginable proportions seized me. I had returned to a time before my life had truly begun. But I clung to this explanation because it at least retained the hope that my life and my world would one day be as I remembered them.

Hurrying downtown, I had to pass 1112 East Collier Street. I stood for a minute just watching the old house. Lights burned in the windows. For the first time in my life it was a comforting presence.

Then Kurt stepped out onto the front porch.

"Josh! Where the heck have you been?"

In a daze, I went to him. My mouth might have been hanging open but he was gentleman enough not to mention it. He'd been reading the newspaper and regarded me curiously over the top of his half-lens reading glasses.

"We were just talking about you," he said.

"Kurt!" I blurted.

"We were worried, brother man."

A woman I didn't know came out on the front porch behind my brother. She was flustered and pretty, with a curl of honey-blond hair over one eye that she brushed away.

"Lee is going to tan your hide this time, mister," she scolded me.

I just stood there, stupefied. Lee?

The woman placed her hand on Kurt's shoulder. "Come in and dry, please," she said. She gave me a last pitying glance and went back inside the house.

Kurt hopped down the steps and threw an arm around me.

"Your shirt's all wet, buddy," he said.

I put my hand on his chest. He was clean-shaven, his eyes kind and wise and intelligent. "And you smell a little ripe," he said. "Why not go home?"

I didn't want to scare him by asking where that might be.

I stuck with what I knew. "Where's Flo?"

"Flo who?"

"Flo—" I hesitated. Clues arranged themselves: the two apple trees. A wing of our house gone. Flo who? I had never been more frightened in my life.

"Flo Garner," I said.

"Vaughan's sister? Boy, I haven't thought about her in years."

"How's Vaughan?"

"Haven't seen him since high school."

I knew better than to go on, but I couldn't help myself. "And Jock Itch?"

"You have jock itch?" he asked, mildly aghast.

"No, Jack Ketch. Jock Itch."

"I don't know a Jock Itch. Don't know Toe B. Fungus or Bud Breath, either." He laughed and squeezed my shoulder. "Go home, Josh. And this time, *stay* home."

He pulled open the screen door. "We've been worried sick about you, Josh," he said. "Where have you been?"

"I don't know where to begin."

He gave me a benevolent smile, and then left me there, at a loss. I had a home somewhere nearby, with a woman named Lee. My brother, Kurt, was apparently accustomed to viewing me with some bemusement.

But what had I done to Flo?

I retreated at a dead run, back to the nearest perp walk mouth. I tried to think of nothing, but of course that was impossible. A mind clear of my true intentions was a luxury that I did not expect to possess any time soon. I tried to think about Penny, where she was, the danger she was in, as almost a preferable alternative to thinking about my wife—still alive—lost to me.

I began to run down the walk. It didn't take long for nothing to happen. Then I was at Clover Street again and I knew that for the time being the fate I'd triggered for myself was mine.

Downtown Euclid Heights was unchanged from what I remembered. The square remained, a corner cut off by the railroad tracks. But the jail hadn't moved. It stood where it always had.

I hurried north. People I didn't recognize called out to me. Coming around the corner of the library, I stopped. The orphanage was gone. I wasn't sure if I should be relieved or not.

I collapsed on a bench. A man in a car honked and waved. He did not seem the least surprised to see me, dirty clothes, bare feet, and all. I waved back. Maybe in this life I was the lovable village idiot. Maybe I was the eccentric who backed up his oddball ways with charitable donations and good deeds. Maybe I was the bighearted citizen who gave selflessly of his time and money. I didn't feel any different. I certainly didn't feel married to anyone named Lee. I felt married to Flo—and I missed her. I missed Penny and the L-shaped house and the small novelty of traveling fifteen minutes through time.

I vowed to stay on that bench until I was asked to leave, and as it happened I was there all night. A cop cruised past at midnight. He waved to me.

I was the first person into the library when it opened. I found a phone book. No listing for Flo Garner. Of course, Flo was probably married to the male version of Lee. A woman as smart and lovely as Flo would not remain alone in any life.

On a hunch, I looked up Vaughan Garner and found the address of Dr. Vaughan Garner's office on Euclid Heights Road.

A doctor. Vaughan, spared drowning at the hands of Jock Itch, had grown up to be a doctor, just like his sister. It was the first time I felt proud of what I had done, of what changes I had inadvertently set in motion.

I put the phone book down. I could go into the microfilm reels and begin reading at August 1918. But the story of what had happened probably wouldn't be in the paper: John Ketch, paralyzed by awareness, by a sure thing, misses his destiny; and I, in turn, miss mine.

I found Dr. Vaughan Garner getting out of his car at his office. I recognized him immediately. He didn't know me.

"I'm Kurt Winkler's brother," I said.

"Okay," he said, taking in my dirty feet and wrinkled clothes. "How *is* Kurt?"

"He's doing great, thanks. Say, I went to school with your sister. What was her name?" I even snapped my fingers, miming an attempt to recall a distant memory.

"Flora."

"Right. Flo. Didn't she become a doctor, too?"

Vaughan lifted an eyebrow. "No. She's a mom."

"No kidding? Who'd she marry?"

"Her high school sweetheart. Doug Vug."

Vaughan excused himself. I thanked him.

Doug Vug. That A in algebra had finally paid off.

He was in the book. A Dragon Hills address.

Flo Vug. It was hard to picture. I didn't feel jealous, only lost. How could I blame her for leading a life without me?

The boy and girl Flo followed out of her house made me tangentially proud. They felt half mine. The girl faintly resembled Penny. The boy was like a son we might have had. Both exhibited energy and laughter. Flo wore her hair longer, frosted to cover the gray. She carried a large shoulder bag, talked to both kids simultaneously, had a cell phone in hand, and appeared to be both harried and contented.

She and her kids swept past in their car. At the moment I was certain Flo would not notice me, she waved.

I wondered if I lived nearby, if I was a neighbor. Maybe she and Lee were friends.

I returned to Kurt's house. He wasn't home. His wife was not reluctant to let me in. Evidently I was harmless. I couldn't figure out a graceful way to ask her name.

"I spoke to Lee," she said.

"Yeah?"

"Imagine my surprise when she said you didn't come home last night."

"I got sidetracked."

"She's going to follow through on her threats one of these times, Josh."

"Threats?"

"Don't play dumb with me."

"I've done this before?"

She gave me a befuddled, anxious look. "Go home," she said.

"The other times. What happened, exactly?"

"You're not funny."

I tried something else. "Where's Kurt?"

"At work."

"When will he be home?"

"He's always on the six-fifteen."

"Can you call Lee and ask her to pick me up?"

She rolled her eyes. "Walk your lazy butt around back and ask her yourself."

A jolt of nervous excitement seized me. Lee was waiting for me in the backyard. She would lead me home, to a shower, a meal, and a pair of shoes. I would surely at least find her likable. We *were* married.

But the backyard was empty. Gas grill. Patio furniture. No Lee.

Kurt's wife came to the kitchen window. I made a helpless gesture with my hands. She raised a finger to me and pointed down.

I noticed the small address plate then: 1112½.

It was over a mailbox, next to the basement door. I went down a few stairs and knocked. A woman opened the door like she'd been expecting me, left it open, and turned away. *Stormed* away. She was short, compact, black hair and pale skin, fine-boned, a type I didn't know was my type until I laid eyes on her. Anger, impatience, and frustration radiated from her like an ill wind. It was a short walk to the far end of the room, where she whirled and came back at me. Her flashing green eyes were two more things I liked about her.

"We're finished, Josh."

"Lee—" I said, just to try out the name.

She raised a hand. "Don't. I've given you a dozen chances. I'm done."

"Let's start over."

"You always say that."

"I do?" I collected myself. "Well . . . this time I mean it. We'll start by moving out of my brother's basement."

"He doesn't charge us rent."

"We can't afford rent?"

"Not on my salary."

"I don't have a job?" I asked.

"You've *never* had a job."

"I'm an artist."

"Con artist, maybe," she said, but not without a trace of fondness.

"I can't believe I'm still living in the basement," I said.

"Pretty pathetic, I'll admit."

"How did *he* get the house?" I asked.

I stepped deeper into the cramped space. There was only room for a bathroom, kitchenette, a small dining table, two chairs, and a sleeping area, which consisted of a queen-size mattress on the floor. When I stood up straight the crown of my head brushed the drop ceiling.

No sign of any artwork. No sign of any art supplies. I recognized the sad, weak light of my childhood.

"Yeah, we definitely have to get out of here," I said.

"I've been saying that since we moved in."

I didn't ask her how long that had been. It wasn't important, that part of my past. There were so many questions I wanted to ask her, things I would know if I were married to her, if I had been paying attention. But there was time to learn all that.

"I'll get a job," I said.

She set her jaw. "That's a start. But it's not the most important thing."

"What is?"

She sighed. "Josh—I'm tired of spelling it out for you."

"I was gone a few days. I'm sorry."

"Even when you're here—you're not here."

"Where am I?" I asked, genuinely curious.

"Some other world."

She went into the bathroom. Water ran. I didn't move. Could I fall in love with this woman? Or had I already? She was definitely patient, and possibly forgiving. And what had she been doing while I was married to Flo? Did she also have flashes of memory opening onto a different life?

"I'm going to work," she said, emerging. She'd run a brush through her hair and put on lipstick.

"Okay," I said. It was not a good sign that I was relieved she would be gone.

"Want to meet me for lunch?"

"Can I take a rain check?"

She bristled. "Busy day planned?"

"I'm going to get to work on the new me."

Lee surprised me by taking me into her arms. She was warm and solid. Her forehead came to the center of my chest. It felt so strange, me holding her. My arms were calibrated for Flo's dimensions and my heart broke all over again.

"I don't want a new you," she said.

As she spoke I was thinking of my other wife. I guess that was the root of Lee's complaints because she dropped her arms and stepped clear of me. She was attuned to my emotional distance.

"Or maybe I do," she said and left for work.

I collapsed on the edge of the mattress. It was the view from my childhood, up off the floor, through a meager window. The furnace coming on kept me awake in winter. I knew that life. No Penny. No Flo. Married to a stranger who knew me perfectly well.

I took refuge in sleep.

I heard someone move above and behind me. The light was too indistinct to gauge the hour, but when I rolled over in bed I saw a girl across the room. She was on tiptoe, in a long dress, feeling for something in the ceiling.

"Constance," I said.

She didn't answer; she didn't acknowledge me in any way.

"You already took Dash's letter."

My remark made perfect sense to me. I kept my mouth shut after that. I was just glad to see her. Even as a ghost she was something solid from that life I'd let slip away.

"Say hello to Penny," I said.

Before she could respond a pain shot through my ribs. When I awoke, Lee was standing over me.

"Who's Penny?" she asked murderously.

I sat up. Constance was just a flicker of hem going up the basement stairs, if that.

"*Who is Penny?*" Lee pressed.

"What?" I said.

"You said 'say hello to Penny.' "

"I did?"

"Yes, you did."

She went to the sink and turned on the water. Something in those few steps brought back a memory of our wedding day. She was in a long, white dress, advancing away from me across a ballroom floor to ask my father to dance.

I tried to fix this memory in its proper framework. A man's face came to me. He was in his late fifties, dressed in an indigo tux, with winglike eyebrows and rosacea splashed across his nose and upper cheeks, disappointment in his eyes. I knew right away that he was Lee's father.

I jumped up and got dressed. As much as Penny's fate pressed on me, I was more troubled by my Flo life being replaced by my Lee life.

"Where are you going?"

I gave her a brave smile. "To look for a job," I lied.

"The day is about gone," she informed me.

I didn't let that stop me.

I hurried to the Dragon Hills, to Flo's new house. She answered when I rang the bell.

"Yes?" she said politely. No sign of recognition. Not even any curiosity about me beyond a tinge of anxiety for a stranger at the door. Her benign expression answered all the important questions. She didn't know me.

"Flo," I said.

"Yes?"

"Josh Winkler."

She waited.

"I went to high school with you," I said.

She smiled slightly, studied me fractionally closer, but with no real interest.

"I'm sorry. I don't remember you."

"Vaughan and my brother were friends," I said.

"You weren't in any of my classes, were you?"

"No."

"Did you know Doug? My husband?"

"We've met," I said.

"I'd love to talk—but I'm making dinner."

"I married Lee Swope," I said, her maiden name just there.

She bit her lip. "I'm sorry. I don't remember her, either."

"You wanted to be a doctor," I said.

That got through to her. "My brother's the doctor in the family," she said coolly.

"But you *wanted* to be one."

"Oh—" She shrugged. "With four kids who tend to get sick one right after the other—it sometimes feels like I'm a doctor."

"You'd have made a great one," I said.

The tenderness in my voice pushed her back to the polite distance between us.

"Any kids for you?" she asked.

"One. A daughter." I hesitated. "Her name is Penny."

Flo blinked. "What a coincidence. My oldest is named Penny, too."

"Mine is fifteen," I said.

She raised a hand. "Say no more. I know exactly what you're going through."

I didn't want to disagree and ruin the mood. But the visit was over anyway.

I drifted out of the Dragon Hills, down Pincoffin Street. The perp walk there was full of commuters taking a shortcut home.

I was downtown when the 6:15 pulled in. Kurt jumped off and saluted the conductor. His necktie was loosened and his briefcase bounced against his leg like it was empty. He held a mixed drink in one hand. I fell in beside him as he headed for home.

"Brother man," he greeted me.

"Hey."

"Four down. One to go."

I was about to ask Kurt what he did for a living, but then I just *knew,* it was right there in my mind, familiar and unremarkable.

"Lee said you didn't come home last night?"

"I did this morning. You're looking at a new me."

"Okay." He nodded. "Not that the old one was so terrible."

"Kurt, do you remember when we were kids—and you taught retarded people how to swim?"

He took a swallow from his glass. "I guess. Why?"

"Did I help you?"

"You might have. I don't remember."

"I think I was there."

"I *do* remember the sunburn I got."

"I wish I could remember if I was there."

"Can't help you, bud. That was *so* long ago."

"Vaughan was there."

Kurt walked on a minute, thinking. Then he laughed. "Could've been. I don't remember."

"Do you ever feel like you took a wrong turn and ended up in a place where you don't belong?" I asked.

"No, Josh. For the hundredth time. I *never* feel that way."

Then we were at 1112 East Collier Street, and Kurt climbed the stairs and let himself in through the front door and I went around back and down into the basement.

The day I was hired to drive a school bus was the day I bought a beginner's set of watercolors and brushes. The process of being approved to shuttle children from home to school and back required two urine tests, a psychological profile, a fingerprint analysis, and a criminal background check. I was curious what they would find out about me. Nothing, as it happened. I was clean. I made no mention of time travel on the essay portion of my psych exam. I must have done okay, because I was given a $250 signing bonus and a contract to drive throughout the school year.

I got lost the first day with a busload of children screaming directions and advice in my ear. But as the days went by I grew to like being around kids. They called me Mr. Winkler, then Josh, then Homey J. Lee banked all my bus pay in an account we called the Apartment Fund.

Every morning I had a one-hour window between one route's completion and the start of the next. I parked during that time on Clover Street, at the mouth of the perp walk, and painted. It was my favorite time of day, sad and rejuvenating at the same time. I wanted to be present if Penny should return—and I was doing something that felt right.

Before leaving home in the morning I filled a lidded baby food jar with water. I painted whatever was close at hand and what was most close at hand was the perp walk—which in my renditions of it again and again was a path vanishing at a point in the distance. Sometimes I painted the perp walk empty. Other times I painted it with Penny coming toward me, or Penny up close. I wished she was there to pose for me—like that long-ago summer that was really only last summer—but even without her standing in front of me she was easy to draw.

I taped the results to the bus ceiling to dry. They fluttered like leaves with the motion of travel. Most of the kids ignored them. The smartest of them—a fourth grade girl named Audrey—pointed one morning to the last thing I'd finished and asked, "Who's that?"

"My daughter."

"Is that her, too? And her and her?" She pointed to other paintings, a whole gallery of them.

"Yes," I said.

"They've been up here since school started."

She was right. Most of them were so dry they might crack if touched.

"Doesn't she want to see them?" Audrey said.

"Who?"

"Your daughter."

I took all the paintings home that night. Lee made dinner and I cleared away the dishes when we were done eating. We heard Kurt's TV through the ceiling. I brought out the perp walk paintings and fanned them out on the table. Most of them contained Penny. In one she was barely a speck in the distance, at that point a step away from vanishing along with the path she walked upon. In others she was in mid-field, but recognizable if you knew her. All the rest were close-ups. Lee focused immediately on these.

"You've been busy," she said with a hand on my shoulder. "You're very good."

"Thanks."

She touched one. "Who's this?" she asked.

"Her name is Penny."

My wife's eyes flashed at me. She had a long memory. *Say hello to Penny.*

She touched each painting with a fingertip. One or two of them she picked up and set right back down. Things had been going well for us. I saw her calculate this fact—weigh it against her need to know the truth about something.

"You told me you didn't know any Penny," she finally said.

"You're right."

"So you lied?"

"I didn't know how to explain . . ." I stopped.

"Penny," she reminded me.

"Right." I thought about that day in Flo's office—a lifetime ago—when I sat on her four-wheel stool and told her about going back in time fifteen minutes. There was much more to come after that moment—but that was when I knocked our life off the rails. I didn't want to do the same to Lee.

She touched one of the watercolors. "You obviously care for her," she said. "These," and she tapped the empty perp walk paintings, "are fine—but the ones with *her* are so much better."

"She's my daughter," I said.

Lee didn't know what to say. She wasn't one to cry easily, but I could see that this was a lot to absorb even for her.

"Your daughter," she said.

"Yes."

"Do I know the mother?"

"No."

"This daughter of yours is just the result of some random unfaithfulness—and *now* you've decided to let me in on it?"

"It's not like that."

"What's it like then?"

"Sit down." I gathered up the paintings, like I was clearing a space for her.

"Have you been giving her money?"

"No."

"Why not? If she's your daughter—you should be supporting her! Did you leave the mom to raise this girl by herself?"

"No. Lee. Listen." I reached for her but she drew away.

"Is she the only one?" she asked. "Do you have other kids I'm going to hear about down the road?"

"No." It felt good to be able to reassure her. "Please sit down."

Halfway through the explanation I wished I had never begun. Better to leave Lee out of it. Save her from it. From me. It would have been easy enough to do. Burn the paintings of Penny, stay away from the perp walk. Let November come and go. Let that other life die off.

To Lee it was just her crazy husband with another crazy lie—this one about traveling through time. First going back fifteen minutes, then more than eighty years. I could see our life together unravel as I told her everything.

But when I finished she looked at her watch.

An hour had passed, but it wasn't the time she was checking.

"Today is September twenty-ninth," she said.

I nodded. I'd felt October coming on like a sneeze.

"She gets sick when?" Lee asked.

"She gets a cough and fever October second. She gets sick for the last time November second."

"Show me," she said, rising.

"Show you what?"

"Everything. Proof. The paperwork. The newspaper clippings."

"It's late. Everything is closed."

"Then you'll show me tomorrow." She made two laps of the apartment, just to keep moving, her impatience, uncertainty, and anxiety like a fuel mixture that burned inside her.

"Show me the path. Now."

"Okay."

"And your old house," she said.

"*This* is my old house."

"The other one. The one where you lived this other life."

We decided to walk. I put my arm around Lee's shoulder but dropped it after a block, feeling her hunched reluctance to believe me—to even be in my presence.

I led her to the mouth of the perp walk at Pincoffin Street. She froze, like she was confronted with a dark hallway in a haunted house. She tested the path with her toe.

"I didn't even know these were here," she said in a low voice.

"You grew up on the west side," I said. I no longer even questioned how I knew things about her. She was my wife. It was just there, a part of me.

"Does *she* live near here?"

I knew whom she meant. "Flo?"

"Yes. *The doctor.*" Jealousy dripped from the last two words.

"She isn't one now," I said.

"But when you were *married* to her—when she was having your *baby*—she was a doctor," Lee said. "Right?"

"Yes." I touched her arm. "She lives in the Dragon Hills."

"Figures," Lee said bitterly. She thought for a moment. "How do you know?" She had me cornered. Before I could tell her the truth she jumped there. "You already checked to see what happened to her! Didn't you?"

"I was going to tell you," I said.

"I'll bet."

"I *was*. Anyway, can you blame me? I come back to all this—wouldn't you check out your old life? Anybody would."

She still hadn't set foot on the perp walk.

"Do you miss her?" she asked.

I thought about this. I was surprised to learn that I didn't—or at least not like I had. Something had changed. Time had passed.

"I *did*," I admitted. "But I don't now—much."

"*Much*. That's just great." She firmed up her shoulders. "Do you miss that other life?"

"I miss Penny."

She pushed past me onto the walk, took a couple steps, and stopped. She stood slightly pigeon-toed, on tiptoe, like someone caught on lake ice during a thaw.

"I could just disappear?" she asked.

"I don't think so. I don't know. It was raining. I was running."

"Would you like that? If I disappeared?" she challenged.

"No!" And I meant it. She was all I had.

She held my hand the rest of the way. The perp walk had a more open feel—wider—with autumn having thinned out the leaves along it. I was reminded in some respects of 1918 and I didn't know if that was a good or a bad thing.

I stopped her before we reached Pine Street.

"This is where the time-traveling dog lived," I said.

She broke out laughing—and I joined her. Wherever that dog was, he wasn't there.

On we went to Clover Street. Even without Flo's wing and my studio, the house was a big step up—spacewise—from Kurt's basement.

"I could live here," Lee said.

I couldn't, I realized. I might park my bus at the end of the walk to wait for my daughter, but telling Lee—taking the step of including her in that past life—had released me from the hold that life had had over me. Flo was gone. That life was gone.

"Where did you paint?" Lee asked.

I gestured vaguely toward the garage. "It's gone," I said. "Or never *was* there."

"And which was your bedroom?"

I pointed to the window.

"And Penny's?"

I pointed it out, too.

"If she came back—I could be her mother," Lee said.

"You'd *have* to be."

I didn't want to think about that, about what Penny would have to deal with if she got back to me.

We stood holding hands on the perp walk long after I was ready to leave.

It was Lee's idea to be at the library when the doors opened. I would have stayed in bed all day if she hadn't been so insistent, not because I wanted to avoid anything but because I felt terrible, maybe suffering from sympathy influenza, although it seemed real enough to me. In bed the night before I had entertained the hope that Lee had seen enough, that the perp walk and my old house had convinced her. But she wanted to see everything. She wanted proof.

"Today's the last day of September," she said as I threaded in the first reel of microfilm.

We spent an hour in 1908. Lee read each report about Constance's disappearance with rapt, squinting concentration. When she finished the last story she said, half to herself, "So *this* is where you've been."

"No. I went to 1918," I said.

I knew what she meant, though.

I held the November 1–15, 1918, reel in my hands so long that Lee almost had to pry my fingers off it.

"Haven't you been convinced?" I asked.

"I'm convinced—but I still want to find out what happens."

There was really only one item left to see. Page 42 of the November 14, 1918, edition. I rolled through the pages, the stream of film and light making me dizzy. The closer I got the slower I went.

"What's wrong?" she asked.

"It may not be here," I said.

"What?"

"The page we need."

I stopped between pages 38 and 39 and explained.

She put a hand on mine.

"You're burning up," she said, and transferred her hand to my forehead.

"We're almost there," I said, more gallant than I felt.

Lee was impressed that I knew page 42 would be missing. She regarded me like a seer.

"Let's get you home," she said.

She put me to bed, poured a delicious, hot liquid down my throat, and left me with the lights down low and the phone beside my head. The last word I said before she left was "Fustus."

It was morning when she dared awaken me. I felt halfway back from death—but not strong enough to get to my feet.

Lee couldn't wait. She shook a copy of page 42 at me.

"You've got to see this!" she said.

I started at the top of the **INFLUENZA VICTIMS** list, reading each name to myself. I was just to *Manger, Constance M.* when Lee couldn't contain herself and said, "She isn't there!"

"Who?"

"Penny!"

I read the bottom half of the list three times before I allowed myself to believe it.

Miller, Ophelia *adult*
Nellisen, Thomas *adult*
Olston, John *beloved child*
Praeger, Arthur *orphan child*
Pzerter, Katherine *adult*
Quinn, Daniel *adult*
Tully, Millicent *adult*
Vincent, William *orphan child*
Voss, E. J. *beloved child*
Winberger, James *adult*
Wisteria, Vitrine *adult*
Wooster, Blanche *adult*
Young, Muriel *adult*
Zook, Kenneth *adult*

No Winkler, Penelope *orphan child.*

"She didn't die!" Lee said.

I wasn't convinced.

"Not *then,*" I said. I crawled to my feet. My head swam. My wife held me upright. "We have to go back to the library."

The next list of influenza victims was in the November 16 paper. Penny wasn't on it. I felt so crummy that I wouldn't have been unduly shocked to find my own name listed there. We found Constance Manger's obituary. Poor Constance. Why hadn't she heeded my warning, as Penny evidently had?

"You said she only had one son," Lee said.

I jumped to the last line of Constance's obituary.

Mrs. Manger is also survived by her beloved sons, E. Wayne Jr. and Michael T. and her father and mother, Peter T. and Faith W. Morceau.

"She had only one the last time I saw her."

"Was she pregnant?"

"No. I mean—I saw her in August. She died—*dies*—in November."

I went back to bed and stayed there for two days. I dreamed of Penny in the orphanage, maybe laid up herself. Playing cards with Bette Andresen. Talking shop with the nurse who would never see China. They were comforting dreams, in a way, with Penny in front of me, alive, as I remembered her. I could keep an eye on her in my dreams.

When I was back on my feet I spent two days searching through the newspapers of November 1918, seeking any mention of my daughter. I was afraid I had only altered her fate by a few days—and that the announcement of her death was hidden deep in some other day's edition, where I could easily miss it.

But I found nothing.

So she was alive, which was a relief, but she felt more lost to me than ever. Her name—even on a list of the dead—had allowed me to keep track of her.

As October deepened I helped Kurt in the yard. He was a little obsessive about getting the leaves up the instant they fell. I urged waiting until they all were down. But I didn't argue. He wasn't charging us rent, as Lee pointed out.

Mixed in with the leaves were sticks and fragments of sticks, dead bits the trees had sloughed off. Most of these I bagged without a thought, but then the shape of one stopped me. Its length or its slimness reminded me of Penny. And once I knew what I was looking for, I found another, and then another.

I got up early the next morning and walked into town. Then I stayed in the basement all day, although it was a Saturday and the leaves cascaded down around my brother's head. Kurt even stood for a while so that the tines of his rake scratched the basement window—in case I'd forgotten that he wasn't charging us rent.

When Lee got home I had finished three dolls, heads and all.

She held each one in turn.

"You are *so* talented," she said, and kissed me.

I put the three back on the shelf. Their clothes were still wet.

"I bet you could sell those," Lee said.

"Kurt will charge us for the sticks," I said.

She touched the hair on one doll's head. "We could call it *Sticks Figure,*" she said. "We could—"

"They're supposed to be Penny."

"I know."

"I don't want to make money off her."

Lee nodded. "Okay. You're right. I'm sorry."

During dinner Halloween night she said to me, "We should go over there tonight."

Over there.

"Why?"

"Because tonight is the only thunderstorm in the entire month of October—in 1918," she said.

I wanted to take the perp walks but Lee worried that Penny might come charging out of 1918 and smash headlong into us. I saw her point.

As we set off, Kurt's wife—Colleen—came out on the front porch. I'd never heard her name spoken aloud—but it was Colleen.

"Kurt's in trouble," she said. Her nose was red-tipped from crying.

"What kind of trouble?" I asked, but then I knew, just like I knew where Kurt worked and everything else about him. It was part of my life. He was my brother.

His wife rolled her eyes at Lee. "The usual," she said. "Could you go get him?"

I didn't have to ask where he was.

"I'd go—but I'm frankly sick of all this," she said.

"I'll go with you," Lee said.

"No. He's my brother."

"And you're my husband," Lee said. "I'm going with you."

A police officer was on duty behind a glass enclosure in the lobby of the jail. He was young and polite and after I told him our business he passed a form on a clipboard to us through a slot. I imagined Kurt in Dash Buckley's cell, with that low view of life passing by. I lost track of Lee while I filled out the form and then she said, "It's him."

I glanced up. "Hmm?"

She was standing by a framed drawing hung on the wall across the lobby. Even from where I sat I could tell it was Sheriff Ketch. Beneath it was a small gold plate that read *Former Police Chief John "Jack" Ketch, from his estate.*

My eyes scanned left and right. The drawing of Ketch was the centerpiece of five framed drawings. The four others were sketches, really—dashed off just to fill the time—of a horse being shod, a palm reader's door, a milk can maker's billboard, and a moss-covered shed.

"Those are my drawings," I said.

Lee studied me as I came and stood beside her.

"I did them in 1918."

"This is the best one," she said, tapping the frame of the drawing of Ketch.

Even I had to admit it was much better—more assured, more true to life—than my sketches. It was Ketch, but not as I remembered him. Something was different.

"I did all of them but that one," I said.

She winced at me. "Sorry," she said.

"No. You're right."

The frame cut off the bottom half-inch of paper. I tried to lift the picture down off the wall to see if there was a signature or a date but it was bolted to the wall. Of course, I hadn't signed any of my sketches. But I had just been passing through.

They brought Kurt out then. He was bleary-eyed and disheveled. A cop in a windbreaker accompanied him.

"Hey, brother man," Kurt said to me, "this isn't your job."

They handed him over to me in exchange for the form.

"See you, Chet," Kurt said to the windbreaker.

"Crazy Kurt—we don't want to see you in here again," he warned.

The nickname startled me. I checked Kurt's eyes to see which Kurt he was. It was the Kurt who lived above me. He left without waiting for us.

"What do you know about these drawings?" I asked the windbreaker.

"Nothing. The guy was chief here forever. He died at his desk. They found the drawings. Somebody got them framed." He shrugged. "Next time we pick up your brother—he'll need a lawyer. This isn't a motel—" And then he said something that startled me. "Josh."

I studied him as long as I could without being rude. His name came to me.

"Thanks, Cal. I'll tell him."

Cal headed toward the door leading to the rear of the station.

"Did he—did that chief—have any family?" I asked.

"I don't know. I don't think so." He paused at the door. "*I'm* not dying at my desk, that's for sure."

Kurt had stopped on the sidewalk out front. "Can you get the car?" he asked. "I'm kinda woozy."

"We walked," Lee said.

"Walked?" Kurt moaned.

I noticed that his shoes were on the wrong feet. I pointed this out and he flopped down onto a sidewalk bench to rectify the situation.

"I'm still dizzy," he said.

Lee and I each took an arm. A block from downtown he got his sea legs back and insisted on walking unaided.

"What's the mood at home?" he asked.

"Not good."

"She'll get over it. She always does."

Although trick-or-treating had become largely a daylight enterprise, we came upon bands of children—some in costume, some with parents, some with the darting demeanor of highwaymen. A cluster composed of Jedi knights and what appeared to be bridge trolls stood on the top step of Kurt's house, thumping the doorbell although the porch light was off and every window of the house was dark.

Kurt stopped at the bottom of the steps.

"Anybody home?" he asked.

The kids shifted as one in my brother's direction.

"She might not be in a Halloween mood," he warned, fishing out his keys.

They made way for him and he unlocked the door.

He said to us over the masked heads, "At least she didn't change the locks."

Lee and I took Collier to Clover, then turned south. It was a beautiful night, chilly and star-struck.

"This was Constance's birthday," I said. "All Hallows' Eve."

Lee's hand was warm even through her mitten. "Does Penny know Constance is going to die?" she asked.

I couldn't remember.

"Because I think I know how Constance got her second son," Lee said.

I nodded. I'd guessed it, too. *He's like us.*

"The boy on the path," I said.

"Right. Penny put him in Constance's care because she knew she wouldn't be around."

"That would indicate that she intended to come back," I said, though I dared not to hope.

"And that she didn't know Constance was going to die."

We reached the perp walk.

"I'm prepared to wait all night," Lee said.

I'm not, I thought. It was a nice night for a walk but the feeling wasn't right. Penny was too much on our minds. Even if she could clear her thoughts to make an attempt from the other end—we would block her arrival with our one-track minds.

"What did the newspaper say?" I asked.

"An evening thunderstorm."

"It happened or it was predicted?"

"Forecasted," she said sheepishly.

"There's nothing in tomorrow's paper about it?"

She shook her head.

"Lee."

"I know. *I know*. I just thought it would be worth a try."

Still, we gave it an hour. Not a single person used the perp walk in all that time.

Heading home, Lee said, "You have to go get her."

"I've tried."

"You have to try again."

"I warned her," I said. "As far as she knows—she gets sick and dies in November."

"That's why—"

"I mean—she isn't going to get a better reason to come back. It's up to her."

Lee dropped my hand.

"Okay. I admit it. I'm afraid," I said.

We kept walking.

"I like *this* life," I said.

"You owe it to your daughter."

"What if I don't get back? What will you do?"

"I'm used to you being gone," she said. "Even when you're here."

We came up on 1112 East Collier Street from the west. Kurt had not turned on any lights in the house—but the trick-or-treater, or one, anyway, had not given up. Back to us, hand raised to ring the bell, the trick-or-treater wore a shawl that seemed to glisten even in the faint light.

Then I noticed a trail of moisture on the walk.

"Penny?"

She turned and saw me and made a little noise—a peep—and then she flew down the steps and into my arms. Her face was so wet with tears that they might have been enough to slide her through time. I couldn't stop kissing her, sobbing myself, and I didn't dare let her go until she gently, but firmly, pried us apart.

"The thunderstorm," Lee said, proud of herself.

Penny glanced at her. I could see the questions beginning to line up in her eyes.

"Who's this?" she asked me. "Where's mom? What happened to our house?"

"Things have changed," I said.

"I thought I'd come back to the wrong time," she said.

"You didn't."

She stared at Lee. "Where's mom?" she asked me again.

I gave her the short version.

"All the things I warned about—happened," I said. "This is Lee. Your—my wife."

They didn't touch, not even hands. Lee knew enough to give Penny room.

"Your *wife*?"

"Yes."

"I'm so happy to finally meet you," Lee said. "Your dad has been a basket case trying to get you back. Are you hungry?"

"No. I don't know!" She bit her lip. "I want to see mom."

"She named her daughter Penny," I said.

"Tell me about it."

"No, I mean her . . . she has *another* daughter named Penny."

"But *I'm* her daughter!" I reached for her but she pulled away. "She'd *know* me!"

"She didn't know *me,*" I said. "She's married to someone else. She's not a doctor now."

Penny was shocked. "She's not?"

"Her brother became a doctor. She didn't."

She collapsed back onto the steps.

"How did you get back?" I asked.

"I'm completely on my own, aren't I?" she asked.

"You have us."

"But my mom, my friends—I don't exist for them, do I?"

"No."

It took her a minute to take that in.

Then she began to speak. "I got real sick early this month. Felt like I was going to die. Ketch freaked. He was *sure* your prediction about me was coming true. Then I got better. I thought Ketch would make me come back before I got *really* sick and died. But just the opposite happened. He was always around. Eating with me. Taking me for rides. I couldn't get rid of him. Then he found your drawings. He thought they were mine. He offered me a hundred dollars to draw *him*. That's big money in 1918—and I didn't know where my money would come from. I think it was just his way to spend more time with me. While he sat he talked about the future. Asked me what I remembered about it. And he told me what you'd told him. How he was destined to marry and have a son who would become sheriff and how he would have a son of his own. He just didn't know who his wife was supposed to be. When he said he thought it was *me*—I knew it was time to come home."